PRAISE FOR *OUT STEALING WATER*

"You're walking a familiar street when something—the play of light, a child's call far off, tree roots pushing through sidewalk, a perfectly blue robin's egg lying lost on the ground—brings on waves of feeling and of memory and you see this street as though for the first time, with wonder. That's what writers at their best do, and what Roxanne does in *Out Stealing Water*."

–Jim Sallis, author of *Sarah Jane, Will Not, Drive*

"…this book is so timely and well done and I admired it."

–Aimee Bender, author of *The Color Mast, The Particular Sadness of Lemon Cake, Willful Creatures* and others.

"In this novel of a makeshift family facing eviction from their trailers on a dirt lot in the city of Tempe, Roxanne Doty makes disreputable and dishonest teenagers, and the adults who mislead them, into sympathetic characters that you are rooting for by the final confrontation with authorities. Doty writes with skill and compassion, bringing this story of escalating mistakes and desires to a satisfying conclusion."

–Patricia Grady Cox, author of *Chasm Creek* and *Hellgate*

"*Out Stealing Water* is a must read if you have ever wondered what it would be like to become an outcast on land that has been in your family for generations, and is about to be taken from you because you can't produce the stupid piece of paper that says it's yours. Roxanne Doty has penned a brilliant novel that immediately draws the reader into this family's plight."

–Nancy Purcell, author of *Stop Twisting the Knife*, and *Challenges and Chores*

"*Out Stealing Water* begs the heart-breaking question between sin and survival, poverty and pride, and sovereignty rights from before the era of computers. With poetically vivid prose, characters you cry for, and unapologetic justifications, Doty's novel lingers, haunting one's concept of truth."

–Freda Jayne, author of *Awake and Dreaming*

"The current conflicts in our different Americas are an integral part of *Out Stealing Water*, not just touched on but the very foundation that holds the plot together from privilege to poverty, spirituality to doubt, money and power to hardscrabble lives lived on the brink of our cities. The story explores our culture in which losing and winning come down to the dreams and promises on a postcard. Read this illuminating book! It will shine in the dark while you stay awake, hurrying to find out what is next, but slowing down to savor Roxanne Doty's writing and the depth of her novel."

–Kate Green, author of *Shattered Moon*

Out Stealing Water

Roxanne Doty

Regal House Publishing

Published by
Regal House Publishing, LLC
Raleigh, NC 27587

ISBN -13 (paperback): 9781646031979
ISBN -13 (epub): 9781646031986
Library of Congress Control Number: 2021943780

Interior layout by Lafayette & Greene
Cover images © by C. B. Royal

Regal House Publishing, LLC
https://regalhousepublishing.com

Printed in the United States of America

To those who struggle in numerous ways, under various conditions to hold on to family, home and roots in places overwhelmed by redevelopment and revitalization.

1

All things are from water and all things are resolved into water.

Thales of Miletus, 624 BC–546 BC

A dozen empty paint buckets rattle in the truck bed as Emily and her two uncles, Dwight and Jay, head west on Van Buren to the ragged edges of downtown Phoenix. Dwight drives, and Jay dangles his arm out the passenger window, his palm spread wide to catch the wind, his feet tapping on the floorboard. Citrus-scented air blows in, the night dimly lit by a shard of moon and a scatter of stars. It's 12:30 a.m. It's been five days since they had running water. Dwight says the buckets should hold enough water to last them a couple of weeks.

They pass Daddy Wallet's Check Cashing, a squat wood structure easily mistaken for an oversized hot dog stand, just before the 202 underpass. Dark, half-demolished motels and old abandoned buildings are interspersed among new apartment complexes with high wrought-iron gates. Tall security lights ascend from the grounds of these new structures, an announcement that the old will be demolished and replaced, the way Grandma Marilee said the barrio in Tempe was wiped out when she was a young woman, after Arizona State University needed more land for their buildings.

They took what they wanted, Grandma Marilee said. *The university needed more land for their buildings. Seized it from the people who lived there. Paid them a pittance and razed their homes. How do you think they got so big?*

A little farther west, run-down but still-open motels dot Van Buren, their logos lit in dull neon. Babylon. The Paradise Inn. Motel 8. A large vacant lot separates Ajax Liquors from the

Pink Rhino Strip Club. Shuttered businesses stand on either side of Magic Keys Daycare Center in a derelict strip mall. The Blue Moon Nude Dancers building is across the street. A few blocks east of downtown, a pale outline of Phoenix's high-rise buildings appears against the skyline. Dwight turns left at Fast and Furious Used Cars and into a residential neighborhood. Twinkly lights along the edges of the car lot's roof light up the nearest house.

"This where we're getting water?" Jay licks his thumb and index finger, snuffs out his cigarette, and sets it in the ashtray.

"Stuff's always going down in this kind of neighborhood. Nobody cares," Dwight says.

He parks the truck between two small houses. No cars are in the driveways or on the street in front. A dingy yellow streetlight stands a few feet ahead. A dog barks in the distance but otherwise it's quiet. Houses across the street look deserted—no cars, no porch lights, only black curtainless windows. Weeds grow up around a bike that lies on its side in the front yard of one of them. Yellow police tape wraps around the house next to it. They sit in silence and watch for several minutes.

"Jay, grab a couple of those buckets. I'll take another two."

Jay nods. "Where's the nozzles?"

"How the fuck do I know? We're gonna have to find them." Dwight points to one of the houses. "You take that one."

"Don't you want me to do anything?" Emily says. When she'd asked to come along, she thought he might let her help.

Dwight shakes his head. "Just stay in the truck. You hear or see anything that's not us, flash the headlights one time."

Emily looks at the light switch on the dash. "Okay."

"Key's in the ignition. Leave it be unless I yell otherwise."

"I could get behind the wheel, be the driver."

"Not tonight. Just keep your eyes open."

Dwight and Jay get out of the truck and silently close the doors. They each take two buckets from the back and approach the houses. Dwight finds the outdoor faucet, and water gurgles into the bucket. Jay walks to the back of the other house. *Look on the side, stupid*, Emily thinks. Jay reappears swinging empty buckets. He looks at Dwight and shrugs. Dwight points to the other side of the second house. Jay walks around the front and disappears.

A couple of blocks ahead a car moves slowly through an intersection. It could be a cop patrolling the neighborhood. But it's too dark to see any writing on the side or a siren on the top. The car disappears and comes back a few minutes later going in the opposite direction. When the car comes back a third time, Emily reaches for the light switch but stops. Maybe the person inside the car didn't see the truck. A light to warn Dwight and Jay will for sure attract attention. She crouches in the passenger seat and watches out the front window.

South Mountain rises in the distance, a vertical bulge of darkness, as if the earth needed more space and pushed through its outer skin. Emily can barely make out the peaks. City lights dim the stars. What lies beyond that blackness? Beyond the sprawl of Phoenix and its surrounding deserts? Dwight keeps a *Rand McNally Road Atlas* in the glove box, and in it, California's a few inches west of Phoenix. The Pacific runs the entire vertical length of the map.

The car doesn't cross again, and Emily relaxes.

Dwight walks quickly to the truck, arms at his sides, hands gripping the bucket handles. Jay follows. Water sloshes as they set the buckets in the back. They knock over a few of the empties, which bang against the metal of the truck bed. Emily turns the key in the ignition and watches the intersection ahead. When Dwight and Jay are in the truck, Dwight puts it in drive and speeds back onto Van Buren, toward Tempe.

"Holy shit." Jay giggles and lights up his cigarette butt. A lock of dark brown hair falls over his left eye and his head leans that way, as if pulled to the side by that strand. Jay's thirty-two, but sometimes seems closer to Emily's own seventeen years. That stint in prison must have stunted his brain or something. He reminds her of a defective firecracker that sizzles and burns out before it actually does anything.

Dwight keeps his eyes on the road and occasionally glances in the rearview. "Who told you to start up the ignition?"

Emily can't tell if he's angry. "I don't know. Nobody. You guys seemed in a hurry."

He takes his eyes off the road for a second and looks at her, his face always a mask. He's handsome in a battered sort of way; the world's thrown a lot of shit his direction. But, under his brown mustache and short beard, Emily catches that almost-smile of approval on his face.

"Good thinking."

They pull into the Babylon. The parking lot is tiny. One car is parked in front of a room at the end of a twelve-unit, single-story structure, another in front of the office. A handmade cardboard sign advertising a vacancy hangs on the door, but it's dark inside. A bare bulb, mounted on the exterior wall, sputters on and off. Dwight parks under a fat date palm, about twenty feet from the office. Fronds brush against the truck's roof.

"Keep your eyes on the office." He gets out, walks behind the motel, and reappears a couple of minutes later.

"C'mon, Jay. Faucet's in the back."

They fill four more buckets, put them in the truck, and then go back with the remaining empties. Emily waits. The clock on the dash reads 1:45 a.m. She sees movement at the double window next to the office door. A light comes on inside, and a woman in a nightgown pulls back the drapes. Flab hangs from her upper arms like flesh-colored jelly. She looks directly at the truck. Emily freezes, feels the woman's eyes on her, and for a second imagines they make eye contact. She taps the car horn once, lightly, but doesn't take her eyes off the woman, who quickly closes the curtains. Dwight and Jay reappear with buckets in each hand, race to the truck, and sling them in back. Emily starts the engine and makes room for Dwight.

As Dwight speeds out of the parking lot, a few buckets fall over and water spills into the truck bed. The traffic signal east of the Babylon blinks red. He stops for a second, then floors the gas and races to the 202 entry ramp. The freeway is empty except for a couple of cars heading in the other direction. It's now 2:00 a.m.

"Hot dog!" Jay wears a big grin on his face, legs dancing as if detached from the rest of his body.

"You think she called the cops?" Emily says.

Dwight concentrates on the road, doesn't answer.

Emily turns to the back window. Nothing behind them.

"Don't matter now." Jay winks at Emily, then leans his head out the window as Dwight exits the 202 onto Priest Road and drives toward home.

Jay's an idiot sometimes, but she feels his adrenaline mix with her own and race through her body. Dwight remains stoic, silent. He turns the truck into the driveway of their two-acre property and parks next to the patio. Water covers the truck bed and drips into the dirt. Dwight lifts one of the full buckets and takes it over to the old Airstream trailer that Emily shares with her cousin, Paula, Dwight's daughter.

He sets it down by the door. "This should do you girls for a while. We'll unload the rest tomorrow." He takes another bucket into the adobe house on the other side of the patio.

The Airstream is dark; Paula's probably asleep. Emily sits on the trailer steps. The light-rail rumbles across the bridge over Tempe Town Lake, curves east, and becomes a smear of illumination. She hasn't showered in a week; her scalp itches, and her long dark hair is pulled into a ponytail. When Emily turned the handle on the bathroom faucet last week not a single drop came out. None from the other spigots on their property either, not even the usual drip from the rusty tap in the kitchen. There must have been some warning, because Grandma Marilee had filled the bathtub to the brim. But the water quickly turned filmy, and gnats floated on the surface. Emily splashed her face but passed on washing her hair or using the toilet, which already smelled from not being flushed. *Only flush once a day,* Grandma Marilee said. *Until we get this figured out.*

At first Emily thought *figured out* meant paying the water bill, but she didn't realize the principle at work in Dwight's mind.

She's been peeing in the yard behind the cab of the old semi to avoid the unflushed toilet. The clerk at Quik Stop up the street gave her the bathroom key for other business. It won't be so easy to wash her hair in those buckets. Even if she has two it will be a pain. Two buckets would be enough to fill the toilet tank for at least four flushes, and Dwight's not about to give her two full buckets just for her hair. She glances at the water beside the steps. Already, bits of debris float on top.

The first thing Emily sees when she wakes up is the poster hanging crooked next to the window in the Airstream. The woman in the two-by-three-foot photo wears black-leather, spike-studded bracelets on her wrist. A red-lipstick smirk stretches across her face as she gives the finger to the camera. Emily got the poster for fifty cents a couple of years ago at a garage sale. When she bought it, she'd never heard of Joan Jett, but she liked the way she looked in the poster—like a lady who wouldn't take shit from anybody.

Emily and Paula share a double bed, which takes up most of the trailer. Paula lies with her back to Emily, but Emily senses she's awake.

"You should've come with us," Emily says.

"How much did you guys steal?"

"*Steal* is a complicated word."

"Not really. It's taking what isn't yours." Paula rolls over onto her back.

"The city's the one who stole our water. We were just getting some of it back. The places we got water from still have theirs. Nobody's hurt."

"You sound like my dad."

Maybe she did. *Goddamn city. Crooks think they own water*, Dwight said on their first day without water. Grandma Marilee agreed. *Sons of bitches,* she'd said and shook her head, her voice like gravel, the first cigarette of the day hanging from her lips. They were right. You don't pay for the air you breathe. You don't pay for rain. They don't pay for water in Ireland. Emily had read that in an old *National Geographic* of Marilee's. Dwight's always saying the government should keep its dirty, thieving hands off people's lives and their property and their paychecks. Water's the latest offense. He's going to bypass the city and get free water, the way it should be. But in the meantime, they need to keep those buckets filled.

Emily's eyes roam the water-damaged ceiling of the Airstream that Dwight patched up with heavy duty plastic and duct tape. "Think about it. Water's a natural thing. Why should anyone get to own it in the first place?"

"Whatever."

"Twelve buckets, minus the ones that spilled over. That's how much we got. There's a bucket outside our door."

Emily props herself up on the pillow and recalls the previous night. "There was this fat bitch at the window, with curlers sticking out of her hair all over the place. Looked right at me with beady little eyes buried in her puffy face. I think she called the cops before we raced out of there." She isn't sure about the curlers or the cops. Or even the woman's eyes. But they add a nice touch.

Taped to the wall in the space between Joan Jett and the window is a postcard of Eureka, California. An aerial view. A pier juts into blue ocean, white popcorn clouds float in the sky, and sailboats of various sizes dot the water. A city spreads out in the background and behind it, mountains. Emily knows the postcard by heart, every detail. She found it in a shoebox at the same garage sale as the poster. On the back, the words: *Eureka, California, largest coastal city between San Francisco and Portland. Located on U.S. Route 101 on the shores of Humboldt Bay.* As they walked home from the garage sale, Emily examined the card and said to Paula, *That's where I'm going someday.* And she is. Figure out how to get some money and take off. Get the hell out of Phoenix.

"So, we're supposed to wash ourselves in those buckets?" Paula sits up in the bed. Short auburn curls messily frame her face. She pulls her knees to her chest and rests her chin on them.

Dwight's right about not paying for water, but it is pretty fucked up they can't shower and wash their hair. "Your dad will figure something out. He said he'd get it back on."

"He wouldn't do this if my mom was still here."

Emily doesn't respond. It's true Dwight would've done anything for Ruth. She would have done anything for him too, so who knows about the water.

"She wouldn't let us go without water. She wouldn't like him going out stealing water. He'd listen to her," Paula says.

Emily's careful about what she says when Paula brings up her dead mom. Emily's own mother left when she was five, probably better than having her die when you're thirteen and she's been there all your life. At least Emily never got used to having a mother around. She waits for Paula's thoughts about Ruth to pass but knows they never really do.

Paint peels from the walls; a piece of balsa wood covers the glassless back window. Dwight had traded rebuilding a friend's Harley engine, plus a couple hundred dollars, for the dilapidated Airstream four years ago, in 2006, when Emily and Paula were thirteen. Right before Ruth got sick.

No more than seventeen feet in length, the back corner dented in a good two feet, the insides water-damaged, it had been destined for the junkyard. He removed the wheels, pulled out everything except the sink and cabinet, cleaned it up, and put in a double bed. Before that, Emily and Paula slept in sleeping bags in the living room of the adobe house. Without plumbing in the Airstream, they use the sink for odds and ends, makeup, hair stuff. Their clothes fill the cabinets. A row of books and DVDs spans the width of the floor under the back window.

Paula's eyes fixate on a space just beyond her feet. Emily can't tell if she's still thinking about Ruth. It was a rush getting the water, but Paula's right about the buckets. They'll never work.

Through the trailer's window, the eight-story U.S. Airways building with its blue glass windows and curved roof dominates the street leading to Mill Avenue, the hip downtown area of upscale restaurants and college hangouts. It's less than a five-minute walk from their place, but it seems like another world to Emily. Even when she walks along that street, pops into American Apparel or Urban Outfitters or the ice cream shop where Paula works a few hours a week, she can never shake the feeling that she's an intruder. "You're right. The buckets are bullshit. We can find somewhere to shower and wash our hair. Let's check out the university."

The sprawling university lies beyond what Emily can see through the window. It snakes through downtown and the surrounding area, like some giant desert creature stretching tentacles in every direction. Emily's never figured out exactly where the campus begins.

"It's so huge, no one will notice us," Emily says.

And if they do, who gives a shit? It's not a crime to take a shower.

2

Beneath Grandma Marilee's unsteady feet, the ground pulses, bears witness to the lives of generations who have resided on the property. Morning sun floods in from the east, the air tinged with heat. She separates parched weeds with the makeshift cane Jay fashioned from a thick mesquite branch, swipes at dried foxtails and dandelions, clears a path in front of her to the headstones east of the big orange tree. Brittle Bermuda grass crunches beneath her steps. Just as well for the overgrown weeds; if anyone from the city knew about the graves, some lackey with a piece of paper and a rule would probably issue a citation telling her what she can't do on her own property.

Six stones line up next to one another, earth grown over their edges, but names and dates are visible beneath the loose dirt that covers them. With the bottom of her slipper she sweeps the dirt away as best she can. Three generations of people who lived, died, and were buried on the property. The newest stone is Jack's, 1992. When he died, it had been twenty years since the soil was dug up for a grave. Dwight said it might be better to bury his dad elsewhere. They had just received that first notice from the state and maybe shouldn't risk calling attention to the property by putting another grave on it. Marilee would have none of that. Her husband was going to stay right where she could feel his presence. Later, as time passed, she found things he left in her path—a perfect white rock, not a mark on it, the size and shape of an egg, smooth as shell. And the tiny rose bush that sprang up near the railroad tracks, all on its own with two crimson roses in full bloom and not a single thorn. The dead do things like that, send you little messages.

Marilee supports herself with the mesquite cane and carefully lowers to her knees, feels the hard earth against her old bones. She pushes strands of gray-white hair from her wrinkled face, the rest clipped in a turquoise barrette that slides down the back of her head barely connected as if it's been there for decades, held in place by some off-kilter gravity. Marilee can't remember when she last took that clip out. She leans forward and brushes the remaining debris from Jack's stone, tracing the letters and numbers Dwight chiseled into the stone—Jack Larson, 1925-1992.

She sits back on her heels, catches her breath. The piece of paper Dwight gave her two days ago almost slips from the pocket of her worn cotton dress, material so thin a tug could rip it to shreds. She tucks the paper back in and proceeds to wipe the stone next to Jack's. Maria, her grandmother who raised her, 1892–1972. Marilee continues down the line, cleaning off the remaining stones with her hands, sensing an endurance to the dead, their continued existence in a time parallel to her own, no past or future, everything occurring in the same eternal moment. There's Great-Grandmother Constance, whose brothers, Martino and Alberto, came from Sonora with their parents back when unused land could be claimed. They built the adobe house for Constance and James Baker as a wedding gift. There's Marilee's own parents, Helen and Devin, who died before she really knew them. All of them give a heartbeat to this property. Their breath is in the wind, the dry heat, the monsoon moisture—as if these things hold the segments of time called years and decades and centuries. Nobody's going to raze this family's history like it's some old, dilapidated building. Nobody's going to take this property. Of this she is certain, convinced beyond doubt and rational thought. As long as she lives, this property will stay in the family.

With difficulty, she rises from her knees, presses the mesquite cane into the ground, and stands. She wipes her hands on the sides of her dress, feels for the paper still in her pocket. Dwight usually doesn't show her correspondence from the state. Ever since that first notice, less than a week after Jack died, saying they had no legal claim to ownership, Dwight has handled the property stuff. “I’ll take care of it, Mom,” he said. And she let him. He tore that paper up and put the pieces in the fire pit. A giant cloud of dust rolled in slowly from the south. Hot, creosote-scented air blew furiously, and the piece of paper turned to ashes. She felt a presence on the property as that paper burned, a sense they were being watched over. Those seemingly separate spheres of time fell away.

She rests for a moment, then walks a few feet to the Virgin Mary shed, a ten-by-twelve-foot structure made of wood and corrugated metal with a dirt floor. She sits on a wrought-iron bench in front of the old statue of the Virgin, its left arm broken off, nose chipped away, paint faded. Nearly as tall as Marilee, it leans against the shed’s wall shelves, plastic tarp at its feet. Marilee feels for the half-smoked cigarette in her pocket. She inhales deeply as she lights it, remembers the times Maria knelt on a small rug on the dirt floor to say the Hail Mary. As Maria whispered the words, Marilee stood in the doorway. Her family never went to church or talked about religion, but she watched her grandmother squeeze each little rosary bead as if some essence passed from them into her fingertips. One after the other until Maria reached the end, blessed herself, stood, and pretended to notice for the first time that her granddaughter was watching. At one time Marilee had known all the words, but now she has forgotten most of them, except for the last line, which goes through her head whenever she sits before the statue, smoking a cigarette as she’s done several times a week since Dwight was over in Iraq and she asked for his safety. Not a prayer really. She doesn’t believe in a higher entity to which she might make a plea; she has faith only in what remains of those buried in the graveyard, what continues in that other dimension of time and space. But she asks anyway, doesn’t think too hard about who or what she’s asking. Pray for us sinners, now and at the hour of our death.

Marilee rises from the bench, lets her cigarette fall to the dirt, snuffs it out with the sole of her slipper, and walks back to the patio. On tracks, adjacent to the light-rail that runs parallel to the property, the much older, rickety Union Pacific boxcars clank by from Los Angeles, headed to El Paso. They jangle and rattle and sound like a pile of collapsing metal.

Emily and Paula are on the patio, sitting in plastic chairs, while Dwight and Jay unload the rest of the water buckets from the truck and line them up next to the back door of the adobe house. Jay picks up two of the buckets and takes them inside.

"Put one of those in the bathroom," Marilee calls after him. "And dump some water in the toilet bowl."

"Okay, Mom."

Jay returns and takes another bucket to the makeshift lean-to structure he and Dwight rigged up with a patchwork of wood panels and corrugated metal. Jay sleeps there until it gets too hot in the summer. Then he moves to the sofa in the living room.

Marilee settles into the old Naugahyde recliner, her near-permanent spot on the patio. Another one of Dwight's finds. A string of Tibetan prayer flags, which Jay found in a box of junk Dwight brought home, hangs from the rafter at the edge of the patio's rotting wood frame and wraps around the vertical beam, the fabric nearly disintegrated, the flags little more than strips of rags, most of the color annihilated by the sun, the black letters and symbols faded—a sign that positive energy has been dispersed. Three have come unwound and lie on the concrete.

"Paula honey, pick up those prayer flags, will you."

Paula rises from her chair and walks to the edge of the patio. "You think the prayers have floated away?"

"They don't float," Emily says. "The wind carries them."

"What's the difference?" Paula says.

"Nothing. Forget it."

Float or carried by the wind—Marilee doesn't take sides when the girls bicker.

"I think they might linger," Marilee says. "Maybe that's why nobody's been able to take this property."

She gestures with her hand in as much of a sweeping motion as she can make with arthritis eating at her joints and accidentally knocks two books off the plastic patio table beside her. Emily picks them up and puts them back, next to a blue metal ashtray full of half-smoked cigarettes.

"They're not supposed to touch the ground though, those flags." Marilee lights up one of the half-smoked cigarettes and coughs, a permanent smoker's hack which feels and sounds as if an ugly substance might dislodge from her throat and shoot out her mouth. "It's a sign of disrespect."

Paula lifts the flags and wraps them around the vertical patio beam, tucking the end of the string inside the wrap. Along with the smoke, Marilee inhales the smell of citrus. The orange tree at the northeast edge of the property by the graveyard stands nearly twenty-five feet tall, the biggest one she's ever seen in Phoenix and the only one left from what Maria told her used to be a small grove before they damned up the river, back before Marilee was even born. But she knows what the riverfront used to look like from photos Maria showed her, the images as real as what lies before her eyes this late spring morning. Except for the berm around the orange tree, the north half of the property is now all desert scrub and overgrown weeds scratching their way to the chain-link fence that runs along most of the northern perimeter. Beyond the fence, Tempe Town Lake.

Marilee imagines the rolling river licking the shore just over the rise of earth where a dock and big ferry boat used to stand. Women in long dresses with fancy umbrellas shield their faces from the sun; men with pointy beards and top hats stand by their sides. The images are as vivid as the placid lake bordered by a concrete walkway, a freeway in the background.

The thing Marilee wishes she could conjure right now, bring to life with the clarity of this late April day, is the deed to the property. What hands did it pass through? Where did it come to rest? Did she ever actually see a deed? Did Jack put it somewhere for safekeeping? She can't remember. Until eighteen years ago she never had a reason to think about such a piece of paper. The land was just there, and the family had lived on it for over a hundred years. Nobody bothered them. Nobody cared about the land. The river dried up when Roosevelt Dam opened in 1911, long before Marilee was born. Who wanted a piece of land next to a dried-up riverbed where people dumped their garbage?

"Who wants to take this property?" Emily asks. "You said those prayer flags—"

"Nothing for you girls to worry about," Marilee says. "The state's not going to take anything."

The latest notice Dwight had shown her, the one in her dress pocket, said they had to be off their property by August 31st.

"Why are they trying to take it?" Paula asks.

Marilee snuffs out her cigarette, which has burned to the filter, retrieves another butt from the ashtray, and lights it. "Some stupid mistake about paperwork."

"Did Dad not pay a bill?"

Marilee shakes her head. "It's got nothing to do with paying anything. They're just a bunch of thieves."

She pictures minions of the state descending upon the property like a swarm of insects, official documents in their ugly mouths.

"Same people who shut off our water?"

"No, that's the city. And we're going to get that water back on. Your dad's taking care of that."

It wasn't a complete surprise when the city turned off their water. Dwight had stopped paying two months back. They could have paid the overdue bills and the fee for turning it back on, but Dwight said no. No more. *We're not paying for something we're entitled to. Government's got no right to charge people for it.*

Jack used to say the same thing. *Water's free in some places*, he said. *No bills, no water meters. Folks have a right to it and they get it. Should be like that everywhere*. But Jack never could figure a way around the city and kept on paying. They couldn't be without water. Dwight said it'd be only a couple of days; he's going to outsmart them. He hasn't explained exactly how he's going to get the water back on. Tap into some nearby is what he said. Maybe one of the businesses the other side of the railroad tracks. Marilee doesn't care about the details. He'll handle the notice about the property too. The government can't just take away a thing somebody's had for over a hundred years. She'll hunt again for the title though, the way she did back when the first notice came and like she does every time she sees unopened envelopes from the state lying on the kitchen table. Dwight always says he'll handle them. For the past three years, she's wracked her brain to remember if there was ever any mention of a title, but it's just a blur. She'll start all over, scour every inch of the house, all those shelves of books in the living room and her bedroom and the boxes in the Virgin Mary shed.

When the water starts flowing again, the first thing she's going to do is drench those dried-up clovers that grow wild around the mesquite tree in the middle of the property. Folks say they're weeds and maybe they are, but they're pretty and they remind her of shamrocks. And shamrocks are supposed to carry good fortune.

3

Energy radiates from the concrete and asphalt along University Avenue. Cars, motorcycles, bikes, and pedestrians crowd the streets near the campus. Emily and Paula pass three men and a woman, who could be students, but their backpacks stretch to the limit, on the verge of bursting like Billy's and the backpacks of the other homeless guys who sleep beneath the two paloverde trees on the property. Each man's skin is deeply tanned and leathery, the woman's not much better. A guy in a cowboy hat, white beard to his chest, sleeps on the sidewalk in front of the United Methodist Church, his back propped against a low red-brick wall, a dog by his side.

Emily and Paula stop at the traffic light across from an aqua-blue building that rises above all the others in the vicinity. Emily counts six floors. The morning sun creates a splintered glow from the upper floors to the street below. Silver, all-capital letters protrude from the top to form a seventy-five-degree angle with the street and spell EXCELLENCE.

Emily gestures toward the building. "Let's try that one."

When the signal changes, Emily and Paula cross and approach the building. A plaque in front displays the ASU logo, maroon letters against a gold sun. Men wearing suits and women in stiff skirts enter and exit. They walk with authority, make the air move out of their way. A different species. The kind Dwight warns against.

Inside, a rectangular plaque made of beige wood with bronze lettering attached to a metal column reads: Here We Celebrate Philanthropy. To the left is the women's bathroom. Emily opens the door to a room that is all silver and chrome and marble, with four aqua-blue translucent stall doors that match the outside of the building. A row of four sinks hangs from the wall. The floor looks like glass, as if it would crack under too much weight.

"Jesus Christ. Do you believe this place?"

Paula opens a couple of stall doors. "I don't see any showers here."

"At least we can wash our hair." Emily walks to the far sink. "Where's the faucet? How do you turn the water on?"

Paula shrugs, then presses the buttons on the sink, and water spurts from the hot and cold spigots. "Cool."

Emily pulls the rubber band from her ponytail, dunks her head under the flowing water, and feels around for soap until she locates the dispenser. Soft, creamy liquid spills into her palm; a lemony fragrance fills her nostrils as she massages the soap through her thick hair and into her scalp. Sudsy water splashes her temples and the sides of her face. She squeezes her eyes shut and turns her head from side to side as the grime falls away. When the water stops, she presses the faucet buttons again and lets the glorious liquid wash over every inch of her head and face until all the soap rinses out. She wrings her hair into a long twist and stands up. Water drips down her neck, her chest, and her shoulders onto the glass-like floor. "You see any paper towels?"

"No. Just this." Paula presses the bar on the wall dryer, and warm air blasts from it. Emily puts her head underneath.

"Your turn, Paula."

Paula sticks her head in the same sink and quickly lathers her short curly hair. Emily runs fingers through her own long tangles, takes a small, black comb from her back pocket, and trawls it through. High heels click on the tile outside the bathroom. The door opens. Emily watches in the mirror as a woman walks in and looks at them, startled. She wears a royal blue skirt that comes to just above her knees and a matching blazer. Her blond hair turns under in such a perfect pageboy it could be a wig. Bright pink lipstick. Shiny beige stilettos. The strap from the woman's brown leather bag crosses her chest from right shoulder to left hip. Emily continues combing her hair. Without taking her eyes off the woman, Emily reaches over and nudges Paula, whose head is still under the faucet. The woman moves her pink lips as if about to say something but changes her mind and goes into one of the stalls.

Emily taps Paula's shoulder again.

Paula raises her head from the still-running water and shakes out her hair. Soapy water flies. "What?"

"Let's go." Emily nods toward the stall with the woman inside.

The toilet flushes. The woman opens the door, looks at them again, and proceeds to the sink farthest away from where they stand. They walk quickly out of the bathroom and through the doors to the street, Paula's hair dripping.

"We'll stay away from that building."

"I've still got soap in my hair."

"Here, comb it through." Emily passes her comb to Paula.

They've been inside the perimeters of the university only once before, inside a building called Gammage Memorial Auditorium. Grandma Marilee and Ruth took them to see *The Nutcracker* for Christmas when they were six, the year after Emily's mom, Phyllis, left. Every time she passes that building, Emily thinks of the Nutcracker-turned-prince driving his sleigh through a glittering forest, snowflakes turning into dancing maidens. This image is permanently linked to that of the snow globe with the white flakes Phyllis sent from Las Vegas shortly after she left.

The campus extends in all directions, a maze of old and new buildings, some with lots of windows, several stories high, others low and windowless. Walkways branch to the left and right. The path Emily and Paula walk is wide and packed with pedestrians, bikers, skateboarders, and small motorized carts. All these young people, not much older than she is, with backpacks casually slung over shoulders, making their way through this campus, big as a city. This world so close to home, a world Emily has prowled the edges of, always sensing a foreignness, an off-limits place where she doesn't belong. The people here walk through life as if under some special light that bestows them with material things out of her own reach. And other stuff, harder to name.

Up ahead, water. A fountain shoots an arc of silver spray into the air. Circular concrete benches surround the fountain. Students sit with open books and laptops, the misting water behind them. Emily imagines walking past the students to the center of the fountain, crystal spray washing over her.

A few feet from the fountain, a large two-story structure displays fast-food logos on its exterior: Taco Bell, Pizza Hut, Jimmy Johns, Starbucks. Shade panels mounted on tall poles cover the patio in front of the building. Thick chains wrap around the legs of the tables and chairs and attach to metal inserts in the concrete. Beyond, a rectangular, single-story, older brick building with "Physical Education" over the double-door entry.

"Let's check this out." Emily stops in front of the building and pushes open one of the doors to a large, empty foyer with a hallway to the right. Inside, it smells like rubber. On the wall near the entrance is a bulletin board filled with flyers and announcements. One of them catches Emily's eye. *FRESHMEN WOMEN, EARN $25 AND A CHANCE TO WIN AN ADDITIONAL $75* in large red capital letters. Emily tears off one of the slips with the contact information and sticks it in her back pocket.

Emily points to the hallway. "C'mon. Let's see what's down there."

At the end of the hallway is a beige door with a WOMEN sign on it. She and Paula enter and find a locker room, which is full of girls in gym shorts and T-shirts or wrapped in towels, fresh from the showers, their skin glistening with beads of water. Tanned bodies and shaved legs so smooth and shiny they could be life-sized dolls. Whiffs of fragrances radiate from them. Emily touches her now-dry, clean hair, but feels sticky sweat on her skin and thinks of the stale smell of the homeless, the filthy tub water back at the house.

Two chatty, giggly girls look at Paula and Emily as if they are trespassers. Emily meets the eyes of one, a blond with a perky ponytail and flushed cheeks. Emily levels her gaze the way Dwight did when that guy from the City of Tempe came to the door last summer about all the junk on the property and the overgrown weeds. She wants to say, *Fuck you, bitch. What are you looking at?* Instead, she smiles.

"What team are you girls on?" the ponytail girl asks. "I haven't seen you in here before."

"No team. We go to Tempe High. We're just visiting," Emily says.

The girl gives Emily the kind of smile an adult might give a child. "Oh, you're with that new student tour?"

Emily nods. "Yeah. We'll be here next year. We got separated over at that Starbucks and Taco Bell building."

"You mean the Memorial Union."

"Yeah."

"Well, the gym's over there." The girl points to two double doors. "If you want to take a look."

"Thanks."

"And that other door goes outside to the track and field."

The two girls pick up backpacks from one of the benches and leave. Emily and Paula hang around the locker room until it is empty. Steam still rises from the stalls, and Emily can almost feel the hot water on her skin.

"Do you want to rinse your hair now?" she says.

Paula shakes her head, runs her fingers through her curls. "It's okay. I think the soap is all combed out."

Gym shorts and ASU gold and maroon T-shirts lie on the benches along with backpacks. Several of the lockers are open, clothes strewn over their doors.

Emily takes a T-shirt and a pair of shorts from the bench, rolls them up, and puts them under her arm. She passes another shirt to Paula.

"We'll blend in better with these," she says.

"We're just taking them?"

"You think these girls can't get another pair of shorts and a shirt? They probably get them free."

"Yeah, but—"

"Shit, Paula. Just take it for fuck's sake."

Paula takes the shirt.

Emily grabs a pair of shorts hanging from one of the lockers. "We should get out of here." She shoves them at Paula.

A silver chain with a locket on the floor catches Emily's eye. She scoops it up. As they pass the bulletin board, she takes the entire flyer about the chance to earn twenty-five dollars.

"That was easy," Emily says as they walk through campus.

"We could have gotten caught. Like you and Jay and my dad could have."

Emily ignores Paula's comment. "What team are you girls on?"

"What?"

"That girl asked us what team we were on. What team do you want to be on, Paula?" Emily laughs. "You can be on my team."

"You're nuts."

Emily smiles. "We can come over here a couple times a week. Until your dad gets our water back on."

"What if we run into those girls again?"

"We'll go at different times. Don't worry so much. Did you notice a lot of those lockers were unlocked?"

"So?"

"Nothing." Emily takes the silver chain out of her pocket and hooks it around her neck.

"What's that?"

"It was just lying on the floor."

They reach the edge of campus, cross Mill Avenue, and head toward home.

Emily takes the stolen T-shirt and pulls it on. It smells like lilacs. At first it makes her think of the perky ponytail girl, but she gets used to it and begins to think of it as her own. Nobody owns the smell of flowers anyway.

4

A rush of wind through the gun shed's open door scatters fine grains of powder over Dwight's work counter. Late afternoon heat has made the shed stuffy. For a second, he's back on that highway of dust and smoke in Iraq. Images of burning vehicles surge to the surface, the endless char and sprawl of bodies forever ingrained in his head. He brushes away the gunpowder and shuts off the load press. He pushes his stool away from the counter, steps outside, and locks the door.

He settles into one of the plastic chairs under the mesquite tree, tamps tobacco in his pipe, and lights it. He puffs deeply, watches the swirl of cherry-scented smoke rise. An Austin Healey convertible pulls up to the curb and parks. Dwight recognizes the car and the driver's hat, a Panama fedora with a black silk band. Wilkins.

Wilkins unfolds his legs, steps out of the small car, and waves to Dwight. Dwight nods as the man walks toward the mesquite.

"What now?" Dwight says as Wilkins approaches.

"They've been trying to get this land for a while, haven't they?"

"They can try all they want."

Wilkins gestures toward a chair. "You mind?"

"Be my guest."

Wilkins sits down, takes off his hat, and puts it on his lap.

"I love this godforsaken desert." Wilkins's dull brown hair, streaked with gray, lies flat against his skull, moist with sweat from the hat. Wiry strands hang behind his ears. He wipes the back of his hand across his forehead. "It can't get hot enough for me."

"I guess you're in the right place."

"Came here thirty-three years ago. Fresh out of graduate school."

That makes him older than Dwight first thought. Mid-sixties maybe.

"No one cares about Central America anymore."

"What?"

"That's my area of expertise," Wilkins says. "At the university. Political risk assessment."

Dwight doesn't bother to ask what the hell that is.

"I'm irrelevant now. It's all design and sustainability. Young baby faces with big data sets."

"Man, I don't know what the fuck you're talking about."

"I'm talking about real estate."

"You got an interesting way of putting things."

"Something concrete. A physical thing a man can build on, make creations. Like this place you got here."

"Nobody's building anything here."

Wilkins gazes at the adobe house, the sheds, the Airstream, the street leading to Mill Avenue. "I already own some land down off State Highway 79. Picked it up cheap in 2008. The crash killed any dreams of a sun corridor connecting Maricopa to Pinal counties. They're dead now, those properties, but who knows in a few years. This whole desert's a gold mine."

"You mind getting to the point, Wilkins? I already told you I'm not selling."

"I've got some other places in Superior. Some rentals in Phoenix and Apache Junction." Wilkins looks at Dwight. "You couldn't sell even if you wanted, could you?"

"What the fuck do you want, Wilkins?" The guy's starting to ruin Dwight's pipe-smoking time.

"I'd like to buy a small piece of your property."

"You already told me that."

"You could sue for the title. Make them give you a deed to the property."

Wilkins wears a different smile now than last week. Almost a smirk, but the arrogance doesn't appear directed at Dwight.

"What makes you think I don't already have a title?"

Wilkins runs his hand through his hair, still wet with sweat that trickles down his temples. "Well, I don't think you'd be in this trouble with the property if you had a title. State ever try to collect property taxes?"

In fact, they hadn't. Dwight didn't believe in taxes; he might not have paid them anyway, at least not after Ruth was gone. The government's scrutinized just about everything, but Dwight's never seen one tax bill. He shakes his head.

"That's because they think it's their property. If you don't own the property, they can't collect taxes from you. As far as they're concerned, you don't own it."

He should have thought of that. But when it comes to bull-shit from the government about the property, Dwight mostly tries to push it out of his mind, ignore it. The way he'd burned up that first notice after his dad died.

"I know that. What do you want, Wilkins?"

"I get you a lawyer and pay the legal expenses. You get your title. In return, you sell me a piece of your two acres. Minus the legal fees."

"Why would the state give me a title if they think we don't own the property?"

"Your family's been here all this time. A long time before the state said anything, tried to take it. There's a legal concept, laches. It means they delayed too long."

"You think I can't get my own lawyer?"

"Sure you can. I notice you haven't done it though. Must be a reason."

Dwight doesn't respond to this. He doesn't like lawyers, doesn't trust them any more than he trusts the government. And they cost money. Why should he have to pay to keep his own property?

"Which part of my land do you want?" Dwight reaches into a cooler and pulls out two cans of Budweiser. He offers one to Wilkins.

"I've been thinking about that." Wilkins takes the can of beer, hesitates as if waiting for a glass to be offered, then pops the top and drinks.

"I bet you have."

Wilkins points to the spot he took pictures of the week before. "That area over there would be perfect for some kind of small establishment."

Dwight takes a swig of beer, contemplates the area where the homeless guys sleep. For as long as he can remember there've been homeless on the property. They come and go, never more than three or four at a time. "This family's always been kind to the less fortunate," Marilee told him and Jay and Phyllis when they were growing up. "We got plenty of space." Sometimes his dad hired them for odd jobs.

"All those tenants when those condos across the street are completed." Wilkins looks at the construction site. "Maybe a convenience store, or bar. A café. Maybe I'd just hang on to it, let it appreciate. I'd separate it off from the rest of your property, of course."

"You'd cut down those paloverde, wouldn't you? To build your little establishment." He and Ruth had planted them a few months before Paula's birth.

Wilkins shrugs. "Maybe, maybe not. Depends on what I put there."

What he puts there—as if the earth were an empty Monopoly board just waiting for little pieces to be placed on it, moved around, traded for other little pieces. Dwight's eyes go again to the construction site. Nearly a block long, rising like a fucking monument. He's read that the university bought up the land for a retirement community. When they're done, that's all he'll see when he looks west. When did space become a thing to be used up, filled in, put a price on?

"I need to think about this, Wilkins."

"Absolutely. And, please, call me Gene. You still have my card?"

Dwight nods. Wilkins stands up to go, puts his hat on. He finishes off the beer and sets the can on the ground. "They call it adverse possession, Dwight. You and your family have been here a long time. You've got certain rights. Squatter's rights."

"I know I've got rights, Wilkins. And we're not squatters."

Dwight watches Wilkins get in his Austin and drive away. He snuffs out his pipe and lights up a cigarette.

Wilkins first showed up a week ago. Dwight had been working on the old yellow school bus when he saw the man walking along the sidewalk. He'd gone to the end of the cul-de-sac, on an expanse of grass before the concrete pathway and the lake. He stopped and looked out at the water, then turned around, pulled out a cell phone, and snapped photos of Dwight's property and surrounding area. He backtracked a few feet, stood in front of the two paloverde, and snapped photos of the three rolled up sleeping bags that rested on the ground.

Dwight approached him and said, "I notice you been eyeballing my place. There something you want here?"

The guy extended his right hand. "Eugene Wilkins. Gene."

His handshake was limp, maybe the man feared the dirt and grease on Dwight's rough hand would rub off. In contrast, Wilkins's hand felt soft. It was clean, nails manicured, a large gold ring with a ruby stone on his left ring finger. The guy probably hadn't done a real day's work ever. He wore a tweed jacket even though the mercury already hovered above one hundred degrees. The man's denim slacks, so precisely and firmly pressed, resembled lengths of cardboard encasing his legs.

"Nice spread you got here," Wilkins said. His shoulders pitched forward as if in preparation to take off in flight. "Ever think of selling?"

"Nope. You a developer?"

He reminded Dwight of one of those long-necked herons down at the lake.

"Not exactly. I just dabble a little in real estate. I'm a professor. Over at the business college." Wilkins gestured toward the university as if Dwight might not know its location.

Dwight nodded in the same direction. "You got a pretty big spread over there yourself."

Wilkins laughed. Not a real laugh, more like when a person

thinks they're being polite, sharing a little joke with you, but really, they're standing off in another world high above yours, a world they think you wouldn't understand a thing about, wouldn't have the capacity to comprehend, and that you wouldn't recognize as an insult because you are an uneducated idiot. Arrogant fucker.

"Seems you guys wanna take over the whole town. You and those banks and insurance companies lined up along the lake. And that airline."

"You've got a lot of land. Even a small parcel would be worth a bit of money. The area's prime. Lots of opportunity."

"Right, it's prime for my family's home. Nothing else."

Wilkins looked around the property. His eyes stopped at the school bus. "What are you doing with that bus?"

"Refurbishing."

The bus had been on the property for fifteen years. Dwight bought it from a guy he served with in Iraq. Leroy Barnes from El Paso. Leroy's family owned a business, buying and selling used school buses and old Greyhounds. "You'd be surprised, the market for them," he'd said to Dwight. "Folks gut 'em and turn them into campers. Some even live in them." The idea appealed to Dwight. The bus became one of his many projects.

He had pulled out all the seats except the driver's; most still lie on the ground around the bus, frames rusted, cushions ripped up. A couple over by the paloverde. He starts up the engine from time to time, moves it a few feet back and forth. He's going to take Emily and Paula on a trip when he gets it all renovated.

"Nobody's complained about all this stuff?" Dwight followed Wilkins's eyes as the man surveyed the other in-process and not-yet-started jobs scattered about the property. A couple of motorcycles, a semi minus the engine, an old Mercedes body Dwight isn't sure what he'll do with. Maybe he'll sell it for scrap metal.

Wilkins probably pegged him as some kind of hoarder. Fuck him.

"Like I said. I'm not interested in selling anything. Unless, of course, you're interested in a bicycle." Dwight pointed to a pile of old bikes leaning against the side of his gun shed. They were covered over with fallen palm fronds. "Maybe you dabble in those too?"

That laugh again. "Just in case you ever rethink." He handed Dwight a card and extended his hand again, before sauntering back to his Austin.

Dwight took the card and glanced at it, then put it in his back pocket.

The guy had riled Dwight. One of those people who thought the place was filled with useless crap, like that asshole from the city with the notice to clean it up—or cover his projects with tarps, or put them behind a solid fence so they weren't visible from the street. But every goddamned thing can be made worth something. Enough to make a living on. Potential always catches Dwight's eye; the possibility of salvaging what others think is junk. Like the Airstream.

Wilkins also brought to mind things Dwight didn't want to think about—the property and the disregarded order for his family to get off their own land. It's become too valuable to ignore, fucking high-rises and condos and upscale everything all around them. Maybe he should have handled it differently. His mom in such a state over the loss of Jack, just handed him the notice. He said he'd take care of it, but what the hell was he supposed to do with it? "You got the title?" he asked her. She didn't know. Didn't remember. "There must be one somewhere. We've just always been here, Dwight." The state's threat had been feeble. Downtown Tempe wasn't a destination point back then; the lake didn't even exist. He took over his dad's business, married Ruth, and put the notice out of mind. The state seemed to forget about it too. Until three years ago, 2007, when that official from the city started digging. Said Dwight's family never even owned the property. Said they'd been squatters all this time, still were. Squatters. That's when his mom started looking for a title. Tore the house apart, couldn't find one.

5

Paula points to the sign in front of True Lord Rebirth Church. An invitation to *join our loving community for the grand-opening service. Celebrate the resurrection of Christ. Easter brunch following the 10:30 a.m. service, April 25.* "Let's go there tomorrow."

True Lord, a one-room, single-story building that was once Sombrero's Taco Shop, now transformed into a place of worship, stands three blocks south of the property. Freshly painted sandy beige, the colorful drawing of an oversized sombrero on the front door replaced with a crudely sketched crucifix that covers most of the surface. Streaks of the faded yellow, green, and fuchsia sombrero brim show through the new paint. Above the crucifix, bright purple letters spell True Lord Rebirth.

"Church?" Emily sounds as if Paula has asked her to step in front of a light-rail barreling through downtown.

"We can check out the Easter food. We're not doing anything else."

They have been inside a church only once before, for the service for Paula's mom. What would a service be like if it weren't for someone who died?

Emily shakes her head.

"C'mon. You like exploring, Emily. What are you afraid of?"

"I'm not afraid of anything. I just don't like bullshit. Religious bullshit. Why do you want to go to church anyway?"

"I don't know." Churches make Paula think of her mom. There's another one on the way to Tempe Library, bigger than True Lord. Attached to a school with a playground. Every time she and Emily ride the bus to the library, Paula looks at that church and thinks of her mom. As if some eternal, ethereal part of her inhabits all churches.

"Aren't you even a little curious? Why people go to church?"

Emily looks at her, the way she does sometimes, boring into the deepest center of Paula. "You mean when it's not for a funeral?"

"Yeah."

"I don't care why they go to church. People do lots of stupid things."

"Forget it, if you think it's so stupid."

That look again, then Emily's face softens. "Okay, Paula. Okay, I'll go with you."

The service for her mother had been at a big church in Phoenix. Out of respect for Ruth's parents, Paula's dad had agreed to let her mom be buried at a cemetery near the church. Or maybe he was just too devastated to put up a fight. They all went, even Jay. They hadn't had much contact with her mother's side of the family. Grandma Marilee said they didn't approve of Dwight's lifestyle, whatever that meant. Paula remembered her mom taking her to her grandparents' house in North Phoenix once, an older place with a manicured desert landscape, tall palms in the front, citrus trees in back, and a dog, a little yippy one with wiry fur that growled at Paula and peed at her feet. One Christmas they sent Paula a green sweater with red trim and a silver tree embroidered on the front.

The funeral service was the clearest memory Paula had of her grandparents. They looked younger than Grandma Marilee, but somehow seemed older. Her grandfather was tall and skinny and wore his hair shaved so close to his scalp that from a distance he appeared bald. Her grandmother hugged Paula tightly, then placed her hands on Paula's shoulders and held her there, looking at her face and into her eyes. "You look just like her," she said sadly, then let her hands fall from Paula's shoulders and turned away. The minister spoke of her mother as if they were close friends. His eyes scanned the congregation, which seemed like a lot to Paula, people she'd never seen before. She sat between her dad and Grandma Marilee in the front row. Grandma Marilee occasionally reached around Paula and squeezed Dwight's shoulder, then laid her hand over Paula's.

"I know most of you," the minister said. "Some of you are strangers." His eyes came to rest on Jay, Marilee, Emily, Paula, and her dad. "But we are all God's flock today and we are all here for Ruth." He looked directly at Paula or at least she thought he did. "Her soul lives on in each of us," he said.

Paula had turned and looked around the nearly full church. The minister made her think that all those people had known and loved her mother and that she had been the center of a close family whose shared grief would now bring them even closer.

"Ruth possessed a pure heart," the minister said. "Now she's in a better place, a place of eternal peace."

As he spoke, Paula tried to visualize the physical surroundings of that place of eternal peace, but all she could conjure were vague, hazy images of white clouds and shadowy figures. And only for a minute did she fathom the thought that her mom might be in a better place. As soon as the minister took a breath and stopped speaking, the whole thing became incomprehensible. How can someone just not exist anymore?

Her dad's face was pale and drawn through the whole service. He held his right hand to his temple, his eyes on the floor in front of him; occasionally he looked up at the open casket at the front of the church, a long beige and white box that contained Ruth's body. Paula only dared to look at the bottom half, which was closed, and the flowers which appeared to her as colorful, distorted monster faces. More than once Paula saw her dad wipe his eyes. Before the service was over, he got up and walked out of the church and waited for them near the front door. On the way home, he said the preacher had never even met Ruth. The funeral was the last time Paula saw her mom's parents.

True Lord is nothing like what Paula remembers of the big church in Phoenix, but it still makes her think of that day. The first thing she sees when they walk through the door is a large crucifix hanging on the wall, a real one, not a painting like out front. A Jesus figure made of metal hangs its head; hair falls over the shoulders, hands and feet nailed to the cross.

Tracks of red paint representing blood drip from his wounds. At the big church, Marilee had nodded toward a similar one and whispered to her, "That's the crucifixion of Jesus." At True Lord, two smaller crosses with men whose ankles and wrists are bound with rope hang on either side of Jesus. Beneath the crosses, three lavender candles flicker on a rectangular card table covered with a white lace cloth. Metal folding chairs are arranged in rows, the small room about two-thirds full. Emily and Paula sit in the back.

The man who seems to be in charge, a priest or whatever he's called, stands behind the table, dressed in a long, dark-purple robe, trimmed in gold. He speaks of death and resurrection. And transformation. "After they killed Jesus and buried him behind a huge stone, he came back," the man says. "Moved that boulder and rose right up into heaven." The people in the metal folding chairs nod.

"His disciples had scurried away like rats. Betrayed Jesus, our savior Lord, son of the Father, but they were transformed. Reborn."

All eyes fix on this man in purple, the room silent except for a small boy in the seat next to Paula. He picks his nose and periodically kicks the leg of his own chair and the one in front of him, which is empty and moves a little each time his foot makes contact. Paula waits to hear more about this resurrection and transformation. The preacher takes a deep breath, closes his eyes for a second, then opens them widely. "Metamorphosis," he shouts, "is a supreme work of nature." He looks around the congregation as if waiting for the depth of this statement to fully sink in. "The monarch butterfly is an example," he says. "But the earthworm is different. It will never transmute."

Paula glances at Emily whose face is twisted into a what-the-fuck frown.

"We are butterflies." He spreads his arms like wings, the purple robe flutters as if hit by a gust of wind. "Earthworms slither along the streets of our towns and cities. Don't ever forget that. They will never achieve salvation."

Paula looks around the room, an expression of intense focus on most of the faces, as if the meaning of this man's words requires concentration. A couple of women in the same row as her and Emily have their eyes closed, chins raised toward the ceiling and the heavens beyond. "Faith takes time," the minister at her mom's service said. "It grows from seeds, like vegetables in a garden." These people must have planted their seeds a while ago. Their faces look peaceful. Grandma Marilee said her mother's face looked peaceful after she died, but Paula could only think about those mocking flowers at the foot of her mother's coffin.

"Ezekiel 36." The preacher's voice booms.

The boy next to Paula has dozed off but awakens abruptly.

"Root transformation." The priest turns and gestures to the three crosses on the wall behind him. "Jesus and the two thieves. He gave them redemption before they died. A new spirit, and a new heart to take to heaven."

Several people in the room murmur sounds of agreement. And without further explanation, the preacher continues almost in a whisper. "Then the resurrection." He folds his hands in prayer, his head lowers to his chest. The people in the metal chairs bow their heads.

"Amen," they say in unison, the service over.

Everyone moves to the small backyard of the church where women scurry about laying out food on two folding tables, cold cuts in Safeway wrappers, a large cake with white icing, and a lavender crucifix made of gum drops on top. A bowl of miniature chocolate bunnies sits in the middle of the table. Emily and Paula take some food. Emily picks a few gumdrops off the crucifix. They sit at one of the smaller tables.

"What the fuck was all that?" Emily whispers to Paula.

Paula elbows her in the ribs.

A woman wearing a faded orange and blue scarf wrapped around her head sits next to Paula. "I think there must be a creator who understands all the chaos in the world," she says. "Does that make sense?"

Paula nods and pokes Emily again before she makes a comment.

"We're all equal in this heat." The woman wipes her forehead. "Trying to get cool, right? Does that make sense?"

"Yes, it sure does."

The woman reaches for one of the chocolate bunnies on her plate. Paula counts six of them. They've begun to melt. The woman puts one in her mouth and says, "I received my faith three years ago. Before that…" She shakes her head. "Does that make sense?"

Paula nods and tries not to stare at the chocolate ringing the woman's mouth. The woman wipes her mouth and doesn't speak again. She stares at a piece of ham and American cheese on her plate and picks at them. The woman is still staring at her plate when Emily and Paula finish eating and get up to leave. As they step away from the table, an elderly woman approaches them. She places a hand on Paula's shoulder.

"You girls come join us anytime." She smiles and hands Paula a card.

"Thank you," Paula says.

"That prayer's worth thirty days off purgatory," the woman says.

Paula smiles and thanks her again. The woman smells of roses and talcum powder.

"Let me see that," Emily says as they walk away from the church.

The card contains a scene of people surrounded by flames with their arms extended into the air above them. On a flat cloud, Jesus stands with a staff, the Virgin Mary beside him. Two angels hover over the burning people, one angel's hands reaching for a woman on fire. Paula turns the card over. At the top are the words: *Pray for the holy souls in purgatory.* Beneath that a prayer. Paula passes it to Emily.

"This is just bizarre shit," Emily says.

"I know." Emily's right, the whole service was pretty weird, but maybe it isn't always like that. "Maybe if we knew more…"

Emily returns the card to her, and Paula puts it in her pocket.

"Do you ever feel like you want to believe in something, Emily?"

"I believe in lots of stuff."

"Like what?"

"California. I believe in California. I believe I'm going there."

"I mean other things. Bigger things."

"Like those people at the church?"

Paula shrugs. They pass their property and walk to Tempe Town Lake. "Maybe it was just an Easter thing. Maybe all the services aren't like that."

The boat rental kiosk is ahead, and several people stand in line. The old lady at True Lord was so nice and she made Paula feel like she belonged there. Something about the place felt safe, as if those people shared something. Maybe they understood the preacher better than she did because they went all the time. Maybe you had to give it more time, listen to more of what he had to say.

"Metamorphosis," Emily says loudly as they pass the kiosk.

"What?"

"Metamorphosis!" She practically screams it, then laughs.

"What are you talking about?"

"That book Grandma Marilee had us read when we started homeschool."

When they were thirteen, Dwight decided they should be homeschooled. Ruth and Marilee would figure out the details. But when Ruth got sick, everything fell apart. Except the books. Grandma Marilee has shelves of them in the living room, and more were stacked floor to ceiling in her bedroom. Their homeschooling became one book a week, then two. Marilee checked up on their progress once a week at first, asked questions about what they had read. Apparently, she had read every single book in the house. *You don't need permission from a school to read,* she said.

When Ruth got sick, Paula read to her. Ruth said she liked listening to the sound of Paula's voice. She closed her eyes and smiled as Paula read to her. That's the face Paula tries to picture when she thinks of Ruth.

"The first book we read. Remember? About the guy who turns into a roach. Isn't that what the weird guy in purple was talking about? That stuff about transformation?"

"He was talking about Jesus and the thieves."

"Yeah, but the thing was transformation." Emily again shouts the way the man at True Lord had. "Metamorphosis!"

"Okay, okay. The preacher was weird. That book creeped me out."

"People are like that. Underneath what you think you see. Like those girls we saw in the gym locker room. It was like they had some kind of power, like they could just step on us. What kind of insects are they? After their metamorphosis? I think they're roaches, like the guy in the book. A squashed roach, scaly with icky white stuff that oozes out when you step on it."

"God, Emily. What the heck are you talking about?" But Paula pictures the girls in the locker room with roaches' heads.

"I'm talking about transformation. Today's topic is transformation."

Paula shakes her head.

"That minister or preacher, or whatever he is, was talking about transformation like it's a good thing. It might be a shitty thing, something ugly underneath what people show."

"So?"

"I'm just saying, is all."

They're almost to the end of the lake. High-rise office buildings, some completed, some under construction, line the street to the south.

"What about us, Emily? What about my dad and Jay and Grandma Marilee? What are we?"

Emily frowns a little, then says, "Jay's a daddy longlegs."

Paula laughs. "Perfect. And Grandma Marilee's a Queen Bee."

"Your dad's a hard one. I need to think about that."

"And you. And me. What are we?"

Emily thinks for a minute. "You know those tiny green bugs

that come around in the summer? With the sheer, almost see-through wings?"

"Yeah."

Emily calls them fairies, says never to kill one because they live only a couple of years. Then they come back as stars and live forever. "That's what we are, Paula. Fairy bugs."

"I like that."

"I thought you would." Emily smiles.

Emily talks crazy shit sometimes, dark stuff that makes Paula feel the world is total crap. Like the Phoenix bird story Grandma Marilee told them a couple of years ago.

That's where this city got its name, Grandma Marilee said. In Greek mythology, a bird with gold and red feathers and eyes like blue sapphires dies in a shower of flames and is reborn the next day.

Here. Marilee pulled an old *Smithsonian* off one of the bookshelves in the living room. A painting of a Phoenix bird filled the cover. She held it out to Emily and Paula. Emily took the magazine back to the Airstream and read it later in bed. She passed the article to Paula. *There's another version of that story. In that one, the bird travels from one void to another, then just dies and decomposes.*

Sometimes Paula feels like that Phoenix bird—Emily's version, traveling from one void to another. But then Emily comes up with something lovely and magical like the fairy bugs.

"And what about my mom?" Paula starts to ask—because she so wants to believe that something lives on, that Ruth is more than whatever remains of her in that beige and white box buried in the big Phoenix cemetery. She's afraid of what Emily might say, afraid to be reminded that she will never get back those pieces of herself that fell through a hole in the universe when her mom died, afraid that anything could fall through that fissure at any time, afraid that the ground she stands on could open and swallow her.

Emily looks at Paula as if she can read her mind. "A spirit, Paula," she says. "Your mom is a beautiful spirit that will never leave you."

6

Dwight, Emily, and Paula have been driving nearly an hour, dropping in and out of washes, creosote bushes scraping the side of his truck. The jagged Silver Bells rise up ahead. Dwight senses the girls' restlessness and turns into a clearing, shuts off the engine, and opens the door.

"Where are we?" Paula asks.

"Ironwood National Forest."

The mountains loom close, backbones of this desert, Dwight's anchor. Tohono O'odham land stretches to the nearby Mexican border.

"This doesn't look like a forest to me. More like the middle of nowhere."

"It's a different kind of forest."

Dwight doesn't make it out here very often, but Ironwood's a favorite spot. Saguaros and mesquite sweep the land, not a man-made thing in sight. The arroyos are dry now, but they'll fill when monsoon comes. Air's like a tonic, purges the poison.

Emily opens the door and gets out. "How did you even find this place?"

"My dad used to bring me and Jay here when we were kids."

Dwight came out here a few times after he got back from Iraq. Walked the trails the first time, then returned and wandered far into the desert, almost to the base of Ragged Top Mountain. Didn't even bring any of his guns or those his dad left him, weary of things that could kill.

He camped for three days under an ironwood tree, no recollection of even packing the water and grub he had with him. The only life he encountered was a bighorn sheep early one morning and a couple of rattlers. It was June and hot as hell; sweat poured out of him like dirty water wrung from a rag.

He headed back to his truck on the fourth morning and didn't reach it until end of day, the last sip of water long gone.

"Your grandpa taught us how to shoot out here." Dwight lifts two gun cases from the cab and sets them on the front driver's seat. "You girls ready?"

"Sure."

"Okay, Dad. Whatever."

The first time he took Emily and Paula shooting they were ten. They went out in the open desert near Apache Junction, but it's hard to find space for target practice anymore. Too many new housing developments and mobile home parks.

"Look at that." Two paloverde, about ten feet away, are snapped at their bases. A fifteen-foot-tall ironwood stands several yards in front of them, full of bullet holes, and the desert floor around it is littered with casings. "Assholes think this place is just a wasteland. Come out here and shoot up the trees, leave their trash." Dwight picks up the casings and puts them in a shoebox-sized ammo crate in the pickup. He pulls a three-by-five-foot target from the back of the truck.

"Aren't we using cans?" Emily asks.

"Found this sticking out of a dumpster in the alley the other day. No point it going to waste."

The target's an outline of a human torso with concentric circles over the breast, an X in the center of the smallest circle where the heart would be, tattered around the edges, but it looks like nobody's ever shot at it.

"It's gross. We're going to shoot it in the heart?" Paula says.

"It's just a target board," Emily says. "Don't worry, you won't make the heart."

Paula gives Emily the finger. Dwight walks past the broken paloverde, finds a fist-sized rock, and uses it to drive the target board into the hard desert floor. He bends over and picks up an empty Red Bull can, a bullet hole piercing the yellow dot between the two bulls. Dwight tosses the can into the back of his truck, takes a Mossberg 100ATR from the truck, and passes it to Paula.

"Remember, visualize. You want to picture the bullet hitting the target." He stands behind her. "Steady."

The rifle wobbles the way it always does when Paula positions it. She flinches as she pulls the trigger. The rifle hops to her right and the bullet hits the upper edge of the target.

"Give it another try. It's natural for the gun to want to move when you press the trigger. It just takes practice."

When he decided on homeschooling for Emily and Paula, Dwight told Ruth he'd show them the math behind shooting. And he did a couple of times, figured the necessary firing angle from the distance of the target and the height of the gun from the ground. Wrote it all down and gave it to Ruth. The girls didn't show much interest. Emily likes the guns, neither of them the math. Paula aims again and pulls the trigger. The gun moves to the right again, the bullet barely misses the ironwood.

"I'm done." She passes the gun to Emily.

Emily's a natural. Dwight doesn't need to tell her anything, but he does anyway. "Shoulders straight to the target. Let your body absorb the recoil." More for Paula's benefit than hers.

Emily holds the rifle as if it's an extension of her arms, trigger finger at a ninety-degree angle so it comes back straight, and the gun doesn't move. He recognizes the look on her face, as if a taut thread ran between the bull's-eye and somewhere deep in her center. Reminds him of himself. That thread pushes everything away, makes the world still and silent. She fires. Doesn't take her eyes off the target until the bullet hits.

"Holy shit. You made a bull's-eye," Paula says.

Emily smiles. Paula gives her a half-hearted thumbs-up. Emily repositions herself and takes another shot. She misses the bull's-eye but hits the ring closest to it. She takes three more shots. Another bull's-eye and two just above it.

"You want to try again?" Emily holds the gun out to Paula.

"Or you can use the .22 long rifle in the truck," Dwight says.

Paula shakes her head and walks toward the truck, shuffling her feet in the desert dust as she moves. *She doesn't like shooting,* Ruth told Dwight. *All the more reason to learn to shoot,* he said.

Ruth didn't like guns either but appreciated they might be necessary. Became a pretty decent shot. But he never pushes Paula too hard.

He places the Mossberg in the open truck bed and takes a Winchester from the rack. He faces the target, mountains in his peripheral view. He takes take aim, exhales slowly, and pulls the trigger. The bright muzzle flash, the earsplitting bang. The acrid smell of gunpowder fills his nostrils, blood rushes to his brain. Then the calm. The calm he waits for every time. He senses Emily and Paula watching but doesn't turn around. Takes another shot. Another bull's-eye. He shoots again and again until all fifteen rounds are used up. The center of the target is gone, a gaping hole with fragments of cardboard hanging.

"You think you hit that target enough?" Paula's voice sounds far away. Dwight turns and she's right behind him. "We're getting hot out here, Dad."

He places a hand on her shoulder. "Okay. Let's get going."

It's close to noon, the afternoon heat's moved in. Dwight gets on Interstate 10 at Avra Valley Road and heads west toward Phoenix but exits at Marana. He passes a Circle K and the Sun RV Resort, a large dusty lot with about a dozen run-down trailers scattered at odd angles. Just beyond it, he turns into a gravel driveway that leads to a 1960s ranch house on a few acres of hardscrabble desert land. A skinny horse ambles inside a fenced-off section of the property.

"You girls wait here."

"What are we doing?"

"I'm dropping off a couple of guns to the guy who lives here." Dwight reaches into the back of the cab for his black rifle case. "I'm selling two Walther P22s."

The house's trim and front door are newly painted, but the exterior stucco is chipped and cracked. A man answers the door in camo pants and a muscle shirt. The guy's a friend of Dwight's buddy Claude Evans. Frizzy red hair hangs to his shoulders, a matching wiry beard and mustache hide the lower half of his face, freckles cover his nose and cheeks.

"Shane Russell." He extends his right hand, smiles broadly, teeth white and straight like a toothpaste commercial. A homemade tattoo runs across his left bicep, U.S. CONSTITUTION in blue ink. Below it, a crude American flag.

"C'mon in." Shane chews something. At first Dwight thinks it's tobacco or gum, then he notices the bright red between Shane's lips when speaks. A thick red rubber band.

"I got my girls." Dwight nods toward the truck.

Shane pulls a wad of cash from his back pocket, counts out $400 and hands it to him. Dwight unzips the black case and passes him the two Walthers. "Come meet my daughter and niece."

Shane follows Dwight to the truck and pokes a large rough hand through the open window and shakes hands with Emily, who sits in the window seat, then Paula. A woman comes to stand in the doorway to the house. She wears an orange sundress and calf-high brown cowboy boots. She walks to the truck.

"This here's my wife, Shawna," Shane says.

Dwight nods. "Nice to meet you, Shawna."

A large tattoo of a snake, poised to strike, runs from her right shoulder to her elbow. Emily and Paula give her a nod. Shawna smiles at them, then looks at Dwight. "Beautiful girls."

Dwight surveys the mountains behind Shane's place. "Nice spread, breathing space."

"Yeah, pretty quiet out here. Nobody bothers us."

Dwight hears the motorcycle's roar before his friend Claude rides up the front drive and parks near the mesquite. He gets off, takes a six-pack of Bud from the back pouch, pulls one can off as he walks toward Dwight, then puts the rest in a cooler under the tree.

"How you doing?" He pops the top and takes a swig.

"Not too bad. Met your friend Shane today."

Claude sets his beer on the ground and removes his black leather vest with the words Sovereign Riders, Arizona Chapter embroidered across the back, an image of a bike underneath. He hangs it over the chair under the mesquite. "Everything go okay?"

"Yeah."

"He's a good guy. Someone you can trust."

"Nice place he's got."

"Yeah. Developers haven't moved in down there yet." Claude gazes at the shell of high-rise condominiums across the street.

Dwight met Claude six years ago when Dwight sold him a Harley he'd picked up at an auction and rebuilt. He's the closest thing to a friend Dwight allows into his life. They were over in Iraq at the same time, on that same highway of burned-out metal and mangle of armored cars and tanks and trucks. Highway 8, Iraq to Kuwait City. February 1991. They didn't know each other then and only talked about it one time. Claude lost his wife to cancer too; they don't talk about that either. Dwight's never mentioned anything to him about the government trying to take this property, but it's crossed his mind Claude might have some ideas.

Dwight lights up a cigarette and finishes half his beer in one guzzle. Nods toward the condos. "They're trying to get my place too."

"Oh yeah? Who?"

"Fucking government. State of Arizona. I'm sure they want to sell it off to developers." Dwight tells him about the notices they've gotten over the years. About not being able to find a title. About Wilkins and his offer.

Claude shakes his head. "I know people who might have some ideas if things don't pan out with this Wilkins."

Then Dwight tells him about the water. "Thought I'd be able to get it back on by now. I didn't plan on making my mom and the girls go without water for more than a day or two." It's been three weeks since he and Jay and Emily made their first water run.

"Now that would be a little easier to fix than your property situation," Claude says. "I might be able to assist."

"You've bypassed the city water before?"

"Yeah. I helped a buddy tap into a neighboring water line a couple years back."

"That's pretty easy to trace, isn't it?"

"Yeah." Claude smiles, a little sheepishly. "We fucked that one up. He ended up getting caught and paying a big fine."

"That's the thing. Figuring a way authorities won't find out about. I thought I could plumb a pipe into that meter box."

Claude shakes his head. "That's the mistake my friend made. What you want is to divert water from an unmetered source." His eyes go to the street south and west of the property. "That hydrant over there. We could probably tap into that water supply."

7

"We could use some of that stuff in the locker room. It'd be easy."

The college girls are careless about what they leave lying around. Purses, cell phones, backpacks, and notebooks are crammed into unlocked lockers, as if their world's a sweet place, a safe place where you don't have to worry about losing things or somebody taking from you.

Emily and Paula walk past the field outside the PE building. Students, in a game or practice session or whatever they do out there, mill about.

"Steal?" Paula says.

"You took that T-shirt and shorts, didn't you?"

"That was different. Like you said, we need them for mixing in. Stealing for no reason's a sin."

"Sin? Where do you get that shit?"

"Nowhere."

"That weirdo church? I'll tell you what's a sin. It's not having any water in your house. What do you think that Easter Jesus on the cross would say about those assholes in the government who turned off our water?"

"I'm not talking about that."

"And the assholes who want to take the property?"

"I'm talking about taking somebody else's stuff from the locker room."

"Shit, Paula. They have way more than they need and they can always get more." Emily nods toward the girls on the field, dressed in shorts and T-shirts like the ones she and Paula wear now, the ones they took a few weeks ago.

"I don't care what they have. Why can't we just wash our hair and shower?"

"Whatever. Do what the fuck you want." Emily walks ahead

of Paula, slams through the front door to the PE building and into the empty locker room. She strips, goes straight to the shower, and turns on the hot water. Steam fills the stall, then she switches the water to ice cold. It washes over her until she can't bear it. Fuck Paula. She never gets it. Who needs her anyway? Emily opens the stall door and lets the air dry her skin, wrings the moisture from her hair, and steps out.

Paula squats under one of the dryers on the wall; heat blows through her curls. Emily dresses quickly. She sees an ASU towel, which she rolls up tightly and places on the bench. In one of the unlocked lockers she finds a backpack and rummages through it. There's a cell phone and a wallet. She put them next to the towel. She continues going through the lockers and finds another wallet and cell phone.

Paula stands at the end of the bench watching. "You're taking that stuff?"

Emily yanks a towel hanging from another locker door, tosses it to Paula. "Here, for drying next time."

Paula throws the towel back at Emily. It lands on the floor.

"Just fuck off, Paula." Emily kicks the towel back to Paula. "Go on. Get out of here. I'll come alone from now on." The hurt look on Paula's face makes Emily turn away.

The shrill of a whistle sounds from the field and after a couple of minutes, they hear loud voices outside the door.

"Let's get out of here." Emily takes the towel and the wallets and cell phones. Paula picks up the towel from the floor. She looks close to tears. Emily walks toward the door. "You coming?"

As they leave the locker room, Emily drops one of the wallets. She stops to pick it up, but Paula beats her to it.

"I've got it," Paula says.

They exit the PE building and walk toward home. When they get to the student union building, Emily picks up her pace. Adrenaline races through her body.

"C'mon, let's run."

Emily blows through the campus like a gust of wind, the

surroundings a blur, her arms in rhythm with her legs, her body light but full of power as if her limbs could propel her off the ground, thrust her into flight. She could climb a mountain, a thousand mountains. Bolt to the summit without stopping. She crosses Mill Avenue and stops in front of Chipotle, not even out of breath. She waits for Paula, who is far behind her.

When they get back to the Airstream, Emily hides the cell phones under their mattress. She opens one of the wallets and counts out thirty-five dollars in cash, pulls out a driver's license and Visa card. The other wallet contains ten dollars in cash, another driver's license, and an ASU Sun Card.

"What are you going to do with all this?" Paula says.

"Keep it, of course. We'll get rid of the wallets." She counts out twenty dollars and passes it to Paula.

"I don't want it." Paula raises her hands in the air, refuses to take the money.

"Shit. Why do you have to be like this?" Emily puts the bills on the bed between her and Paula.

Paula doesn't answer.

"Do you remember that house we went to just before your dad took us out of regular school? That real big one? In that new development?"

"For the Girl Scout meeting?"

"Yeah. You wanted to join, and I went along with you."

"Kelsey Davie. Her mom was the troop leader. What about it?"

"Remember all those rooms? Six bedrooms. And the downstairs like a whole other house. They had that humongous flat-screen."

"Yeah, it was cool."

"Only two kids, Kelsey and her brother."

"Yeah?"

"All that stuff they had."

Paula shrugs. "I remember. And I remember that CD you stuck down your shorts. Backstreet Boys. Kelsey's mom was nice."

"That doesn't matter. They had so much stuff."

"So?"

"Those college girls are like Kelsey and her brother. They have everything."

"But it's their stuff, not ours."

"You're missing the point." Emily examines the two driver's licenses, one from Arizona, one from Utah. "And you may think they're nice people, but you can be sure they think we're shit. How can you be so—"

"Stupid?"

"I didn't say that. Naïve. How can you be so naïve?"

"Whatever, Emily. You got what you wanted from the locker room."

"*We* got it, Paula. Half of it is yours." Emily pushes the twenty dollars to Paula's side of the bed.

The next morning Emily jogs to Tempe Town Lake. It's early, and the area is empty except for someone paddling a kayak under the train trestle. She tosses the wallets, watches them float, then disappear, in the blinding dazzle of the morning sun.

By the second week in May, they have a collection of cell phones and wallets, a couple of iPad minis, and an Acer laptop. They keep the credit cards, driver's licenses, and other IDs under the mattress, and the cash behind the pipes under the sink in the Airstream. Everything else goes under the bed. Emily takes six ASU Sun Cards from their collection of wallets, looks through them, and passes two to Paula.

"The new us."

Paula examines the IDs. "These don't even look like us."

"Don't be so negative." Emily takes the two cards and looks at them. A girl with short, curly auburn hair smiles at her from a shiny maroon-and-gold surface. She hands this card back to Paula. On the other card, a girl with long, dark, wavy hair parted on the side looks at the camera, a bored expression on her face. Emily keeps this one for herself.

"They'll do for now."

Paula places hers on the cardboard box next to the bed. The holy card the old woman at True Lord gave her lies next to it.

"What's that other one?" Emily says.

"The one from the old lady."

"You don't believe any of that shit, do you?"

Paula ignores her.

"Seriously, sometimes I wonder about you."

"It's just a card."

"We need to think bigger."

"We're lucky we haven't gotten caught already. Besides, what are we going to do with more stuff?"

"Make some money off it."

"How?"

"I'm working on that. And it's not as risky if we branch out, work some different places."

"Like where?"

"I don't know yet. There's Wells Fargo Arena where they play big basketball games. And that swimming place."

"Mona Plummer Aquatic Center."

"Yeah. Both are places where students change clothes, leave things lying around. And the parking lot at Sun Devil stadium. We can check that out."

"I still don't like this."

"Look. I want to get some money together for Eureka."

"You could get a job at the ice cream shop. Or somewhere else."

"Are you serious? How much do you make? Do you know how long it'd take to get money for California? I'd be as old as Grandma Marilee."

"Sorry my job is so dumb to you."

"I didn't say that. It just wouldn't be enough money. Look, do you want to come with me?"

"To Eureka?"

"Yeah."

"You want me to go with you?"

"I figured you would. We always do stuff together."

"You never asked me."

"I'm asking you now."

That afternoon, they check out the stadium parking lot: an abyss of cars, with no surveillance cameras, a mile or so removed from the rest of the campus. They walk up and down the aisles, trying the vehicle doors.

"Idiots. They don't even lock their doors." Emily opens the glove compartment of an older model gray Honda Civic, and pulls out a stack of papers. Nothing worth anything. Then she sees the rolled joint in the corner and tucks it in her bra.

"ID," the guy at the Mona Plummer reception desk says. He wears a bright-gold, silky-looking shirt with a collar and the letters ASU printed in maroon across the front. His hair, cut short and parted on the side, nearly matches the color of the shirt.

Emily puts her Sun Card on the counter. He barely looks at it and waves her through. Paula drops hers, picks it up, and hands it to him. The guy examines the card, looks at Paula, then passes it back to her.

"Chill," Emily says as they head to the locker room. "That panicky shit will make people notice you."

In the locker room, Emily's eyes go to a notice posted about a girls' swim meet the following Saturday and the times of all the practice sessions leading up to it.

"This place will be full of swimmers."

"Perfect opportunity."

Emily smiles. "Catching on, cousin."

Paula shrugs. "Maybe."

For the first couple of days, they just watch and don't take anything. The ASU girls wear solid black bathing suits and maroon bathing caps. They fill the largest pool at the aquatic center all week, their stuff strewn over the locker room. What would it be like to be one of those girls?

"Someday we're gonna come back over here and swim in one of these pools," Emily says. The smell of chlorine makes her skin feel cool.

They make their move on the Friday before the meet. Each of them takes one of the gym bags left on the benches and dumps out the contents, mostly clothes and towels and underwear. Emily goes through three purses in unlocked lockers and takes the wallets and cell phones from each. Paula doesn't bother sorting through the purses. She dumps the contents of two into her gym bag. On their way out, Emily grabs an oversized backpack.

When they get back to the Airstream, they dump everything on their bed.

"We've got to do something with all this. And the other stuff."

"You said we could sell it. Isn't that why we're doing this? To get money for Eureka?"

"Yeah. But where do we sell it?"

"A pawnshop?"

"Maybe."

"That's not a good idea," a male voice says.

Jay stands in the doorway. A red-and-white Diamondbacks T-shirt hangs loosely on his tall lanky frame, a cigarette balances on his lower lip.

"What are you doing spying on us? How long have you been standing there?"

"I'm not spying, Emily. I seen you come in with all this stuff is all," he says. "You two have done this before, haven't you?"

Emily doesn't answer.

"Do you think my dad saw us?"

"He was never around when we came home with stuff." Emily hadn't worried about Dwight seeing them. He was either away or in his gun shed each time.

"We didn't know Jay was around either," Paula says.

"Don't worry, he didn't see us. We'd have known by now." Emily turns to Jay. "So, what's wrong with a pawnshop?"

"First place cops look for stolen stuff. Pawnshop owners would get suspicious you bring in all this stuff."

"We're not going to take it all at once," Paula says.

"I know someone who could help you out."

Jay spent three years in a Florence prison for the Circle K thing, which is why Dwight had to get him a lawyer. Emily and Paula were ten at the time and no one gave them details on exactly what Jay had done. They just knew it as the "Circle K thing." Dwight says he's not allowed to carry a gun because of it. They all went down once to visit him, but kids weren't allowed in, so Ruth took them over to the 7-Eleven across the street and they sat outside drinking cherry Slurpees while Dwight and Grandma Marilee visited Jay. Emily's not sure about letting him in on their operation. But he could be useful, help them sell all the stuff. He's older and that might come in handy.

"So, what brilliant thing would you do with this?" Emily nods toward the stuff on the bed.

"I know someone who buys IDs, driver's licenses, credit cards; stuff like that. Cell phones too. He knows how to unlock them, bypass security codes."

"Who is this guy?"

"You don't need to know that."

"Yes, we do," Paula says.

"Yeah, Jay, we need to know who we're dealing with or just forget it."

"His name's Steve. I met him in Florence."

"We need to think about this."

"What are you going to do, just keep piling up stuff? All your hard work for nothing?"

"I said, we'll let you know. Right, Paula?"

Paula nods.

"Ponder away." Jay turns to leave, then pauses. "Might want to think about the big basketball tournament in a couple of weeks too. Girls' teams from all over the Southwest and West Coast. Wells Fargo Arena. Saw it in the sports pages yesterday."

Emily looks at the treasures on the bed—driver's licenses, ASU Sun Cards, credit cards, social security cards, a few passports. She likes the cards with photos. They give life to this little business. Brigitte Marmelo, Penelope Hartwell, Ashley Baer, Shannon Simmons, Theresa Milliford, Grace Hollander. What would it be like to be Ashley or Grace? Or Katrina Anne Myers, born March 6, 1990, twenty years old, 5' 3", with brown hair and hazel eyes? A California driver's license. Emily's seen cars with California plates in the Sun Devil lot. She had opened an unlocked door on one and taken the registration from the glove box just for the heck of it and tossed it in a recycling bin. Only people who had so much they didn't have to worry about their possessions getting stolen could afford to be careless. Who knows? Maybe it was Katrina Anne's car. The potential connections in the world fascinate her.

Jay's right. What good is all the stuff piling up in the Airstream when someone will pay money for it? Why not send Katrina Anne and Brigitte and Ashley out into the world, let someone else enjoy their identities? Get some use out of their cell phones?

8

"Don't leave anything to chance," Jay said when they agreed to his plan. "Get there early, learn your surroundings. Find the locker rooms and the exit doors."

"We've done this before," Emily said.

"You ever been in Wells Fargo Arena?"

"We haven't." Paula twists her index finger around a lock of curly hair, something she has begun to do recently, like a baby sucking its thumb, minus the peaceful, serene expression.

"Okay, okay. We'll case the place."

"And they might check your purses. Don't carry anything suspicious in them. Not even cigarettes."

"We're not idiots."

"You two are underage. A simple pack of smokes could fuck everything up."

"I said we're not idiots. And we won't need purses at all."

The game begins at seven. Emily and Paula stand in line at the circular building, which has four entrances.

"Those girls must be on the teams." Paula gestures toward a group of girls in ASU shorts and T-shirts, heading toward the north entrance. They all carry gym bags or backpacks slung over their shoulders.

Emily and Paula reach the front of the line and hand their tickets to a guy behind the counter. He passes them each a program.

The inside of Wells Fargo smells like rubber. People fill the wide, rounded corridor, making their way to the bleachers. Plaques, framed photos of teams, and old news stories about team victories hang on the walls. T-shirts with ASU logos from the past are framed in glass.

"Okay. Let's find the locker room before we sit down," Emily says.

They pass two south-facing exit doors. Emily stops and checks each one of them; both are unlocked, at least from the inside. The girls' locker room is a few feet ahead. She opens the door to a din of female voices and closes it quickly. Four teams are scheduled to compete in the tournament. That seems like a lot for one night. Whatever. Maybe the games are short. A little farther down the hallway, the men's locker room has been converted into another locker room for the girls; a sign with WOMEN, painted in black letters, is posted on the door.

Emily cracks the door and sees more girls. "Okay, let's go to our seats and wait for the game to start."

They enter the arena, an enormous room with seating that begins on the ground level and rises all the way to the ceiling. The highest seats are empty, but the rest of the arena is full. Emily looks at their ticket stubs. They are three rows from the back on the lower level. Girls wearing gym shorts and their team T-shirts—Arizona State, New Mexico State, University of Nevada Las Vegas, University of California–Riverside—occupy the two front rows.

A woman dressed in ASU team colors walks onto the court and places her right hand over her heart. A deep voice booms from loudspeakers. "Ladies and gentlemen, we will now rise for the national anthem." Everyone stands in unison and places their hands over their hearts. The national anthem, sung in a deep male voice, resounds throughout the arena. When it ends, the first two teams take to the court. New Mexico vs. Nevada. Emily and Paula stay through the first forty minutes of the game, until the large clock on the wall says 7:40 p.m.

"Now." Emily rises from her seat. Paula follows, finger twisting through her hair.

The corridor is empty.

"We need to be selective," Emily says in a low voice as they walk toward the girls' locker room. "Cash, licenses, credit cards first. All we can get. And cell phones. Bigger things only if we have time and space."

"Okay. I know."

Emily double-checks her back pocket for the tiny cloth shopping bag Paula had stuffed into her backpack at the aquatic center, folded up so small it could almost fit into a change purse. She slowly pushes the locker room door halfway, and then stops and listens. Quiet. They walk in. Empty. Emily pulls the shopping bag from her pocket and shakes it open. She catches Paula's eye and points to the lockers on the left side of the room. Many of the lockers have heavy metal combination locks on them, but some are unlocked. Paula picks up a gym bag from the bench, empties it of its contents—a towel, a pair of jeans, and a T-shirt. She opens and closes unlocked lockers, quickly dumps out purses and puts the wallets and cell phones in the gym bag. Emily does the same. Neither speaks. Periodically Emily glances over at Paula. She worries about her messing up, getting freaked out, and doing something stupid. She seems okay though. Emily thinks of Halloween as she fills her shopping bag, stuffing it full of treats. They work fast and methodically.

"Okay," Emily whispers when her bag is full. "I think we're done here."

She picks up a backpack, doesn't even check what's inside, and slings it over her left shoulder. They walk out of the women's locker room and head toward the other one. The roar of the game fills the background. Cheers. One of the teams must have scored. As they approach the other locker room, a female security guard exits. The girls stop. The guard walks in the opposite direction without turning to look their way. Emily's heart pounds; she can almost hear Paula's thumping. She looks back. The exit doors are not far behind them. No one in sight. The female guard has rounded the corridor and disappeared.

"Let's go," Paula says. "We've got enough."

They could get more. With three minutes in the other locker room, they could just grab the first things they see and split. But Paula's right. And that guard could come back any second. "Okay."

They walk quickly to the door and exit into the night. Emily doesn't look back. She wants to get far away from the Wells Fargo Arena as quickly as possible. She and Paula run toward the big parking lot. The plan is for Jay to borrow Dwight's pickup and wait for them. They'll head to Steve's with their loot. Jay has the items from previous jobs. Emily's not one hundred percent comfortable with Jay having their stuff, but it's a risk they need to take.

Diffuse light from Mill Avenue and the parking structures near the arena illuminate the area. The mountain with the letter *A* looms on the periphery. An accomplice. Or a spy. Emily looks for Dwight's truck but doesn't see it. Jay said eight o'clock. Maybe they're early, not having done the second locker room. She moves to a shadowy spot in the parking lot, out of the light's reach.

"Let's wait right here."

A car comes toward them. A late 1990s model Ford Escort. It pulls up and stops. Emily's on the verge of dropping her bags and running when Jay leans over and opens the passenger side door.

"C'mon."

"Jesus fuck. You scared the shit out of us."

Emily drops her load on the front floor and hops in. Paula gets in the back. Jay races out of the parking lot.

"Where's the truck?" Emily says.

"We haven't unloaded the damn water buckets we got last night. They'd have swooshed all over the place. Besides, Dwight would've wanted to know why I needed it."

"Where did you get this car?"

Jay jerks his chin toward the parking lot.

"You stole it?"

He smiles. "Let's get out of here."

A gun handle protrudes from Jay's side pocket.

"I thought you weren't allowed to carry a gun."

"I thought you weren't allowed to steal cell phones and credit cards." Jay shifts into fourth gear and heads down Mill Avenue toward US 60. "Next stop, AJ."

"AJ?" Emily says.

"Apache Junction."

They pass the exit Dwight takes for the shooting range at Usury Mountain, the sign with an arrow pointing to the Renaissance Festival held every spring. The lights of new housing developments and strip malls dot the landscape. Across the street from a Circle K gas station, a large billboard with a picture of praying hands says: Paradise—You'd Think It'd Be So Much Farther.

"There you go, Paula." Emily points to the religious billboard. "It's your friend, Jesus."

Paula ignores her. The highway darkens; the glow of suburbia fades into the night.

"You said Apache Junction." Emily's not sure where they are.

"Just a little past it."

"What's his last name?" she says.

"Who?"

"Steve. What's his last name?"

"Look, you don't need to know that. He's probably going to be pissed I even brought you two."

"We can wait in the car," Paula says.

"No, we can't." Emily goes through the stuff in her bag, separates out the cash and puts it in her back pocket. Does the same with the backpack she grabbed on the way out. Then Paula's bag and the one on the back seat from earlier jobs.

"We need to stop somewhere, Jay. Before we get to Steve's."

"What for? We're almost there."

"Sort this stuff out. We'll look like dumb fucks with everything all mixed together. Just pull over or turn off somewhere before we get there."

Jay exits onto a dark road just before the Highway 79 Florence interchange and turns off the headlights.

"We need some light," Emily says.

Jay pulls out his cell phone, holds it close to the seat as Emily separates the driver's licenses, credit cards, ASU Sun Cards, and social security cards. She puts them in a bag with a couple of passports. The cell phones go in another bag.

"Okay, let's go," Emily says.

Jay gets back on the highway and drives another mile before exiting at the Florence interchange. Lights from a couple of trailers in the desert are the only relief against the starless night. He turns onto a narrow, paved street with a few houses sprinkled on the dark expanse of land and stops in front of a small house, where a man stands in the doorway and motions them in.

Steve is a small man. He wears a pair of black slacks and a short-sleeved white cotton shirt; his hair is cut in an old-fashioned crew-cut style. He looks more like that preacher at the True Lord Christian Rebirth Church than the big-time criminal Emily imagined. Beneath black-rimmed glasses, his pale blue eyes appear almost colorless, his right eye wandering uncontrollably. Emily can't tell where he's looking. Jay motions for her to unload the goods. She takes out the cards and arranges them on the table and dumps the cell phones next to them. Steve passes his hands lightly over the cards as if he's a fortune-teller. His wandering eye seems to be on her. He nods and smiles in approval.

"Tell you what," he says to Emily. "I'll give you two thousand for all of it, including the phones."

Emily has no idea what the stuff is worth. She looks at Jay.

"C'mon, Steve." Jay suddenly seems wiser. "These girls went to a lot of trouble to get this stuff. Took some risks. And you got a shitload of IDs there."

"It's small-time stuff."

"You're a small-time operation."

"Twenty-two hundred."

"Twenty-five hundred, and it's a deal," Emily says.

Steve looks from her to Jay. When he walks into a bedroom, Emily sees a handgun protruding from his belt. She watches as he opens the top drawer in a chest. Paula stands by the front door, twisting her hair rapidly as if she might pull it out. Emily thinks briefly of telling her to stop. Steve comes back with an envelope and starts to hand it to Jay but changes his mind and gives it to Emily instead.

"Let's go," Paula says. It's the first thing she's said since they got out of the car. She turns and opens the door.

"Wait a sec." Emily takes the money from the envelope and counts it. Ten fifty-dollar bills, the rest in twenties and tens. $2500 total. She puts the money back in and stuffs the envelope into her pocket.

They get back on the highway. Emily doesn't notice the flashing red behind them until Paula points it out. It's a ways in the distance; maybe it's not even for them. She looks at Jay; his eyes are on the rearview mirror.

"Get us out of here, Jay."

He slams the gas pedal and turns out the lights. They fly. Everything is black except the far away flash of red behind them and the lights of the East Valley up ahead. A sensation rushes through Emily, same as the day she ran through ASU, stolen wallets and cell phones in her hands, the same rush she gets as the bullet leaves the gun when Dwight takes her and Paula shooting.

The locket she picked up off the floor that first day in the locker room hangs around her neck; a photo of a young girl on one side, and a tiny handwritten piece of paper with the name Julie on the other, had been inside before Emily took them out and replaced them with a photo of herself on one side, Paula on the other. It occurs to Emily she can be anyone she wants. Steve didn't look so smart, she could figure out how to do it. And there are other places besides ASU, lots of places. She looks at the flashing red behind them, closes her eyes. She's lifting off the ground, soaring.

The blare of a siren engulfs them. An ambulance screams past. Jay turns the headlights back on.

"Holy shit," he says. "That was close."

Emily turns and looks at Paula in the back seat.

"Count me out next time," Paula says.

"Let's get rid of this car." Jay slows down as they approach central Mesa.

He exits and drives to the parking lot of the Mormon Temple. They dump the stolen Escort and walk a couple of blocks to the light-rail station on Main Street.

It's after midnight and the light-rail car is empty except for a man in a red baseball hat with a black-widow spider on the bill. A grayish white beard hangs past his chest. The man looks like an oversized elf. His belly folds over the top of his pants, rising and falling with each breath he takes. Emily sits a few feet away from the elf man, and Jay and Paula sit across from her. Jay's legs bounce up and down, and he's grinning. It's the first time Emily's ridden the rail. Its energy and power rumbles through her as it moves along dark streets.

The elf man holds a filthy-looking plastic bag of grapes in his lap. He puts one in his mouth, swirls it around with his tongue, and then chews and swallows. His head falls forward and he dozes for a few seconds, then rouses himself and eats another grape. At first Emily thinks he's looking at her as he chews, but his eyes are blank. He stares straight ahead as if he can see something invisible to everyone else.

Jay stands. "Mill Avenue's the next stop."

The elf man struggles to rise from his seat. His bag of grapes falls to the floor; a few tumble out and roll like marbles. He looks at them sadly, almost in tears. Emily gets up, squats near the floor and gathers the grapes into her hands. She puts them in the bag and hands it to the man. His eyes meet hers for a second, then become blank again. As they exit the car Emily sees him pull out a few more grapes and put them into his mouth. Maybe he rides all night, periodically trying to get out of his seat. Maybe he lives on the light-rail and gets off only to pee. That's what someone who doesn't have any money or a place to stay looks like.

As the rail pulls away Emily catches a glimpse of a large advertisement on the outside of one of the cars. Years ago Grandma Marilee gave her a photo of her mother. Emily had examined the face carefully, then ripped it up and tossed it in Dwight's fire pit. The ad on the train shows a woman with dark shoulder-length hair and a black sweater against a lavender background. It doesn't really resemble Phyllis, but still, it makes her think briefly of her mother.

"Are you coming, Emily?" Paula says.

Emily turns away from the disappearing light-rail. Jay and Paula are already crossing the street, heading toward home.

When they get close, Emily stops. The streets are quiet and empty.

"Hold up for a minute." She counts out five hundred dollars and hands it to Jay. She splits the rest and gives half to Paula.

"You like having a thousand dollars?" Emily says to Paula as she closes the door to the Airstream.

"Yeah, I like the money. But Jay's nuts stealing that car. And that Steve guy gives me the creeps."

"But we're okay, aren't we? Better than okay."

"We almost got caught."

"We didn't almost get caught. You freak out over every little thing."

"Every little thing? Like a vehicle with a red light on top? And us in a stolen car?"

"You panic, that's a good way to fuck things up."

"Whatever, Emily. Count me out next time."

"We don't have any more stuff to get rid of anyway. And it's end of semester."

9

Emily walks toward Marilee in the graveyard, the excitement of the previous night still coursing through her veins. Marilee's always up before dawn, walking around the property as if to make sure it's still there. Sometimes she drags a rake behind her, maybe with the intention of clearing weeds and overgrown patches of grass, but her body is too stiff for that and she leaves a vaguely visible trail as the rake's prongs scrape along dirt and scrub. As Emily approaches, Marilee steps away from the stones and looks in her direction.

"Take my arm, Emily. I'm not so steady on these old legs the way I used to be."

Emily goes to her side, wraps her hand around Marilee's skinny arm, and leads her back to the patio. She waits by her side as Marilee lowers herself into the recliner. Marilee settles into the chair and sips her morning coffee. She reaches for a cigarette and lights it. Emily imagines Marilee as her younger self, the way she is in the black-and-white photo of her and Jack, long dark hair flowing in waves over her breasts as she looks straight at the camera. Emily sees that face for an instant, then it changes like the images in one of those flipbooks that create an illusion of motion as the pages turn. Marilee, a withered queen of the desert, an ancient storyteller.

"You sure you want to see her?" Marilee says.

Emily nods. Dwight said he'd take her up to Tonopah, Nevada, to see Phyllis after he and Claude got the water back on. *Soon,* he said, which could mean tomorrow or the next day or three weeks or six months from now.

Emily barely remembers what her mother looks like, but a few images, maybe from the photos Marilee gets out from time to time, have permanently engraved themselves in her psyche, and these are what come to mind when she thinks of Phyllis, which she's made a conscious point of trying not to do for nearly thirteen years, since the day her mother left with Wayne Crowley. Marilee told Emily the truth when she was seven years old. She didn't mince her words. Emily appreciated that. Why sugar-coat the truth with bullshit, even to a kid?

He came back to Phoenix three times, Marilee said. *The third time he talked your mom into going with him. She wanted to stay here. With you. Wanted Wayne Crowley to stay too.*

Emily didn't ask why they left. She couldn't.

Dwight was going to build onto the house if they stayed. Said Wayne could work with him. You remember that third time, don't you, Emily? Grandma Marilee asked as she took Emily's small hand in hers.

Emily remembered. She remembered Wayne Crowley wearing a baseball cap with the bill half covering his face. And she remembered more. Remembered when she was seven and remembers now. Her mom smelled of perfume that day, the perfume she dabbed behind her ears, on her wrists, and along the contours of her neck. *It's called Beautiful*, Phyllis said when she saw her daughter watching. For a long time, Emily thought that the word for perfume was *beautiful*. Phyllis placed Emily's index and middle fingers on her wrist at the perfume spot. *Pulse point*, she said. *Can you feel it?* Her mother's vein pumped ever so slightly under Emily's fingers. *That's life*, Phyllis said as she inhaled deeply on her cigarette and smiled at Emily.

Emily watched her mom fill the red suitcase. Jeans, T-shirts, underwear. Two dresses from the closet: a plain black one and a lime-green halter dress with yellow-and-orange flowers. Emily followed her to the bathroom. Lipstick, a cylinder of eye make-up, Phyllis's special shampoo and crème rinse, a toothbrush. The bottle of Beautiful. All thrown quickly into a plastic zip bag which went into the red suitcase, which she zipped shut and stood up on its wheels. Ready to go.

Where's mine, Momma?

Phyllis didn't answer. She rolled the suitcase out the door of the adobe house, over the patio, to the end of the driveway, where Wayne Crowley had parked on the street. He stood by the open driver's-side door of his maroon Chevy Malibu with a broken left taillight, smoking a cigarette, the baseball cap over his eyes. Phyllis lifted the suitcase into the trunk, which was opened wide as if waiting to swallow up Emily's innocence and slam shut on the hurt she'd learn to deny.

Momma, Emily said again. *Where's my suitcase?*

Wayne Crowley closed the trunk, looked briefly at her, then turned to Phyllis. "You ready?"

Phyllis walked back to Emily.

Momma, I'm coming too. It wasn't a question. Then it was. *Am I coming with you?*

Phyllis squatted in the driveway, took Emily into her arms, and put her face close to her daughter's. Emily felt the tears running along Phyllis's cheeks mix with her own. She opened her mouth to ask again but stopped, understanding finally that she was not going, knowing this even as she imagined running into the house and filling her Little Mermaid backpack with her own clothes, imagining this as Phyllis held her so tightly that she had trouble catching her breath. Eventually she felt Marilee's hand on her back. Phyllis released her, stood up, and got into the car.

I'll be back for you after we get settled, Phyllis said as she slowly pulled the door closed and Wayne revved the engine.

They pulled away from the property. Emily watched until they rounded the corner and disappeared. Even then she pictured herself running into the house to fill her backpack.

Marilee lifted Emily's chin, pushed away the hair that fell over her eyes, and kissed her forehead, her cheeks, and every inch of her wet face. *You're my girl,* she said. *Don't ever forget that.*

At first Phyllis sent postcards, every two weeks for almost a year. And the snow globe with white flakes falling onto a saguaro cactus that had chips in its green paint. Then a dress on Emily's seventh birthday, two sizes too small. After that, the years passed with nothing. Marilee called Phyllis when Ruth died. Phyllis asked to talk to Emily. Marilee held the receiver out to her, but Emily said no. She had practically run from the phone, in case she changed her mind, put the receiver to her ear, and heard the voice she both loved and hated.

Phyllis called Dwight two years ago after Wayne Crowley got sentenced to a fifteen-year stint, for armed robbery at an old Vegas Casino and a convenience store. Phyllis needed some money and a ride to Tonopah; she couldn't afford Las Vegas with Crowley in jail.

You drove all the way up there just to give her a ride?

Yeah.

That's pretty fucked up to make you come all that way. Doesn't she have any friends?

She's my sister, Emily.

Whatever.

She asked about you, Dwight said. *Wanted a photo.*

Big deal. Did you give her one?

I only had that one of you and Paula with me over at South Mountain. I didn't want to give that one away.

It doesn't matter anyway. She didn't give a shit if Phyllis had a photo of her or not.

But now, Emily wants to see her. Maybe out of curiosity. Or maybe for some kind of closure before she turns eighteen. Maybe to say fuck you. Who the hell knows why?

Marilee reaches out and takes Emily's hand. "It broke my heart when your mother left," she says. "Phyllis is my daughter, my little girl, and I love her no matter what she's done."

Emily looks away.

"It may be selfish of me," Marilee says. "But it would have broken my heart more if she'd taken you. I don't think I could have stood it, losing both of you."

Emily gently pulls her hand from Marilee's and walks back into the Airstream. She's not going to cry; she doesn't remember crying since she was little and she's not going to do it now. Not over someone who abandoned her. And not over the love she hears in Marilee's voice, which is a thing maybe even sadder than Phyllis leaving, maybe the saddest thing in the whole world.

"Hallelujah! Emily, come look." Paula stands in the doorway of the Airstream, poised to step outside. A week has passed since they sold their stuff to Steve.

"What?" Emily rises from the bed and stands next to Paula at the door.

"Look." Paula points to Marilee, who holds a hose. A rainbow-colored arc of water shoots from it and lands on the dead shamrocks. It puddles on the hard ground under the mesquite tree, running along the grooves in the dirt, away from its roots. The yellow-orange morning sun is just over Marilee's shoulder.

Emily and Paula step out of the trailer and walk to where Marilee stands.

"They might come back to life," Marilee says.

"I can do that for you." Emily reaches for the hose.

"I like the feel of it." Marilee holds the hose with both hands, waters the shamrocks for a while longer, then leans forward a little, raises the nozzle to her mouth, and drinks. Water streams down her chin, down her wrinkled neck, and over her faded purple-gray cotton-print dress. Marilee laughs and, for a second, Emily again sees the young face of her grandmother. Marilee passes the hose to her.

Emily takes it and waits until Marilee has gone back to her recliner. Then she laughs and shoots the water straight up into the air, over herself and Paula. Emily squirts Paula and laughs, then sprays herself.

"Hold on," she says and passes the hose to Paula.

Emily goes into the Airstream and returns with a container of shampoo, pours some onto her head and then Paula's. Paula sets the hose down at the base of the mesquite and they lather their hair. Emily picks up the hose and rinses both of their heads, then turns off the faucet. They are both completely soaked. Marilee watches them, book closed, hands folded on her lap, an unlit cigarette hanging from her lips. A smile spreads across her wrinkled face. Emily catches a glimpse of Dwight standing in the doorway to the kitchen, coffee cup in his hand. He lifts the cup in a wave.

10

The ride up to Tonopah takes nearly nine hours. They are quiet in the truck, the hum of the engine and spin of tires on the road the only sounds as Emily, Paula, and Dwight travel west out of Phoenix. Flat desert scrub surrounds them, dull rock formations in the distance. Emily thinks of Eureka and the blue water on the coast, a contrast to the ugly dry landscape.

Dwight's preoccupied as always; Paula sleeps, her head falling toward Emily's shoulder. Emily closes her eyes. Speed and motion ripple through her. The highway feels like a promise that might come true or might not. What the promise is doesn't matter; it's the idea of a promise that counts. She doesn't want to think too much about seeing Phyllis, tries not to imagine what she looks like now or how she'll react to Emily. Does she still wear that perfume? The whole trip could be a bad idea.

"You girls want to see the strip?" Dwight turns off Highway 93 and onto the towering hotel and casino line-crawl of Las Vegas Boulevard. "All these high-rises weren't here before. Just a wide street with casinos."

Emily wonders about the places Wayne Crowley robbed. "When were you here?" she says.

"Right before I joined the army and went over to Iraq."

"Why did you join up, Dad?"

"I was twenty-six and stupid. Seemed like the right thing."

"You changed your mind? About it being the right thing?" Paula says.

Emily looks out the window at the Mandalay Bay and the purple pyramid-shaped casino next to it, Luxor. Of course he changed his mind.

"Damn right. Your mom didn't want me to go, and I should have listened to her."

It's the most he's ever said about it. Emily turns to look at him, wants to hear more, but Dwight becomes quiet and she knows he's finished talking about Iraq.

After a few minutes, he points to a fifty-foot-high Coke bottle attached to a building. "Take a look at that."

"Cool," Paula says.

"Looks stupid to me." Emily gazes up at the bottle and the Hard Rock Cafe next door, all that glass and glitter even in the daytime. So this is what Phyllis left Arizona for.

They stop at the Nugget Café, an unglamorous box-shaped brick building at the end of the strip. A middle-aged woman with orangish-blonde hair nibbles on french fries at the end of the Formica lunch counter while an old man at a booth holds a sandwich, his head bent over a newspaper spread out on the table in front of him.

"Losers must come here," Emily says.

"Most lose in this town. You just can't see it with all those fancy casinos and hotels."

On their way out, Dwight buys a deck of playing cards, packaged in a box printed with gold nuggets against a black background. He tosses them in the truck's glove box. About twenty-five miles past Vegas, a road sign announces the town of Indian Springs. A long gray concrete wall stands in the distance, three guard towers with searchlights rising high above it.

"Is that where he is?" Emily says. Grandma Marilee told Emily that Wayne Crowley is in High Desert State Prison, Indian Springs, Nevada. An image of half of his face under a baseball cap flashes as she gazes at the prison in the distance.

"Yeah."

"What casino did he rob? Was it on the strip where we were?"

"No. The older part of Vegas."

"And a convenience store?"

Dwight nods.

"Idiot." Emily looks at the guard towers and wall, wondering what it's like inside.

Farther down Highway 95, Dwight points to a large expanse of land to the west. "Nevada Test Site."

A stucco building stands off the road with "Nude Girls" hand-painted on the front. Open desert lies beyond.

"What's the Nevada Test Site?" Paula asks.

"Government sets off bombs and stuff. Then there's Area 51 next to it. That's the real secret stuff. Some say there's UFOs out there and bodies of dead aliens." Dwight laughs. His eyes twinkle a little.

Emily laughs too.

"You can only get into Area 51 on special, unmarked planes," he says. "God knows what they do there."

Highway 95 becomes Main Street and runs smack through the center of Tonopah, Nevada—all two miles of it. A large blue billboard with the words "Clown Motel," in red letters superimposed on a clown face, greets them. Next to it, a life-sized clown figure with curly orange hair holds a cardboard sign containing hand-printed room rates. The motel itself is a single-story row of rooms with a restaurant at the end. Ugly gray-and-brown mountains rise behind the motel. They look like giant mounds of vomit or shit; Emily can't decide which. Not a tree in sight. A few feet past the clown figure, Dwight turns into the Silver Queen Motel and parks facing the puke-colored mountains. He gets a suite with a separate bedroom and pull-out sofa in the living room. A faded painting of a mountain, in a broken frame, hangs on the wall. In it are two shacks surrounded by an assortment of machines. On one of the shacks are the words Belmont Mining Company. The room smells of stale cigarette smoke, even though a No Smoking sign dangles from the doorknob.

"I'll sleep out here." Dwight points to the brown-and-beige striped sofa.

"What's the plan?" Emily says.

"I'll go pick up Phyllis. Bring her back here."

"I want to come. See where she lives."

"I do too," Paula says.

They head back down Main Street and turn onto a gently inclining road, which leads to a single-story brown brick building with Nye County Jail painted above the door. Dwight pulls into the parking lot, turns off the engine, and gets out. Air drifts into the cab of the truck, a little cooler than Phoenix, but not much.

Emily gets out of the truck. “What are we doing here?”

“I tried to get a hold of Phyllis a couple of days ago, Emily. No answer on the number I had for her. I kept trying and nothing.”

“Are you kidding me? We’re not going to see her? Why did we come all this way?”

“We’re going to see her. One of the sheriff’s deputies is a friend of mine.”

“And?”

“I gave him a call, asked if he knew anything about my sister.”

“Let me guess.” Emily looks at the Nye County Jail sign.

“They picked her up the night before last. Said he’d hold her until I got here.”

“That’s why you wanted us to wait at the motel? So I wouldn’t see you get her out of jail?”

“I’m sorry, Emily.” Dwight lights up a cigarette.

“What did she do?”

“Too much to drink. Vagrancy.”

“What’s vagrancy?”

“It means you don’t have any place to go.”

“They put you in jail for that?” Emily thinks of the guy on the light-rail.

“They throw people into jail all the time for stuff that doesn’t hurt anybody. This time it worked for us, finding Phyllis.” Dwight gets out of the car and walks toward the brown building.

Emily and Paula wait in silence. Emily doesn’t want to talk. Paula seems to sense this. Except for the Las Vegas strip and that huge dam, everything she’s seen today has been either a shithole small town or a vast, dull expanse of nothing. Tonopah looks like a crappy place too. Small, ugly. Why would Phyllis want to live here? She could have come back to Tempe. Waited out Wayne's prison term there. Grandma Marilee would have let her stay.

They're walking out of the brick building now. Dwight and Phyllis. And the sheriff. Phyllis approaches the truck; Dwight and the sheriff hang back. She's taller than Emily imagined. Nearly as tall as Dwight and he's over six feet. But she seems a little hunched over as if her height is a burden, too much to hold erect. She wears jeans and a faded red T-shirt. She carries a multi-colored cloth purse.

Emily gets out of the truck, and Phyllis looks at her in a way Emily can't put a finger on. She can't tell if she's glad to see Emily, embarrassed, or sad. Emily can't identify her own feelings either. She remembers the face, those dark brown eyes, the gentle smile that would form gradually and the burst of laughter that followed. She remembers the feeling of a hand holding hers, like a lifeline, something strong and firm and secure. Emily's held on to that in some hidden place inside. Doesn't remember the circumstances, or what they were doing, just the feeling. Close up, lines in Phyllis's face stand out, tension around her mouth, two missing teeth on the bottom right. She looks older than she should. Tired, drained. Nothing like the woman in the light-rail ad. Her hair, a washed-out blondish brown, falls past her shoulders. It was darker in photos. It's greasy and hangs like wet strings; an inch of her dark roots shows. She tucks it behind her ears and approaches Emily. She touches the side of Emily's face, runs her fingers along a strand of Emily's hair, looks at it as if she's trying to remember something. Emily starts to pull away but doesn't. She freezes the way a child sometimes does before an adult. For a second, Emily feels the breath sucked out of her.

"You turned out beautiful." Phyllis's voice is raspy, a smoker's voice like Grandma Marilee's. Her hand trails from Emily's hair and she runs it down the length of Emily's arm. When she reaches Emily's fingertips she stops for a second as if she is going to grasp them, but then lets her hand drop away.

Paula joins them.

"And you," Phyllis says. "All grown up too."

Paula smiles. "Hi, Aunt Phyllis."

"I was sorry to hear about Ruth's passing." Phyllis touches Paula's shoulder briefly and then glances at both girls. "Me and your mom got on real good when you two were little."

Dwight returns. "How about we go back to the motel?"

When they get back to the motel, Dwight and Paula play cards in the bedroom. Phyllis sits on one end of the sofa, Emily on the opposite end. They sit in silence. Emily gets up and opens the bedroom door. Dwight and Paula are spreading cards all over the bed.

"I want you guys to come out here with us," Emily says.

"Why?" Paula says.

"I just do. I don't hardly know her." Emily doesn't care if Phyllis hears her.

"We need to finish this game," Paula says.

Dwight looks at Emily. "We'll be out in a while."

Emily hesitates, then closes the door and goes back to the sofa. Phyllis gets a Styrofoam cup from the counter by the coffee maker, sits back on the sofa, and lights a cigarette. She positions the cup between her legs and flicks the ashes into it.

"I don't think smoking's allowed in this room." Emily nods toward the No Smoking sign on the door.

Phyllis shrugs, goes on smoking. A cell phone buzzes in her bag and she reaches in to retrieve it. She looks at the screen and puts the phone back in her bag. It rings a few more times, then stops.

"You still in school?"

"I'm done with that."

"Boyfriend?"

Emily shakes her head. "What do you do here?" Emily asks. She doesn't add, *in this shithole.*

Phyllis looks surprised at the question. "I just live here."

"It doesn't look like there's much to do."

"I work over at the Clown Motel. In the café."

"Do you like it?"

Phyllis shrugs. "It's okay. They don't give me enough hours. I could show you inside. They got a room with a million dolls."

Phyllis lights up one cigarette after the other. She's on her third one, and Emily notices the quiver in Phyllis's cigarette hand.

"You are almost eighteen, right?"

"Yeah. August."

"August 24th," Phyllis says.

Emily nods. "Paula turns eighteen on the 27th."

"I remember. Two babies on that property."

"Where do you live?"

"Down the road a bit. With some friends."

Emily doesn't bother to ask why the vagrancy charge if she has a place to live. Maybe Phyllis is lying. Maybe she's homeless.

Emily thinks of her $1,000 back in the Airstream. How far will it take her? How much more can she get for Eureka?

"How much longer is Wayne Crowley in prison for?"

"Eight years, maybe less."

"You staying here then? When he gets out?" Emily doesn't know why she's asking these questions. She doesn't give a shit when Crowley gets out or where Phyllis lives. An impossible story plays in the recesses of her mind. Maybe she could be five years old again and they could come back to Tempe and just pick up their lives. Some alternative, do-over world.

Phyllis looks out the window and then back at Emily. "I don't know what I'm gonna do one day to the next, sweetheart. I don't know what we'll do when he gets out."

"I'm Emily. Not sweetheart."

Phyllis nods. For a second Emily's sorry she said it.

They sit in silence. Paula giggles in the next room. She hardly ever giggles around Dwight.

"How's your grandma doing?"

"Okay."

"She still talks to the dead people on the property?"

"Yeah, she does."

"Jay?"

"What about him?"

"He all right?"

"Yeah. Still Jay."

Phyllis smiles as if she knows exactly what Emily means. The bedroom door opens, and Dwight comes out.

"You guys hungry?"

Emily doesn't have much of an appetite, but nods.

"Dwight," Phyllis says. "Would you guys mind if I take a quick shower. I feel like a leftover something."

"Go ahead."

Phyllis disappears into the bathroom with her bag. The shower runs, then after a while, the blow dryer. When Phyllis comes out, she's wearing a navy-blue tank top that looks clean and a denim jacket over it. Her hair is full and soft around her face; silver hoop earrings hang from her ears. Emily smells vanilla from the shampoo. Phyllis has put on mascara and cranberry-colored lipstick. No perfume.

Dwight smiles at her. "When did you become a blonde, sis? Or partly a blonde?"

A picture flashes before Emily's eyes, like a flashback in a movie. Grandma Marilee as a young mother. Dwight and Jay and Phyllis as little kids running around the property. She almost smiles but catches herself.

Phyllis runs her fingers through her hair, holds her lower lip over her bottom teeth when she smiles so the gap from the missing teeth doesn't show.

On the way to the Clown Motel café, Paula points to an old graveyard. "Look at that."

"This whole town's supposed to be haunted," Phyllis says. "Nevada's full of haunted places."

Phyllis's cell phone buzzes three times during dinner. The third time she gets up and stands by the café's front door with the phone to her ear. Emily watches her. Phyllis smiles at whatever the person on the other end of the call is saying, and then she throws her head back and laughs. She returns to the booth, a hint of a smile still on her face. Emily can see how she could have been pretty. The waitress brings a check. Dwight gets up to pay at the register and the girls follow. They all stand awkwardly in front of the café.

"When are you all leaving?" Phyllis asks.

"Tomorrow morning," Dwight says.

"Do you want us to drop you off at your friends' house?" Emily asks.

Phyllis shakes her head, looks at Dwight. "You could give me a lift just down the road a bit."

"Okay. Let's go."

They get into the truck.

"Where to?" Dwight says.

Phyllis points down Main Street. They drive almost to the end, where Highway 95 heads back into the Nevada desert.

"Here. This'll be good."

Dwight pulls over. Phyllis turns to Emily, puts her arms around her and squeezes. Emily can feel Phyllis's bones, fragile as if she might break were Emily to hug her back. Emily doesn't. Phyllis touches Emily's hair the way she did outside the county jail, running her hand along the side of her face. She starts to say something but doesn't. Emily turns away.

"Thanks," Phyllis says to Dwight.

She walks a few paces down the street and turns into a building lit up with a neon sign that says Bug Bar. Then she's gone.

When they arrive back home, Dwight lets down the tailgate to unload their backpacks and an old-fashioned screen door he'd picked up at a yard sale on the side of the road in one of those shit towns in Nevada. Emily walks over to the tailgate, and he passes her the backpack.

"Don't hate her, Emily. She fucked up big time," he says. "Didn't do anything right by you."

Emily's chest tenses. She holds her body rigid, her way of stilling emotion, holding back any threatened flood of feeling. She focuses her gaze on the ground in front of her. She doesn't want Dwight to say anything else, but he keeps talking.

"But don't think she's not going through her own hell. And for a long, long time."

Emily raises her eyes for a minute. Dwight touches her arm briefly, gently, like a light brush of wind. Then, he picks up the screen door and carries it over to the side of his gun shed.

11

The flyer that Emily took from the wall of the PE building protrudes from the pages of *Slaughterhouse Five*, which lies on the floor next to the bed. She'd nearly forgotten about it, but now she pulls it out and examines the photo of three college girls in jeans and T-shirts, facing the camera, each with an armful of books. In print underneath, the psychology department is recruiting freshman undergraduate women who are at least eighteen years old. *We are looking for a good representation of diverse cultural groups for a study of stress in college. Interviews will take place between the end of spring semester and June 30. Ideal candidates will be taking summer classes. Participants will receive twenty-five dollars and be entered into a drawing for an additional seventy-five.*

She passes the flyer to Paula.

"Twenty-five dollars isn't that much."

"I know. But I might win the drawing. I need to get more money together for Eureka."

"You could do it too."

"No, thanks."

They take the bus over to Tempe Library, where Emily uses one of the computers to sign up online. Five days later, she stands in front of Paula, her hair pulled back in a high ponytail. She's dressed in a pair of new jeans and an ASU T-shirt from the Mona Plummer locker room, nicer than the first one she took. The Sparky logo covers the front. She whips her ponytail from side to side.

"Well?"

Paula nods. "You look like a college girl. With a lot of eye makeup."

Emily takes out her stolen ASU Sun Card and driver's license, holds them up next her face, one on each side.

"You'll pass. You want me to walk over with you?"

"That's okay. I don't know how long it'll take. Maybe an hour."

"Okay. I'll wait here."

Emily places her hand on the Airstream's door handle.

"Emily?" Paula says before she opens it.

"Yeah?"

"Are you glad you saw her? Your mom?"

Emily lets go of the handle, turns around. "My mom? Why the hell would you call her that?"

"Sorry. Phyllis. Are you glad we went up there?"

Emily doesn't answer at first. "I don't know. I don't give a shit one way or the other really."

It's late morning; the campus feels deserted. Summer classes haven't started yet. Emily finds the building—Administration Building C—an older two-story building with stairs on the outside. She climbs the stairs, enters through a glass door, and finds room 208 at the end of a short corridor. Inside is a rectangular conference room with a long table that takes up most of the space. Two girls sitting at the table look up when Emily comes in. Emily takes the seat closest to the door. Through a row of windows on the opposite wall, she sees the tops of palm trees and the sky behind them. This should be a piece of cake. But the walls feel confining, the way classrooms did before Dwight pulled them out for homeschooling. She squirms in the seat, can't get comfortable. A guy comes in, dressed in black pressed denim and the typical maroon polo shirt with Sun Devils in gold letters across the pocket.

"Hi, I'm Pete Henderson," he says, as he passes a questionnaire to each of them. "I'm going to ask you to fill out this questionnaire. When you're finished, I'll collect them and then we'll conduct open-ended interviews with each of you. You'll be out of here in less than forty-five minutes. Any questions?"

The girls shake their heads.

"Okay. I just need to verify IDs and we'll get going."

Emily is nervous as Pete walks around the table and checks each one against a list on his clipboard, but he doesn't check to see if the pictures match the girls. He places a Sun Devil cup full of Bic pens on the table and Emily takes one. It matches the cup and everything else on campus—maroon, with Sun Devil spelled in gold. The survey contains thirteen questions.

Age: Emily writes seventeen then crosses it out with heavy lines over and over and writes nineteen.

Gender: Female
Major: She leaves this one blank.

Semester Hours: What does this mean? A semester's a few months long. How many hours would that be? Emily looks at the other two girls, but they sit too far away for her to see what they're writing. Emily thinks back to junior high, how many classes did she take that semester before they started home school? There was math and English and American Government. Beginning Spanish. Geography. She writes five.

Employment: She thinks of the IDs and cell phones and the drive out to Steve's. She leaves this one blank.

Boyfriend/Girlfriend: The kind of question Dwight would respond to with *none of your goddamn business*. She leaves it blank.

GPA: She leaves this one blank too.

Commute or on-campus housing: Commute

Live with parents: No

Death of a loved one in the previous twelve months: She writes in YES in all caps. She starts to cross out the word but leaves it.

Change in living conditions: Emily thinks of the water and discovering the PE building and getting the water back on. The property thing. She writes Yes.

Have you felt anxious during the past semester? Yes. Why the fuck not? They're looking for people who are stressed.

Do you have trouble sleeping? Ditto.

By the time Emily finishes the survey, the other two girls have also finished. The one across the table smiles at her. Emily smiles back.

Pete returns and collects the surveys. "If you girls will come with me please."

They follow him down the short corridor to room 202. There are two other people there, who Pete introduces as the two other researchers, Alex and Shondra.

They pair up—Pete with Emily, Alex and Shondra with each of the other girls—and they go to separate rooms. In the room Emily and Pete go to, there is a desk and Pete motions for Emily to sit.

He's cute, reminds Emily of Jack in the *Titanic* DVD she and Paula watched over and over when they were twelve or thirteen. Ruth had told them all the young girls were crazy about Leonardo DiCaprio, the actor who played Jack. For a second Emily sees Jack at the bow of the *Titanic*, standing on the rail with Kate Winslet, wind blowing through his hair, face full of dreams, the soundtrack playing in the background.

Pete places Emily's completed survey on the desk, reads it over, and raises his eyes to her. When he smiles, he has dimples like Jack's.

"You took only two classes spring semester?"

"Five."

"So fifteen semester hours."

"That's what I meant."

"Are you registered for summer classes?"

"Not yet, but I will."

"Second session in July, right?"

"Yeah."

"How many semester hours?"

"Two classes."

"Okay, so six hours."

"Right."

Pete looks down at the questionnaire again. His hair's a light brown, with gold strands. He looks up at Emily. He seems much older than a college student, his eyes all serious and full of concern.

"I'm sorry about the death of your loved one," he says.

"What?"

"You wrote yes to 'death of a loved one.'"

"Oh yes. Thank you."

"Do you mind if I ask who died?"

"My mother."

"How long ago."

"A couple of weeks."

"Oh, I'm so very sorry." He seems taken aback. "That's pretty recent."

"Yeah. She lived in Tonopah."

"Arizona?"

"No, up in Nevada."

"I'm sorry," Pete says again.

"I hadn't seen her in a long time. We were going to visit each other. Then she just up and died." Emily looks down at her lap.

Pete pauses and then asks, "Are you okay for the interview?"

"Yeah, I'm fine." Emily looks at him. His eyes are blue. "We weren't really that close. She'd been in jail for a while."

"Oh, wow, really?"

"Do you want to know what she did?" Emily examines Pete's face. She can't imagine him doing anything that would land him in jail. Or even knowing anyone who would commit a crime.

"You don't have to tell me." But he looks curious.

"Okay."

"Of course, you can if you want to. If you think it's relevant to any stress you've experienced as a college freshman." He pushes his chair back from the desk, crosses his legs.

Emily shrugs. "It might be relevant. Like I said, though, we weren't really close."

Pete turns once again to Emily's survey. Emily wonders about his age. Over twenty for sure. His skin is smooth, but she detects the tiniest of stubbles on his chin.

He's quiet for a minute, and then he says, "You said you've felt anxious during the past semester. What kinds of things at the university make you anxious?"

"Oh, just stuff. Grades and homework, things like that." Emily looks around the small room. The walls are painted the palest of beige, almost white; not one thing hangs on them. There are no windows, and she thinks a prison cell must be bare like this room, stark. Can you put pictures on the wall in prison? Maybe Wayne Crowley has a picture of Phyllis on his cell wall. "She robbed a convenience store up in Las Vegas. With her boyfriend. She was just the get-away driver. Waited outside in a car, but he had a gun, the boyfriend. He got twenty years; she got less. I don't remember how many. She could have come home when she got out, but she didn't. Wanted to stay in Nevada near him. Then she died."

When Ruth died, Emily couldn't help thinking it would have been better if it had been Phyllis. Ruth and Paula loved each other so much. How fair was that? To just snatch Ruth away?

"I'm really sorry, Amber."

Emily barely hears him.

"You ever been up to Tonopah? It's a total shithole. I don't know how anybody could live in a place like that. Way worse than Phoenix. They have this fucking clown motel with a dumb clown figure out front that waves to people; well, if there were people, but there aren't many people in that dead place, but that clown holds a sign with prices like they're expecting tourists to flock in and stay awhile in that manure heap. It's actually named The Clown Motel. And this stupid-looking bar called the Bug Bar down the street—the whole friggin' town is about a block long, so everything is down the street from the fucking clown motel and full of dust and dirty brown air, brown like shit, even the mountains look like piles of shit and it's in the middle of fuck-all nowhere at the end of—"

"Amber."

Pete's voice sounds distant, like background noise.

"The boyfriend was my father. He couldn't think of anything more original than robbing a convenience store or casino. She stayed up there so she could be near him, Dwight said—"

"Amber?"

Emily looks at him. Who the fuck is Amber? Why is he calling her Amber?

"Are you okay?"

Tears spill down her face, her neck. Fuck. She swipes at them, rubs the back of her hands under her eyes; they come away streaked with black mascara.

"I need to go now." Emily gets up from the chair, turns to the door.

"Wait."

She stops.

"I owe you twenty-five dollars." He hands her an envelope. "And we need to do a quick debriefing."

She takes the envelope, squeezes it in her right hand, and puts it in her pocket without even opening it.

"I'm sorry," Pete says. "The university has a counseling service. I don't know if they're here all summer, but I can give you the number."

"I don't want their number."

"Okay. The debriefing will take only a few minutes."

Emily ignores him, walks out of the interview room, through the reception area, down the hall to the double glass doors, and down the stairs two at a time.

"Fuck!" she screams as she walks away from the building. She finds an outdoor water fountain and splashes water on her face. Amber. The name on her fake ID.

Almost noon, the heat of the day is in force, but Emily runs to the edge of campus and, instead of crossing to the west side of Mill Avenue, begins to jog around the perimeter of campus. She circles it twice, faster than she remembers ever running. Buildings and people are a blur. Vehicles flash silver and shiny metal. The aqua-blue glass building is a distorted smudge. She stops at the traffic signal on Mill and University. Her heart races, sweat pours down her temples, runs behind her ears, and soaks her T-shirt.

"What's wrong?" Paula says when Emily walks through the Airstream's door. "I thought you'd be back in an hour. It's been over two."

"Whatever. It took longer." Emily is parched. She picks up the gallon of water from the floor, twists the top off, and gulps down the lukewarm water.

"Did they pay you?"

"Yeah." Emily tosses the damp, crumpled envelope to Paula, takes her shoes and wet T-shirt off, and lies down.

Paula opens the envelope. "It's a check made out to Amber Nelson. Did you know it would be a check?"

Emily doesn't answer. She closes her eyes.

Paula moves the square floor fan to Emily's side of the bed. The air blows wisps of hair around Emily's face. All that trouble for a check she can't even cash.

12

Paula and Emily are in the Airstream when Jay comes in with a cigarette dangling from his lips. Emily looks up from the book she's reading. "Ever think of knocking?" she says.

"Door's wide open."

The doorknob broke six months ago. Emily tied one end of a piece of rope around it and wrapped the other around a hook on the wall, but it's come undone.

"What do you want?"

"Steve's got something we might be interested in."

"You think we're partners or something now?" She lays her book on the bed.

"Always the smart-ass, Emily." For a second Jay looks hurt.

"Sorry. What is it?"

"He's not gonna tell me on the phone. That's something you should learn."

"I don't have a phone, so I guess I don't have that problem."

"All those cell phones you guys stole and you didn't keep any for yourselves? You should buy a couple."

He's right. They should get some cell phones.

"Anyway, Steve's picking me up at the lake tomorrow. He asked for you two. Think about it."

"No way, not me," Paula says.

Emily gives Paula a look. "We'll let you know."

"Two o'clock." Jay steps out and tries to pull the door closed, but it swings wide open when he lets go of the knob. Paula closes the Airstream's door and reattaches the rope to the wall hook. "I told you I'm done."

"C'mon, what the hell else do we have going on?"

"I've got something else going on."

"What else do you have going on?"

"Nothing. Just something you'd think was dumb."

"C'mon, what is it?"

"A retreat."

"What the fuck is a retreat?"

"What did I tell you? You don't even know what it is, and you think it's dumb."

"Tell me what it is."

"I saw a sign out front of True Lord last week."

"You went back there? To another sermon?"

"No. I was just walking by. That nice old lady was there in the front yard and a few other people." Paula takes a sheet of paper from her makeshift bedside table and passes it to Emily. "She gave me this."

True Lord Christian Rebirth Retreat. 3 days, May 30—June 1 on the exquisite Verde River. $300.00 lodging, meals, and prayer service. Below the words, a photo of a river and two cabins.

"That's next weekend."

"I know. I'm going. I paid the money yesterday."

"You paid three hundred? To pray for three days? To listen to that weirdo preacher guy? Jesus, Paula."

Paula grabs the paper back from Emily. "Fuck you. I won't be praying and listening to that guy." She places the flyer back on the table.

"So what are you going to do there?"

"I don't know. What are you doing down here? What are you doing with the money you have?"

"Get a cell phone for one thing."

"Yeah, me too."

"Look. We'll be eighteen in a couple of months. We can do anything then. Take off for Eureka. And there's other places too. Places not full of ugly shit-pile mountains and dead little towns."

"That's great. What's it got to do with me going to the retreat? Or meeting that Steve guy again?"

"It takes money to go places."

"I know that."

"So just come with me to check it out. We don't have to say yes."

"I already know I won't like it. Steve's creepy."

"He's not as creepy as that True Lord preacher."

Emily pulls back the curtains, opens the window, and props open the door with a stack of books. The floor fan barely blows cool air. The outside air is hotter than inside, but the open window makes the Airstream less smothering. She puts her face to the screenless window and breathes deeply. Bright afternoon light splashes on the U.S. Airways building.

"You could come too. To the retreat. We'd be in a pretty place by a cool river."

Emily laughs, but for a second she's touched that Paula would like her to go. "Thanks. I don't think I'd fit in with those people. We can just check out the thing with Jay. Find out what Steve's got going. It won't hurt to see what it's all about. And you can still go on your retreat."

"I know I can still go on the retreat. I don't need your permission."

"I didn't mean it like that. You're so sensitive lately."

The following afternoon they meet Jay at the Rio Salado parking lot. Jay stands next to the open passenger door of a white Camry. Steve sits behind the wheel. Jay motions for them to get in the back.

When Steve turns to nod at Emily and Paula, his wild eye strays over the back seat and out the rear window. Emily wonders how he can drive without bumping into other cars. But it doesn't seem to affect him. He takes Interstate 10 to Phoenix and gets off at Nineteenth Avenue, a busy commercial-industrial area near the state fairgrounds. A large billboard underneath it advertises the Crossroads Gun Show on Memorial Day weekend.

"Where are we going?" Jay says to Steve.

Steve doesn't answer. He turns west off Nineteenth Avenue and into a neighborhood of warehouses, salvage yards, and empty dirt lots. Linden Street. On the corner, a small stucco building, Southwest Recollectors, stands in the middle of a yard with a mountain of aluminum cans, old computers, and scraps of metal. On the property next door, skeletons of rusted-out vehicles slump on the ground next to a double garage with two cars up on jacks. A Doberman paces and barks as Steve parks the Camry on the opposite side of the street, in front of a house. When they get out, the air smells of hot dust and engine oil.

Emily looks around the street. The house next door is vacant; awkwardly placed panels of wood cover the windows. A run-down one-story apartment complex sits a few yards from the empty house. She's never been to this part of Phoenix. It reminds her a little of home and all of Dwight's in-process projects. But it also gives her the sensation of stepping into a crack, an invisible crevice between the city's spaces of new high-rises and upscale apartments, gated communities, freeways, and the university. A world underneath the visible one.

Steve lifts the latch on a gate to the house. The whole front yard is a brick patio. A man behind the screen door opens it as they approach and steps onto the porch. Steve nods to him, his right eye drifting off in the direction of the house next door. The man looks at Jay, real serious for a second, as if he might punch him in the face, then laughs and gives him a bear hug.

"Stone, man," Jay says. "How the fuck are you? Steve didn't say we'd be working with you."

Stone smiles but doesn't say anything. He looks at Emily and Paula and tips his porkpie hat.

"Mic Stone," he says. "Stone to my friends." He wears a beige shirt with tiny navy-blue dots and a silk scarf around his neck, navy with tiny beige dots, the reverse image of his shirt.

Emily offers her hand. "Emily."

"And?" Stone looks at Paula.

"This is Paula." Emily nudges Paula with her elbow and Paula extends her hand to Stone.

"My nieces," Jay says.

Stone's eyes go again from Emily to Paula, then back to Emily. She keeps her eyes on him as well. He does look sort of like a stone, a rough, pock-marked one. Deep lines cross his face at various angles, as if his face were a recently put-together jigsaw puzzle. Quite a bit older than Dwight. But his eyes are sharp, wouldn't miss a beat; you wouldn't try to put something over on him. Two small gold-hooped earrings hang from his left ear, one from his right. A mix of near-black hair with streaks of gray protrudes from under the hat. Black eyeliner rims his lower eyelids.

"Let's go inside." Stone holds the screen door open and gestures for them to enter.

The cavernous living room is empty except for a sofa. Thick aluminum panels cover the front window, a strip of sun cuts through the gaps. The house feels as if no one lives there. Stone motions for them to follow him down a short hallway that ends in a small bedroom. Stone flicks the light switch on the wall.

"Holy donkey scrotums." Jay giggles like a little kid. "What's all this?"

"Looks like suitcases to me," Steve says.

Suitcases in a variety of sizes and colors fill the room. Emily counts them, twelve neatly lined up against the wall, another row of ten in front of them, and a third row with maybe half as many. Then order gives way to suitcases randomly shoved against one another and she loses count. The panes in the only window are painted black. A few feet from the window is a metal-barred external security door.

"Those are new." Stone points to the haphazardly tossed suitcases. "They came in last week."

"Came in from where?" Jay asks.

Tags hang on the newest arrivals, some with dark bar codes and numbers, others with names, addresses, and phone numbers. Emily moves closer, touches one of the name tags. Jeffrey Garner, Paradise Valley, Arizona 85283, 602-555-4129. The name gives the suitcase meaning the way the names on the stolen IDs do. Who is Jeffrey Garner? What does he look like?

Emily turns to Jay. "They came from the airport. Where do you think?"

Stone smiles. "Airports don't check baggage claim tickets. They've got more important things to worry about. Nobody gives a shit about baggage claim."

"Besides," Steve adds, "TSA doesn't have authority there. You just walk up to the bag belt and take what you want." He looks at them. "You girls ever been in an airport?"

Emily has never been to an airport. "No, but we can check it out though," she says.

"Airports aren't like other places, Emily," Jay says.

Emily ignores Jay, turns to Stone. "Like I said, we can check it out."

Stone laughs. "I like this little niece of yours, Uncle Jay. How old are you girls?"

"Almost eighteen."

"They got surveillance cameras at Sky Harbor," Steve says.

"Well." Stone pulls a cigarette from a pack in his shirt pocket and holds it unlit between his lips. He looks at Emily. "I guess there's nothing unusual about picking up suitcases at baggage claim, is there?"

"Why do you need us? And what do we get out of it?" Emily says.

"Steve will tell you on the way home."

The dog is still barking as they pull away from Stone's house.

"Stone's a hands-off kind of guy," Steve says as they drive back to the lake parking lot. "He likes to interview who works for him though."

"Interview?"

"Yes, Emily. That was your interview. You passed or he wouldn't have told you anything at all."

"He didn't even ask me any questions."

"No, but he watched you in that room with all the suitcases."

"Whatever. Why does he even need us?"

"You, Emily," Paula says. "Why does he need you?"

"He needs you because, like I said, he's hands-off. And he's got me doing other stuff. And he don't trust a lot of people. And he likes your uncle Jay." Steve takes his eyes off the road for a second and looks in the rearview mirror at Paula. "You passed the interview too, Paula."

"I didn't do anything."

When he drops them off at Tempe Town Lake, he says, "I'll be in touch with you, Jay."

On the way home Jay walks with a gait, as if he's about to start skipping. "He's something, that Stone, huh?"

"Yeah," says Emily. "What's with the eye makeup?"

"Thinks he looks like Keith Richards."

"Who?"

"The Rolling Stones guy. The one in *Pirates of the Caribbean*."

"He's as weird as Steve," Paula says. "Worse."

"What now?" Emily asks Jay.

"Like Steve said. Wait for him to contact me and I'll let you guys know what's up."

"You mean let her know." Paula points to Emily. "I'm not getting involved in this." She walks quickly ahead, toward the Airstream.

"Just come with me to Sky Harbor," Emily says later that night. "We'll take the light-rail. It'll be an adventure. We're not going to do anything."

Paula stays quiet.

"I went to that church with you, didn't I?"

"That's different."

"How's it different? I went along on something you wanted to do. We'll just take a look at the airport. I know you don't want to work with those guys."

"Fuck, Emily. You always do this."

Emily checks the time on her new cell phone, a Target special, pay as you go. It's two o'clock in the afternoon. She and Paula wait at Forty-Fourth Street and Washington for the bus that will take them to the airport. The temperature is record-breaking for May at 111 degrees. The eternal fierceness of the sun scorches everything—the concrete they stand on, the nearby rooftops, the chrome of vehicles scurrying like insects along the arteries of the city. The air nearly explodes from efforts to cool it. The few people who walk along Washington look like zombies in a state of shock, as if they cannot quite fathom the fact that they are still able to breathe and move, and that their bodies have not simply gone up in flames. A man and woman push a shopping cart past the bus stop. A sleeping bag, clothes, a large water bottle, and grocery bags fill it. The couple appear bent as if melted by the heat and then re-formed into slightly different versions of their prior selves. Bus 13 approaches and stops. Four people get off and then Emily and Paula board for the airport.

Stone said Terminal 2, the older part of Sky Harbor. "It's easier to get in and out of the parking area."

The ride takes about five minutes; they get off at the end of the passenger drop-off area in front of the terminal. Before entering, Emily walks to the end of the sidewalk outside the terminal and looks at the parking structure across from the sidewalk. Cars pull up and drop passengers off. People stand with bags by their sides waiting for rides. She returns to Paula and they enter the airport at the United Airlines entrance. A blast of icy cool air hits them, a stark relief from the heat but also too cold. Hostile, sterile. Emily rubs her palms up and down her arms. The ticket and check-in counters are ahead. Garbled announcements sound from unseen speakers. Electronic arrival and departure boards hang from a wall to the left of the United check-in counter. There must be a million flights a day and this is just Terminal 2. Jay said there were three terminals at Sky Harbor. Emily breathes in the sense of possibility that comes from all the flight numbers and names of cities. Is that why Phyllis left Tempe? Searching for energy and movement and what life might hold in store? Emily could understand that, but it sure as shit didn't look like Phyllis found it in Tonopah.

"There." Paula points to a sign on their left. Baggage Claim.

Travelers congregate around three carousels. The screen above Carousel 2 announces United Flight 389. A couple dozen or so people watch the luggage roll by on a conveyor belt, some periodically grab their bags and walk away. The belt empties, but half the people are still waiting. After a few minutes, more suitcases shoot out.

"Let's look around," Emily says.

They walk to a large open area with stores arranged in a semicircle—Starbucks, a Mexican restaurant, a shop with newspapers, cigarettes, and snacks. Beyond it a line forms at security. Passengers stand with small suitcases and briefcases at their sides, papers in their hands.

Emily tries to imagine what the area beyond security looks like. "This place is cool."

"Yeah, it is. But I still don't want to work for Steve or Stone."

Emily is annoyed. "Whatever then." She walks away, back toward baggage claim.

Paula follows. "I already told you I don't want to."

"Okay, okay. Go pray with those church people. I'll do the job with Jay."

A throng of people surround the carousel closest to the exit. Emily walks to it and stands amongst the just-arrived passengers. The conveyor belt moves but it's empty.

"What are you doing?" Paula says.

"Just taking another look."

The first few suitcases shoot from the opening. Several people lean forward to see if the bags belong to them. As the conveyor empties and the crowd thins, two bags shoot out—a large brown leather one on wheels and a small black bag, not much bigger than a briefcase. Emily grabs it, sits it on the floor, and examines the name tag. She puts it back on the belt. Easy. She moves away from the carousel and the people standing around it and heads out to the bus stop. Their bus pulls up and passengers get off. She looks around but doesn't see Paula. Two women board. Emily is the only one waiting. She still doesn't see Paula.

"When are you leaving?" she asks the bus driver.

"Soon."

"Can you wait for my cousin? She's coming."

"Five minutes, then I'm off."

Emily is about to go back inside the airport when Paula walks through the exit.

"Where the hell were you? He's about to leave."

"Where the hell was I? You're the one who huffed away from me. You said we were just checking out the airport."

"We did."

Emily gets on first, Paula behind her.

"I thought you were going to take that bag," Paula whispers to Emily as they sit in two seats near the back of the bus.

"I told you we wouldn't do anything. You never trust me."

13

When Emily wakes, Paula's side of the bed is empty and she's not in the Airstream. Rain taps on the trailer's roof. The Airstream's door swings open and closed; the rope hangs loosely from the wall hook. Paula hardly ever gets up before Emily. Maybe she already left for that retreat, but Emily thought the retreat was tomorrow morning. Maybe she got the days mixed up. Paula would have woken her though, wouldn't she? Emily goes to the door and watches the branches of the mesquite tree sway in the wind and the prayer flags whip around the edge of the patio roof. Grandma Marilee sits on the patio under the eaves, sipping coffee, a book in her lap. Emily watches her through the rain's blur, as if looking at her through a film of cellophane. Marilee looks up and waves. Emily smiles and waves back.

She closes the door and puts on her jeans. She squirts a strip of toothpaste onto her tongue, takes a swig of water from the one-gallon container they keep by the sink, and then opens the door and spits onto the ground outside. Marilee looks up and waves. She gestures to the wind and rain. "Early monsoon." She smiles with pride as if the weather is her own accomplishment. "I heard those cicadas singing last week. I knew it'd come early." Marilee always says monsoon starts a week after the cicadas begin singing at night.

Paula packed some clothes for the retreat in a gym bag they'd stolen from the PE building. It's still on the floor by her side of the bed. Emily leaves the trailer, oblivious to the rain, and heads up the street in the direction of True Lord Church. Maybe they had some stupid meeting before the retreat. Maybe Paula met a church boy she didn't tell Emily about. She probably thought Emily would tease her about that. And she would be right. Emily would have.

Traffic from Mill Avenue hums in the background; the Union Pacific whistles and clunks. Emily's soaked, but the rain feels soft on her skin, comforting like bath water. She turns on Tenth Street, passes a few houses, and arrives at True Lord Church. Paula sits on the concrete step under the eaves, her back to the door. She doesn't even look up as Emily approaches. A padlock has been placed on the door handle. A large sign announces Bank-Owned, No Trespassing. Underneath, someone has posted a note on yellow notebook paper: *Trust Yahweh with all your heart and don't lean on your own understanding*. Religious gobbledygook bullshit.

Emily sits down next to Paula but doesn't say anything. Paula's auburn curls look like shiny swirls of ribbon framing her face. When they were little, Grandma Marilee used to recite an old nursery rhyme for them. *There was a little girl, who had a little curl, right in the middle of her forehead.* When she said this Marilee would gently flick Paula's curls. *And when she was good, she was very, very good. But when she was bad, she was horrid.* Emily and Paula would giggle and repeat the word horrid over and over. Paula always used to say to Emily, *I wish I had your hair* as Grandma Marilee carefully fixed Emily's thick dark hair into a long braid that hung down her back. But Emily always envied those curls.

"You're all wet."

"So are you." Bits of rain linger on Paula's cheeks, or maybe they're tears.

"I'm sorry about your retreat."

Paula wipes her face with the back of her hand. "You thought it was stupid."

Emily shrugs. "That doesn't mean I can't be sorry."

"I came over here to check on the time. I couldn't remember if we were leaving at eight or eight-thirty tomorrow."

"Who did you give your three hundred dollars to?"

"That preacher. Mrs. Burnstein, the old lady we met on Easter, told me he was the one in charge. She was going too, already paid her money."

"Do you know his name."

"No."

"Maybe we'll see her around. Maybe Mrs. Burnstein lives in the neighborhood. We could find out his name from her. Or we could tell your dad. He knows a lot of people around here."

Paula shakes her head. "He'd ask where I got three hundred dollars. Just forget it, Emily. I don't even care about the money."

"Whatever, it's your money."

To the east, swatches of blue break through the gray sky. The rain lightens, but water streams from the gutter at the corner of the building.

"Emily."

"Yeah."

"Do you wish your mom would come back here to stay?"

Emily picks up a pebble from the ground next to the step and plays with it in her palm. She starts to say, *Don't call her my mom*, but lets it slide. "Are you kidding? I hardly know her. She doesn't give a shit."

"I mean before. Did you used to?"

"No. Mostly I tried to forget her." That's not true. She tosses the pebble toward the street.

"Maybe it's better if you don't get so used to having someone around."

"I never got used to having her around, that's for sure."

Paula doesn't say anything.

"At least your mom stuck around to take care of you as long as she could. She loved you a lot."

"I know. You know what I never thought about before?"

"What?"

"I knew how sad I was when she died. And how sad my dad was. And Grandma Marilee and everybody."

"Yeah. Your mom was great."

"But my mom must have been really sad too. At the end, she must have known she'd never see any of us again. I never thought of that until just a little while ago, sitting here in the rain."

Emily doesn't say anything. There's no good thing to say.

The rain has stopped; the cloud cover disappears from the sky. Their clothes and hair are still damp.

"Do you ever wish our family was normal, Emily? Things always seem messed up."

"We're okay. The world's fucked anyway. Let's go."

Paula stands, looks again at the bank-owned sign. "Let's go swimming tomorrow. Like we used to at Clark Park."

"Okay."

❧

Clark Park Pool is packed with adults, teenagers, and little kids. An elderly couple sits on the side at the shallow end, their feet dangling into the water. Swimmers sit on towels spread out on the concrete around the pool and at tables with shade umbrellas.

"C'mon," Emily says. "Let's do the slide."

The line is mostly ten- to twelve-year-old kids and a few adults with smaller children. Bodies swish down the slide, spray shooting from the sides, making a splash as they hit the water. An image comes to Emily as she watches them. Phyllis is holding her hand in a line like the one today. She doesn't remember how old she was. When they reached the top of the ladder, they stood there for a second and looked out over the park, the neighborhood beyond, the world. Then her mom sat down, positioned Emily between her legs and held her arms around her small body. And they flew, nothing but water and motion and splash at the bottom of the slide. Emily's head went under for a second and popped up. She giggled and screamed and never for a second doubted that Phyllis had her tight and wouldn't let go.

Now, Paula goes first. Emily doesn't wait until Paula hits the water as the lifeguard standing at the top of the slide told her to. Instead, she starts down as soon as Paula shoots off, less than two feet between them. "I'm right behind you," she screams as they careen down the slippery slide. The tips of her feet touch Paula's backside. Paula hits the water, swimming quickly to the right of the slide. Emily hits seconds later and does the same. They look at each other, eyelashes clumped together, giggling.

"Let's do it again," Paula says, catching her breath, laughing.

The line is shorter.

"Not so close this time," the lifeguard says.

Emily smiles at him. Winks. He looks about her age, blond and all tanned. He'll probably go to ASU in the fall. She's ahead of Paula this time. She sits down, ready to push off.

"Hey, Emily."

Emily turns her head enough to see Paula. "Yeah?"

"I'll go to the airport with you and Jay."

Emily gives her a thumbs-up, turns back, and shoots down the slide.

14

"You look almost like a normal person." Emily stands before Jay in the parking lot at the west end of Tempe Town Lake. "Did you get your hair done?"

Jay's hair lies back off his face, plastered against his head with hair gel. He wears new-looking beige denims and a pale-blue polo shirt.

"Funny, Emily." He shuffles his feet impatiently in his polished brown loafers. "Where'd you two get your threads? You look twenty or something."

Emily smiles. She wears a navy skirt and a white silk blouse; her hair is twisted into a French knot. A loose strand falls along the left side of her face. She's sweating in the afternoon heat, and already the blouse feels damp.

"Buffalo Exchange." Paula curtsies in her yellow and green sundress. Silver hoop earrings hang from her ears.

Steve pulls into the lot in a maroon Dodge Caravan, windows deeply tinted except for the front one. Jay rides shotgun, Emily and Paula slide into the middle seat. Steve nods to them. The third seat has been removed, leaving the back vacant.

"Where's your Camry?" Jay says.

"Back at Stone's place."

It's a little after three o'clock when they enter the Red Mountain freeway and head toward Sky Harbor Airport. Jay's legs tap against the floorboard as if keeping time to music only he can hear. He looks a little uncomfortable in his new clothes and slicked-back hair. But his eyes have the sparkly look he gets when he's excited.

"United Flight 2039 from Chicago lands at four o'clock," Steve says. "And a British Airways direct from London lands at three-thirty. It'll take a while for those passengers to go through customs."

"Customs?" Emily asks.

"They check you out when you come from another country," Steve says.

"Yeah, like England," Jay says.

Steve takes the airport exit.

When they exit for the airport, planes roar overhead. One comes in for a landing and flies over the van, so close it seems within an arm's reach. How would it be to shoot into the air in one of those things, straight through the clouds, above everything? Or at night with a million stars in the sky? And what is it like on the inside? Do the seats look like those on the light-rail?

Steve attempts to pull in front of the United sign at Terminal 2, but cars unloading and picking up passengers line the curb next to the sidewalk. He stops the van as close as he can get and double-parks next to a green Corolla. "I'll be out front at passenger pickup," he says. "Get what you can. Use your head and don't be stupid." He looks directly at Jay when he says this.

Jay turns to Emily and Paula. "You hear that, girls?" A grin spreads across Jay's face.

"Whatever," Emily says.

"If I'm not here when you come back out, don't panic, it just means I had to circle."

Outside the terminal the air buzzes. Energy. Motion. And heat. It's busier than the first time Emily was here. Travelers arrive in cars, taxis, and a Super Shuttle van. Up ahead the bus waits to pick up passengers for the light-rail stop.

When they enter the terminal, Emily examines the departure and arrival boards: Los Angeles, Chicago, Albany, Boston, and a long list of cities, some Emily's never heard of. And that's just United. There's Continental and Alaska Air. And more in the other terminals.

"We could go anywhere," she says, more to herself than anyone else.

But Jay hears her. "Yeah. Dwight went all the way to Iraq. Not from this terminal though."

"You ever been on a plane, Jay?"

Jay shakes his head, a little sadly. "You need a passport to go some places."

"I know that."

"Look." Paula points to the arrival board. "There's a flight coming in from Las Vegas."

Emily thinks of the glittery strip and the desolate road to Tonopah.

The line at the TSA checkpoint is longer than the last time. Paula heads for Starbucks. Emily and Jay follow.

"What are you doing?" Jay says.

"Just getting a drink. When we checked this place out last week, I saw a woman waiting at baggage claim with a Starbucks drink in her hand."

"She knows what she's doing," Emily says, though she's a little surprised. She hadn't even noticed the woman with a drink. Paula seems comfortable. Maybe she's really getting into this thing.

Paula looks at the drink menu on the wall behind the counter and orders a raspberry latte venti.

"What the hell is venti?" Emily says.

"I don't know." Paula smiles. "It sounds nice though."

The clerk pours dark liquid, milk, and three scoops of raspberry syrup into a metal container. He puts a top on it and turns it every which way, shakes it up and down, and then dispenses the liquid into a large paper container and snaps a plastic lid on it. He places it on the counter and calls out, "Raspberry latte." Paula picks it up, takes a sip from the tiny opening, and then passes it to Emily.

"Okay," Jay says. "You guys ready to do what we came for? Me and Paula will take United. Emily, you take British Airways."

"Steve didn't say who would take which carousel."

"Look, Emily. Why are you always such a smart-ass? You don't like British Airways?"

"Forget it." Emily turns toward the British Airways carousel.

"Oh yeah," Jay says. "Steve said we should leave our sunglasses on. Just in case the surveillance cameras take our photos."

Emily watches Jay and Paula at the United carousel. Paula sips her latte. She doesn't look nervous like she always had at ASU. She focuses intensely on the suitcases as the carousel moves. The luggage comes slowly at first; the bags tumble out over one another. Emily's British Airways carousel is still empty. A few passengers are waiting for their luggage. Signs instruct passengers not to accept rides from drivers soliciting outside, advise them to verify claim tickets, warn that bag theft will be prosecuted. Emily doesn't see anything that looks like the surveillance cameras Jay mentioned.

Jay reaches for a large navy-blue suitcase with a red strap around the middle. Just as he's about to lift it off the belt, a middle-aged man takes hold of it and looks at him. The man says something, and Jay backs off. A woman next to the man takes a small red bag off the belt and they move away from the carousel. Jay grabs the next suitcase, a black canvas bag, and moves casually toward the door they came in through. Three bags shoot onto the British Airways belt: a grubby brown duffle bag, a large gray metal suitcase, and a green-and-red plaid cloth bag. Emily watches them go by. One, two times. She glances again at the United carousel and sees Paula grab a beige hard-shell suitcase. The British Airways bags go by a third time. None of the passengers reach for them. Two more suitcases shoot out. Emily keeps her eyes on the first three suitcases. Her gut tells her to take one of them. The fourth time they come by, she takes the green-and-red plaid one and heads to the door. She immediately thinks she should have chosen a more ordinary-looking suitcase. *Too late, don't think about it.* Her pulse races, her temples throb. Despite the frigid air from the AC, perspiration drips down her temples. She doesn't take her eyes off the exit door, doesn't stop to see if anyone saw her or is looking at her.

When she steps outside, the afternoon light plays off the roofs of the vehicles and the air dances in flickering sheets. Even the asphalt emits a shimmer. The chill from the AC inside the terminal sticks to her skin, wrapping her in a cool invincibility as she makes her way to the Caravan, which is parked on the curb, its engine running. Jay slides the side door open. Emily passes her suitcase to him and gets in. As they drive away from the airport, Jay gives a whoop. "Holy shit! We did it." Paula is saying something, but they are both muffled background noise to Emily. What is this feeling? Panic? Excitement? She's stepped over some line.

At the driveway on Linden Street, Steve gets out, unlocks a wrought-iron gate, and then drives the van into the backyard. He parks on the grass adjacent to the patio. While he relocks the gate, Jay unlocks the house and Emily and Paula follow him inside with their suitcases and put them in the room where the others were stored. The room is empty now and so are the two opened suitcases tossed at odd angles on the floor in the corner.

"What happened to all the other bags?" Emily asks.

"I guess Stone sold what was worth anything and got rid of them."

Steve walks through the door and nods. "Not a good idea to keep stuff around too long."

The house feels empty.

"Where is Stone?" Emily asks.

Steve steadies his good eye on her, the wild one wanders the room. "He don't tell me everything. I guess we're done here."

"Aren't we going to open the suitcases?" Paula asks. "See what's inside."

Steve shakes his head.

They were the hired help. Why would they need to know what was inside the bags? Emily walks to the plaid bag and looks at the name tag. Stephanie Hopkins. "Can I take this?"

"What for?" Jay says.

"I'm not asking you." Emily looks at Steve.

"What do you want it for?"

"I don't know. I like IDs, makes it personal."

Steve laughs. "I know you like IDs. Be my guest."

Emily rips the name tag and the British Airways flight tag from the bag.

They follow Steve out to his car. He counts out $450 and hands $150 to each of them. It's six o'clock by the time he drops them at the Tempe Town Lake parking lot.

"We've got something else going for next Wednesday. I'll pick you guys up, same place at five p.m. This time Terminal 3."

When they get out of the car, Jay turns toward Mill Avenue.

"Where are you going?" Emily says.

"I don't know. It's Friday. I have some money. Who knows? Maybe I'll go to one of those college hangouts."

"It's summer, Jay."

"So?"

"College girls won't be hanging out."

"Doesn't matter." Jay blushes slightly.

As Emily watches him walk away, his loneliness hits her. He shuffles down the sidewalk by the lake until he's out of sight.

"It sucks we couldn't see what was inside."

"But we got all this money," Paula says.

"I know, but still."

At five o'clock on Wednesday, Steve picks them up. "Delta 2290 from LA lands at 5:45," he says.

Terminal 3 is quite a bit bigger than Terminal 2, several levels high. Steve pulls over at the passenger drop-off. "This is level two. The gates and shops are on level three and the baggage carousels are on level one."

They get out of the van and enter at the Delta entrance. Emily quickly surveys the scene inside and heads for the escalator up to level three. Paula's right behind her.

"Where are you guys going?" Jay follows them. "Steve said we didn't have time."

"We've got time. I just want to see what it looks like up there."

Level three reminds Emily of the Arizona Mills mall, except people pull or carry suitcases. Gift shops and bookstores line the corridor. She steps inside The Body Shop to the display counter.

"Look at all this stuff." Paula dips her finger into a sample container of mango shea butter.

"Can I help you?" A woman walks to the counter.

"Just looking." Emily smiles at her.

"C'mon," Jay says. "The plane is landing now."

"Okay, okay. Let's go down the elevator."

They find the elevators in a small corridor off to the side of the shops. A family with a stroller and two small girls gets in with them. The man hits level one for baggage claim. Emily winks at the older girl, who's about five. The girl giggles shyly and turns her head to her mother.

They each take one suitcase from the Delta carousel, all various hues of black, and walk quickly to the exit. Steve is pulled over to the pick-up curb, engine running, back of the van open. They quickly put the bags in the back and close the doors. This time he drops them off at the Tempe Town Lake parking lot directly from the airport. He counts out another $150 each.

"We're gonna get rich this way," Jay says.

As they step out of the van Emily glances in the back. It's half full of suitcases, which makes her think Stone must have other people working for him.

A couple of days later, Emily watches as Jay pulls into the driveway in Steve's Camry. He goes into his lean-to and comes out with a duffle bag.

Dwight looks up from the motorcycle he's working on. "Where you going?"

"Staying with a friend in Phoenix for a while. Helping him with some construction stuff."

Dwight looks at him funny. "Stay out of trouble, Jay."

Jay gives him a thumbs-up.

Two weeks go by before he comes back.

Emily walks over to the Camry. "Where have you been?"

"Around. Steve's. Stone's."

Dwight's gone off somewhere with Claude. Grandma

Marilee's fallen asleep in her recliner, head drooping over the book in her lap.

"What's up with the suitcase jobs?"

"Nothing. Steve says Stone likes to lay off for a while. You can't steal suitcases every day. Airport people might get suspicious, put on more security."

"Or maybe he's got another team working for him. Or maybe Steve's doing it on his own."

"Steve ain't doing it on his own."

"Did you see all those suitcases in the back of the van last time?"

"Yeah, I did. And it's best to just mind your own business. Do the job they give us and that's it."

"Whatever."

"Aren't you going to live here anymore?" Paula asks.

"Sure. I'm just hanging out at Stone's place for now."

"Are you and Steve doing the airport on your own?"

"I told you, Emily. What's your obsession with the airport jobs?"

The money, of course. That's what she's obsessed with, but she shrugs. "Nothing."

Grandma Marilee lets out a loud snore, then a silence as if she isn't breathing at all. She opens her eyes, looks at Jay, and smiles.

"There's no reason we can't do it on our own," Emily says when she and Paula are back in the Airstream, lying on the bed, the floor fan blowing on them. "We just take the light-rail and the bus, like we did before."

"How do we know flights and times and stuff?"

"We can figure it out. Let's go back to Terminal 2 and check out those overhead screens. See which flights are coming in. They probably come in all day."

"I don't know."

"If it doesn't work out, we just come home."

"Steve and Mic Stone wouldn't like us doing this on our own."

"They don't own the airport. Besides, they'll never know. C'mon. Let's try it."

❧

Alaska Air Flight 159 from Seattle-Tacoma flashes on the screen at Carousel 4. A dark green canvas bag catches Emily's attention. She watches it come around a second time. It has a smaller zipper compartment in the front, average size, no wheels. She looks around. The flight must have just landed, only a few people stand around the carousel. She feels Paula's eyes on her. The bag comes around a third time. She grabs it and heads for the side door—east side of the terminal where the buses come—and doesn't look back to see if Paula is behind her. She walks past the bus stop, then turns around to see Paula about fifteen feet behind her. She's pointing to a bus that has just driven past the front entrance, waving Emily to come back to the bus stop. They board and Emily doesn't even look at the suitcase until after they switch to the light-rail. A name tag is attached to the handle, and Emily can't read the scribbled name.

When they arrive home, Dwight's truck isn't there and Marilee is inside. They take the suitcase inside the Airstream and close the door.

Sweat drips down Emily's chest. She takes off the silk shirt and tosses it on the bed. She and Paula open the suitcase to find it full of men's clothes, neatly rolled up, a row of white Fruit of the Loom underwear next to black T-shirts, a pair of jeans, and a box of Trojan condoms. Nothing else.

"Shit." Emily closes the suitcase, puts it against the wall under the back window.

"We should wait a while before we go back," Paula says.

A week later they try again. "Let's do Terminal 3 this time," Emily says.

"Why? We know just where the bus drops off and picks up at Terminal 2."

"Don't worry, Paula. We can figure it out."

It's Wednesday afternoon, and baggage claim is packed.

They don't waste any time. Paula grabs a small blue cloth bag, and Emily grabs a larger beige one. Back at home, Marilee is sleeping in the recliner on the patio. Dwight is at the far edge of the property, gazing out at the lake. They lay the suitcases on the bed. Emily examines the name tag. Jeanette Karl.

Paula empties her suitcase quickly. "Nothing here." A few items of clothing, a tube of shampoo, women's underwear. "What do you have in yours?"

Emily slowly goes through her suitcase. A hair dryer lies on top of folded clothes, shoes positioned around the edges, and a one-gallon Ziploc bag filled with toiletries is next to the hair dryer. "Doesn't look like there's anything worthwhile here."

Emily removes the shoes: a black pair of Mary Janes about her size, New Balance running shoes, and a small pair of sneakers, no longer than five inches.

"Kid shoes." Paula picks them up. Blue and raspberry with thick white soles. The label says Saucony. They look new.

A pair of socks is stuffed into each shoe. Paula removes them from one of the shoes and something falls out. A cylinder with a red rubber band around it. She shakes the other shoe. Another cylinder falls out. Emily grabs it, pulls off the rubber band.

"Holy shit. This is money. Check the other shoes."

Paula takes the two pairs of women's shoes from the suitcase. Socks are stuffed in each. She removes them and shakes each shoe until more rolls fall out, two from each shoe. Ten rolls total.

Emily lays out the cash from the roll in the kid shoe. "Jesus, there's five one hundred dollar bills here. And some tens and fives."

Paula takes the band off one of the rolls in the other shoes and counts. They set the money in stacks next to one another and toss the rubber bands to the side.

"Holy fuck, Paula. We've got a lot of money here."

"I don't like this."

"What?"

"We should take it back."

"Are you fucking nuts? Take it back?"

"There's a kid involved in this." Paula picks up one of the kid shoes, rummages through the clothes, and pulls out a child's T-shirt.

"So you want to march up to the Alaska Airlines counter and say, 'Excuse me. We stole this suitcase off the baggage carousel and want to give it back.' Jesus, Paula. What are you thinking?"

"We could call the number on the tag. Just say we'll leave it somewhere."

"That money could get us to Eureka."

"God, Emily. We don't need all that money to get to Eureka. And why is it so damn important to you anyway? It's just a stupid postcard."

"Fuck you. It's not a stupid postcard. And the real Eureka will be better."

The fan blows the bills on the bed. Emily starts to roll the stacks back up and put the rubber bands around them. Paula does the same. They don't look at each other.

"We've been taking other suitcases for Stone." Emily lines up the rolls of money on the bed, like little soldiers in formation.

"But we never knew what was inside."

"So? I don't get you. Why do you think this money was all rolled up and stuffed inside the shoes? Why wasn't it in the bank? Or in the woman's purse? Maybe she stole it herself. You don't know anything about her. Maybe she beats the kid those shoes belong to. Maybe there is no kid. We don't know shit about her and we don't need to." Emily shifts on the bed and the row of rolled bills falls over, like dominos. She hears Dwight's footsteps on the patio. "Put these back in."

She and Paula scoop up the rolls, stuff them back in the shoes and into the suitcase. Emily zips it and shoves it under the bed.

15

The white envelope, addressed to Emily, with no return address, is on the patio table with a stack of other mail and advertisement flyers. She picks it up, folds it several times until it fits in the palm of her hand. Aware that Marilee watches her, Emily walks to the sidewalk and heads to Tempe Town Lake.

Three construction workers sit on the back of a pickup. A few others mill about the frame of the towering structure. As Emily walks past, one of the guys in the pickup catcalls. She turns, and a guy with dark hair, cropped close to his scalp, grins at her. She gives him the finger and continues walking, ignores the laughter behind her.

At the lake she sits on one of the benches and gazes out over the water to the freeway beyond. It's late morning; the air is filled with white noise from traffic, the city, and the light-rail moving over the bridge and headed to Phoenix. Emily opens the letter. Scraggly handwriting on stationery from the Clown Motel in Tonopah.

Dear Emily,

Seeing you all grown up but still so young made me think of things I haven't thought about for a long time. Like myself when I had everything before me, like you do now. Before mistakes started piling up, one after the other, until there were so many it was just a way of life figuring out how to keep going in the midst of all I'd screwed up. And that's just about everything for me. I've messed up just about everything I've touched in this world. I know that. Except for one thing. I realized that when you came up here and I saw how you turned out and I realized I'd done one perfect thing. I never knew it until you came up here to

Tonopah. I had no right to call you sweetie, no right to call you anything, and I certainly don't deserve good feelings from you, not one bit. And I know you wouldn't believe it if I said I loved you, so I won't say that. I don't think I even know what that is anymore. If I ever did. But there must have been a teeny little good thing inside of me. There had to be. Just big enough to result in you, though god knows I can't claim to have ever done anything at all for you. That's all Grandma Marilee and Dwight and Ruth. What I mean is just being the one that gave you life, that must mean there was something worthwhile in me back then and I just wanted to tell you this, tell you that I know this now, tell you how glad I am that you came up here to see me. Tell you how perfect you are.

Love, Phyllis

At the bottom, a phone number. Shit. *How you turned out.* What the hell does she know about how Emily turned out? The lake water blurs before Emily. She crushes the letter in her hand and tosses it, then immediately gets up and retrieves it from the grass near the bench. *Dear Mom, Phyllis: Fuck you, fuck you, fuck you.* She walks to the edge of the sidewalk and down a gentle incline to the lake. Again she thinks of tossing the letter but doesn't. Instead, she smooths it out and puts it back in the envelope, refolds it, and stuffs it in her pocket.

Back at home, she sees Marilee drenching herself with the hose, her faded dress clinging to her old body like a second skin, the pattern no more decipherable than the writing on the prayer flags. Before Marilee shuts the water off, she turns the hose on the shamrocks, which had briefly looked as if they might come back to life. Now they lie beneath the mesquite, dry and shriveled, burned to death by the heat and sun.

16

"We're not giving some stranger part of our family land," Marilee says when Dwight tells her about Wilkins.

They're on the patio, just before sunset.

"We're not giving him anything. He's paying for it." Dwight shows her Wilkins's business card.

"He's a professor?"

"Yeah, says he dabbles in real estate."

"That university's been taking land from folks for a long time. How do you know he won't take more than that little corner?"

"It doesn't have anything to do with the university. And he's not taking anything. We'll have a contract that says what he gets. He can't just take what he wants."

"And you trust that, Dwight? Like the government's not already trying to just take what they want?"

Claude said about the same thing when Dwight told him about Wilkins's proposition. *Why the hell would you trust somebody who wants part of your property?* It's not a matter of trust. Hell, Dwight wouldn't trust Wilkins as far as he could spit. It's just a business deal. Wilkins gets the lawyer to save the property, and they give him a little piece of land.

"C'mon, Mom. I don't trust anybody any more than you do. Can you let me take care of this? I'm not going to let anybody take our property."

"You see that article Jay brought me?"

"What article?"

"On the kitchen table."

Dwight steps inside and finds a section of the *Arizona Republic* folded to a story about the retirement community the university is building across from the property. He reads it as he walks back out to the patio. La Maravilla. Lakeside property with a view of Tempe Town Lake, the Superstition Mountains, and Camelback Mountain. Demand is soaring, eighty percent of the units already sold before construction's even finished. Three restaurants inside. Buy-in costs of $400,000–$800,000 and monthly fees of $5,000. Holy shit.

"This doesn't mean anything, Mom." He sets the article next to his mom's ashtray. "I already knew this."

"It means they always want more. And they always get it. Just like San Pablo."

Dwight glances at Emily and Paula, who sit on the step of the Airstream, listening to him and Marilee. Just as well they know exactly what's going on.

"I'm not done looking for the title yet." Marilee picks up the article, looks over it as if something's going to pop out and prove she's right about the university and Wilkins. "What if I find one?"

"I guess that'd solve everything, wouldn't it?"

Dwight's fairly certain now that the family never had a title, despite what Marilee says or thinks. He's looked too, through her dresser drawers, the closet in her bedroom, the boxes in that shed of hers. Nothing.

"But right now Wilkins is our only option. Unless you want to pay money we don't have and get our own lawyer."

Above the lake, gray and white clouds hang heavy over the sinking sun. The last slice of light disappears, and power lines above the property swing as the wind picks up. Dwight turns toward Emily and Paula, but they've gone back inside. The door swings open and closed.

From his truck, parked in front of Gerry's Sandwich Shop, Dwight watches cars pull in and out of Dutch Bros drive-through coffee, on the corner of University and Hardy. He imagines such an establishment on their property—the entire two acres turned into a strip mall. It's worth a shitload of money, but all that means to him is problems.

A few minutes later Wilkins arrives in his Austin Healy. His tall, awkward body unwinds from the convertible like a prehistoric reptile hatching from its shell. He opens the trunk, takes out a beige canvas car cover, and carefully drapes it over the Austin.

Dwight steps out of the truck and stands in front of the Austin. "You afraid your car's gonna get dirty?"

"Sun bleaches the hell out of the paint. Cracks the leather upholstery." Wilkins pulls at the corners of the car cover, tucks them under the front and back bumpers.

"Well, I guess I should get one of those for my truck."

A sound comes from Wilkins's chest, an exhale of air as if he's about to laugh; then he stops. "I don't know if they make truck covers."

"I'm joking, Wilkins."

"Can I buy you some lunch?"

"I'll just have coffee."

They take a seat at a table near the window. It's mid-afternoon, and the lunch crowd has left. Gerry's is empty except for a man and woman sitting at a small round table in the corner, and a disheveled man at one of the larger tables, which is full of dirty dishes waiting to be cleared away by the server. The man picks at the leftovers, makes his way from plate to plate finishing off half-eaten sandwiches and french fries. Dwight recognizes him. Hank. He sleeps on the property from time to time. Disappeared for a while, then recently returned. Hank used to have two long, thick braids of smoky black hair that hung proudly down his back, muscular arms, and a bear-paw tattoo on his left bicep. His hair is short now and his face seems indented as if many teeth are missing. The waiter appears and says something to Hank, then stands behind him and waits while Hank gets up. As he's leaving he looks at Dwight and nods. Dwight nods back.

"You didn't tell me everything, Dwight." Wilkins takes off his hat, smooths the rim, and sets it on the table. He wipes the sweat from his forehead and picks up the menu.

"You're a smart man, Wilkins. I thought you did your research."

"Gene."

"I gave you that folder, Gene. Figured you would actually read what was inside."

"I did read everything. You didn't tell me they sent you an eviction notice."

"Okay, they've sent an eviction notice. It won't mean shit if you get us a title, right? It doesn't change the adverse possession thing, does it?"

"That's the argument we'll go for, adverse possession. That and the fact the state waited so long to make any claims on your property. Still, they sent that notice. I got an appointment next week with a lawyer, David Alyward. Meanwhile, here's a contract between you and me." Wilkins slides it across the table.

Dwight picks it up, reads through it quickly.

"You don't have to sign it now. If Alyward takes the case, we'll both sign with him present."

Dwight lifts his coffee cup, holds it in front of him without taking a sip, raises his eyes over the rim. "My mom doesn't trust you. Says you're probably trying to get our land for the university."

Wilkins laughs. "I'm just an irrelevant professor these days. I wouldn't be the one to get land for them."

"Maybe not." Marilee's suspicions irk him. He folds the contract, slips it in his back pocket.

Outside, Hank has positioned himself near the Dutch Bros drive-through exit. He's holding a ragged cardboard sign that says Please Help, God Bless. It hits Dwight, the way it has periodically over the past few months, that without their land he has no way to make a living. It's not a thought he allows himself to hold on to for more than a few seconds.

Wilkins puts his hat on and extends his hand to Dwight. Dwight refrains from asking what all the fucking handshaking is about and reciprocates. He watches Wilkins pull the car cover from his Austin, fold it neatly, and lay it on the passenger seat.

❧

"They want this land. They're gonna try to take it," Claude

Evans says that night when Dwight fills him in on the meeting with Wilkins.

They sit under the mesquite. It's late. Marilee's gone into the house. Jay hasn't slept on the property for over a month. The girls are in the Airstream. A dim light shows through their window. Dwight tosses his empty beer bottle into the dried-up, ash-filled fire pit. If it weren't so damn hot, he'd light up the pit, watch the orange-yellow flames dance in the night, listen to the kindling crackle and burst. Sometimes he lights it up in the summer, just to take his mind off things. Tonight the air bakes, even at this late hour; it's almost too hot to be outside, but Dwight likes the way the heat burns through him.

"You and your family's got a right to this place. It's yours no matter what the government says. Sovereignty of the soil. You got a right to defend it."

"I know that. That's what I'm trying to do."

"Dwight, didn't the U.S. military teach you anything in that war about defending yourself? Taking on the enemy?"

"What are you talking about?"

"I'm talking about defending your place if they try to take it from your family."

"They're already trying to do that."

"I mean physically. If they send the law to make you leave."

It has occurred to Dwight that the authorities might try to physically force them out, but he's always pushed that thought into the shadows rather than think too much about how it might happen.

"I know some people you need to meet, Dwight."

"Oh?"

"People who think like you. You're not the only one can't stand the government."

"I don't guess I am. Who are these people?"

"Folks with a philosophy."

"Fancy word."

"I'm serious, man." Claude lights up a cigarette, drops the match into his empty beer bottle, and sets it on the ground beside two other empties. "They got a philosophy about the government. And about people like you and me. About sovereign citizenship. Shane down in Marana, the guy you sold the guns to, he's part of the movement."

"Movement?"

"Federal government's trying to enslave every U.S. citizen, rob us of our rights. Government and their lackeys and the rich bastards who support them. Tyranny of the elite."

"I didn't know you were such a deep thinker, Claude. Tyranny of the elite." Dwight takes another beer out of the cooler. "Need a refill?"

Claude nods and Dwight passes him a bottle.

"This ain't a joke, Dwight. You don't believe those assholes take what they want, screw your rights when it suits them?"

"Of course I believe it. I don't need any movement to tell me."

"They might be able to help you with your property issue."

"How?"

"They're not some big organization with a leader. Just local groups. Lots of them all over the country with informal leaders. Some call themselves True Sovereigns. They think like you, Dwight. I'm surprised you don't know more about folks that think like you."

"Always been a bit of a loner, Claude. You know that. I'm not a joiner."

"You don't have to join anything. Like I said, informal groups."

"So, their philosophy is the government's trying to enslave us?"

Claude takes a swig of his beer. "That and they believe there's two kinds of citizens. Some folks are true sovereigns and others are federal citizens. Like the Black people who got their citizenship from the government, from the Fourteenth Amendment. Federal citizens are beholden and subject to the government. True sovereign citizens aren't so beholden."

Dwight rolls this around in his head for a couple of minutes.

Part of what Claude says appeals to him. "The enslaving thing makes sense to me. The second part sounds a little fucked up."

"It's just historical fact, Dwight. The way things went down."

"I met all sorts of folks over in Iraq. Lots of Black guys. We all had the same military IDs. Bled just the same, same bones and guts that got strewn all over the place. I don't see any difference."

"I know that. I was there too. Sovereign philosophy don't say everyone's not human. Just that there's differences regarding their beholdenness to the government. If you're beholden to the government, you're subject to it. Simple as that. True sovereigns aren't beholden."

Dwight looks at the empty fire pit. He thinks of Marilee's stories about the history of the property—the same stories she's told over and over to Emily and Paula, stories about the two brothers, Martino and Albert, their sister, Constance, and the old barrio where the university now stands.

"You know, Claude, my great-great-grandmother and her brothers came up here from Mexico. Would they be federal citizens? Or the other kind?"

"Look, Dwight, for the situation at hand here, the distinction isn't even relevant." Claude waves his hand around the property. "We're talking about the tyranny of the government trying to take something from you, deny your rights. In your case, it's the state government, but same principle—feds, state, city. You're a true sovereign citizen. You lose your property, then what?"

"I couldn't do my work without this place."

"These people I'm telling you about stand up for sovereign citizens. They're not afraid to face down the government."

Dwight doesn't say anything. Doesn't ask what *face down the government* means.

"I ever tell you about my uncle up in Nevada?" Claude says. "You'd like him, Dwight. Don't take shit from anybody, including the government."

"I like him already."

"He owned a ranch up in Nevada. Had nearly 400 head of

cattle," Claude says. "Just let 'em roam and graze like cows are supposed to."

"Yeah?"

"One day the federal government tries to tell him his cattle's grazing on their land. Says he's gotta pay them for grazing rights. Miles and miles of nothing up there around my uncle's ranch, and those fuckers want him to pay for letting his cows walk around on land nobody's using. Eat some grass nobody cares about anyway." Claude opens the cooler lid and reaches for another beer, but it's all melted ice. "So, he just refuses to pay them cocksuckers anything."

"What did they do?"

"Nothing, for twenty years. Just kept sending him notices, which he threw in the garbage where they belonged. Twenty years. Then they sent him a bill for one billion dollars, says it's the debt for all those years his cattle's been grazing. A billion fucking dollars. He tosses that bill too. Right in the garbage."

"That's what I've been doing with the notices about this property, so to speak," Dwight says. "Kept the papers, but just ignored the bastards."

"Then the damn government takes him to court and the kiss-ass lackey judge says they can seize his cattle. Can you imagine the government hauling away four hundred cows?"

"That'd be a sight."

"Well, what my uncle did was round up his buddies to come out and defend his property. I mean really defend it. They came armed. About 150 men, a few women. Took up positions around the ranch and had those weapons ready. Camped out in tents and campers for almost two weeks. My uncle's a peaceful man, Dwight. Got a wife and daughters and sons and grandkids. Some live on the ranch. He wasn't looking for trouble, just wanted to be left alone."

"Did they take his cattle?"

Claude laughs and shakes his head. "The assholes just left. I swear to god they just left, Dwight."

"This uncle of yours is my kind of guy."

"That was three years ago. Good thing those government goons didn't kill anyone like they did at Ruby Ridge. The whole thing drove a wedge right through my uncle's town. Most folks live around there agreed with him, but some supposedly upright citizens who don't know their assholes from their elbow joints got all bent out of shape that the government just left and never even prosecuted my uncle or anyone else. 'You can't just set yourself up above the law,' the mayor said. Fuck that. Some people are so loyal to authorities, but they don't know jack about the Constitution."

"That's some story."

"It sure is, Dwight. Thought you'd like it."

"Your uncle still ranching up there?"

"Sure is. And now he knows who his friends are."

"What about his cattle?"

"Still grazing. Like I said, the authorities just gave up."

"You're thinking I could do something like that here?"

"Possibly."

"This property's a whole lot different from a ranch up in Nevada."

"Let's pay Shane a visit, Dwight. Meet some of the people I'm telling you about."

Dwight tosses his empty beer can into the fire pit. "Truth is, Claude, I'm just about out of options if Wilkins's lawyer doesn't come through with something."

"Shane's good people."

17

Two days later Dwight and Claude head down to Shane's. Past the outskirts of Phoenix, dust devils swirl over the open desert. Dwight feels as if he's gone back in time, once again on that road, thousands of miles away. Melted windshields, incinerated bodies, half a body hanging upside down in the seat of the Kawasaki front-end loader. The highway was blocked at both ends, a death trap for retreating Iraqi soldiers. Over seven miles of bombed-out vehicles—T-55 and T-72 tanks, armored vehicles, fire engines, cars. Objects strewn along the ground around the rubble—anti-aircraft guns, gas masks, grenades, scraps of green uniforms. Photographs of kids. Dwight looked into the eyeless sockets of a scorched corpse, an Iraqi soldier, as if those empty holes held the answer. The soldier's arms reached over a blasted-out windshield. A final futile plea. That face, or what had once been a face, never leaves him. Ruth was right. He never should have volunteered. What fucked-up sense of duty had gotten into his head?

"You okay?" Claude's voice brings Dwight back, nothing before him but Interstate 10.

"Yeah, yeah."

"Thinking about Iraq?"

Dwight nods. Claude doesn't ask for details.

The truth began to sink in after that day in Iraq. Dwight saw the war for what it was, came around to his dad's thinking. Governments are all the same, but some have more money, more weapons, more soldiers. No difference on the inside though. Half man, half beast, his dad used to say.

Sometimes you see the man, Dwight, Jack said before Dwight left for Iraq. *But don't ever forget that the beast is what's at the core.*

You can't always let yourself see the beast, though, even when it stares you right in the face, not if you want to survive and not crack into a zillion pieces. Dwight had forced himself not to recognize it, not until he got back home. Then he cursed the war and the U.S. government, the Iraqi government, all of them. His dad was right, but Dwight never got the chance to tell him.

"You remember how to get to Shane's place?"

"Yeah." Dwight exits the interstate and passes the RV park, the bar, and Circle K, down West Marana Road to Shane's house. Several cars are parked in the driveway and the yard.

Shane comes out the front door with two other guys and walks over to the truck. He smiles at Dwight and Claude; the red rubber band he's chewing on is visible when he smiles.

"This here's my brother Deland. And this is Jerry McFaul."

They shake hands and go inside. An old black lab sprawls on the family-room floor, barely moving except for an occasional feeble wag of its tail.

"You guys want a beer?" Shawna pokes her head around the corner from the kitchen.

Dwight and Claude nod. She brings out two bottles of Bud.

"Claude tells me you got a little trouble up there in Phoenix with your property." Shane picks up a half-empty beer bottle from the coffee table, motions for them to have a seat.

"I sure do." Dwight takes a long gulp, wonders what he's doing here telling these strangers his personal situation.

"Up in Nevada the government owns over eighty percent of all the land," Shane says. "Eighty percent! That ain't right. Who the fuck are they anyway? Did they pay anybody for that land? Did they have to purchase it like you and me?"

"Government owning all that land goes against the Constitution." Jerry McFaul is a short wiry guy with black curly hair. He paces the room, restless energy bouncing off him like sparks of electricity. "They should give it back."

"Especially if a family's been living on it for a hundred years." Shane looks at Dwight. "Those assholes should be trustees of the people, not fucking land grabbers. When did they tell you to be off your land, Dwight?"

"End of the month, August 31."

"Two weeks away."

"Yep."

"You got any plans?"

"No, except we're not going anywhere."

"Delay is the best strategy," Jerry McFaul says. "You keep getting them to delay. That lawyer of yours had any balls that's what he'd do."

"He's not even my lawyer. Not yet. I'm waiting to see if he'll take the case."

Shane rubs his beard. "It's probably too late now anyway with an eviction notice. But we can try to get them to back off when they come to kick your family out."

"They've never actually come out to the property," Dwight says. "Sent notices and then we wouldn't hear from them for a while."

"They ever send an eviction notice with a date before?" Jerry asks.

"No."

"You can be pretty sure they'll come," Shane says. "Unless that lawyer thinks of something real quick."

"Lawyer's not going to do shit," Jerry McFaul says. "First thing you do is hand them a declaration of sovereignty."

"A what?"

"A declaration of sovereignty."

Shane walks over to a small desk in the corner of the family room, opens the middle drawer, and takes out a piece of paper. He hands it to Dwight.

The words at the top in bold letters read, *Declaration of Individual Sovereignty*. Dwight scans the writing. *Under the provisions of the Tenth Amendment of the Constitution of the United States of America I, ________, the undersigned, do hereby declare myself to be a sovereign individual.* There's a line at the bottom for a signature and date. Is this a joke? Did he come down here for a silly piece of paper? "You think this piece of paper's gonna keep those government dicks from coming onto my property?"

"Paper's what those assholes deal in, what they understand," Claude says. "It's just the first step."

"That's right." Shane stops pacing, sets his beer down. "They've got a piece of paper for everything. A declaration of sovereignty is your notice to them you don't accept their fucking eviction notice. Don't accept their authority. It should have been done back when you first got the notice."

"What am I supposed to do with it?"

"Give it to any assholes who come onto your land and try to evict you and your family," Jerry says.

"Then what?" Dwight looks from Jerry to Claude to Shane. These guys seem so sure of what to do. He should have already thought of these things. But how the fuck would he have known about declarations of sovereignty? It probably won't work anyway.

Shane's brother Deland hasn't said a word since he shook Dwight's hand. He gets up from the sofa, walks over to the patio doors, looks out briefly, then turns back to the group. A gun holster with a .44-Magnum revolver in it hangs around his hip. Deland touches the gun handle.

"We stand our ground is what," he says.

"'We'?" Dwight says. "You guys coming up to Phoenix?"

"We sure will," Deland says. "And we got more friends in Phoenix. They'll stand with us."

"I told you it pays to know people who think like you," Claude says.

Out here at Shane's place, amongst all these guys, the property problem becomes more vividly real than ever before, a cluster bomb headed toward his place, ready to release a bunch of bomblets to destroy everything he loves. His ability to sweep the issue into his mind's recesses vanishes. These guys elicit a feeling of reassurance and discomfort at the same time. They've either got a hold on some deep truth, one that's only played around the edges of his own mind, or they're full of shit. Smart guys or incredibly deluded ones.

It's dusk when Shane lights up the grill in his backyard. Two motorcycles roar into the driveway and two guys walk onto the patio from the side of the house. One of them sports a tattoo on his left bicep with the words *LIVE FREE* in bold black letters, underneath in smaller letters, *Without Government.* The other guy is shirtless with the number fourteen in black across his chest. Shane nods their way. Deland walks over and gives them both a cross between a hug and a slap on the back.

"This is the guy Shane told us about," Deland says and nods toward Dwight. "The one with the property up in Phoenix."

"Terry Lee," the one with LIVE FREE on his bicep says to Dwight and extends his hand. "And Russ."

Russ nods and offers his hand to Dwight.

"What's with the number fourteen?" Dwight asks.

"Numerical shorthand," Russ says.

"For what?"

"Fourteen simple words—'We must secure the existence of our people and a future for white children.'"

"White children?"

"Seems like everybody else gets some protection these days, some kind of special treatment."

Dwight's about to ask him what he does to protect white children, but Claude nudges him. "You about ready to head back to the big city?"

"Yeah."

On the drive back to Phoenix, Dwight takes his eyes off the road for a second and looks at Claude. "A future for white children? Who the fuck are these people?"

"Look, I don't necessarily think like Russ and Terry Lee. Not everyone in the movement does."

"Jesus. How well do you know them?"

"They're real tight with Deland."

"And Shane? He tight with them?" Shane seems an okay guy.

"He can take 'em or leave 'em. But he doesn't have much choice. Terry Lee is Shawna's brother."

"Shit, Claude."

"They're okay. You don't have to buy into all their thinking. Got the same philosophy as you when it comes to the government and that's what counts right now."

A line of semis moves like a long locomotive in front of Dwight's truck. He switches into the left lane, steps on the gas a little harder than necessary, and passes them.

Two days later Dwight gets a phone call from Wilkins.

"Alyward says there's no point, Dwight. There just isn't a case this late in the game, with an eviction notice and no documents."

"What about adverse possession?"

"Alyward says it's too late."

"We've been living here all these years. My mom says there's a title somewhere." Even as he says this Dwight doesn't believe it. There's no fucking title. There's nothing.

"Well, unless she's got that title, Alyward says it'd be a waste of everybody's time. Maybe if we'd started sooner. Back when you first got the notices."

Dwight hangs up. August 31st is twelve days away.

18

"You don't want to overthink this, Dwight."

But that's exactly what Dwight does as he and Claude unload rolls of steel mesh, barbed wire, and eight-foot metal posts from the back of his truck and lay it all on the ground at the western edge of the property. He imagines every possible turn of events, when and if the authorities show up on the thirty-first and try to evict them. Even as he holds on to a slim hope that their threats will peter out the way they have in the past, things feel different now.

"Any number of things could happen," Claude says. "You'll drive yourself nuts, you try to anticipate everything."

Something's going to happen, something's going to change. Dwight lights up a cigarette and surveys the material they've just unloaded, considering the work ahead of them. The entire western perimeter of the property, and a section of the north end facing Tempe Town Lake, is open. The rest is already fenced off, except for a twenty-or-so-foot gap at the driveway entrance.

"What about that?" Claude points to the sleeping bags at the northwest corner under the paloverde trees.

"We'll leave that part outside the fencing."

"It's your property, isn't it?"

"Yeah, but I don't want to fence those guys out. Billy's been sleeping there for a few years now. A couple of others come and go. They don't cause any trouble. If Billy shows up, I'll get him to give us a hand."

"Okay, we'll place those top rails at an angle and keep that area on the other side of the chain-link."

Dwight starts at one end, Claude at the other. Dwight thinks of Ruth as he works. What would she have thought about all this? What would she have advised him to do? He'd told her about the first notice right after Jack died, but it wasn't until after Ruth died that the state said his family had been squatters all these years. Ruth was always practical, always thought of the most logical thing to do. But there was no sensible, logical solution to this. She would have stood behind him, though, whatever he decided to do. God, how he wishes she were here now. Somehow that would make it all more bearable.

His eyes go to the yellow school bus. The day Leroy Barnes called him, Dwight had been home from Iraq for two years, Jack dead, Paula a few months old. He'd told Leroy to find him a bus for under $5,000 and he'd think about it. He'd thought his dad might enjoy overhauling it with him. He didn't hear from him for a while and then one day, out of the blue, Leroy called.

The bus was in Las Cruces. Leroy would meet him there. The engine, transmission, and brakes were good, tires so-so, but it would make it back to Phoenix. He and Jay drove down to pick it up. His plan had been to convert it to a camper and sell it. *People don't see a thing's value,* Jack used to say as Dwight worked with him on his many undertakings. *Not unless it stares them in the face.*

The afternoon he drove the bus onto the property, Ruth had gone inside it, walked up and down the aisle. *After you get it converted, let's go up north. We'll take the girls*, Ruth had said. She wanted to spend a whole summer in Flagstaff. They'd talked of the money they'd need to make it happen. Maybe pick up odd jobs there. Within a month, Dwight and Jay had all the seats, except the driver's, torn out. He'd worked on it in bits and pieces over the years, but never got it in shape for a trip.

After Ruth died, he abandoned the project. Then one day he went inside and sat in the driver's seat, the sun slashing through the windshield, and wept until his vision blurred. He wept for the things he and Ruth would never do, never see together, for the memory of her face. Why hadn't he finished the project, taken her up to Flagstaff? He cried until his body shook and his ribs hurt. By the time his eyes cleared and he brushed the moisture from his face, the sun had moved on. Through the front window, Ruth stood in the shade of the mesquite, auburn curls framing her face. Concern and confusion crossed her face. And something else—sorrow. He smiled, raised his hand to wave, then stopped. It wasn't Ruth but Paula, who resembled her more every day.

The following day he resumed work on the bus. Tinkered a few times a week, between his other money-making projects. Promised he would take Emily and Paula on a trip before they were grown. But he knows, and they know, and the rest of the family knows, it's never been about getting the bus ready for a trip. It's about Dwight, about Ruth, about Dwight surviving, not fatally fraying around his edges.

"Looks good," Dwight says when he and Claude meet in the middle, at the western boundary of the property. They've been working several hours. Sweat streams from his temples into his eyes. He wipes his face with the back of his hand.

"It's not every day an opportunity like this presents itself."

"I could think of lots of words for what this is, but opportunity sure as shit isn't one of them."

"I mean an opportunity to support you, Dwight. Take a stand. You can count on Shane and Jerry and the others too. They'll be here on August 31st."

Even as Dwight swears to himself he'll never hand over his family's place to the government, an image fixes itself in his head of everything, including his family, thrown out like garbage, unanchored and drifting in an explosion of renovation and new construction. He's buried that fear for so long, but now it's breaking through with the intensity of the summer sun coming up over the horizon, slow and gradual at first, then slamming the hell out of him.

"I appreciate this, Claude. I really do." He looks around the yard. How much can their work withstand? "But the authorities can surely outnumber us."

"That they can, but it depends on how far they want to take this thing. They could have out-manned my uncle, too, but they just gave up."

"We're in the middle of the city here, Claude."

"More reason they might back down. Trying to take a man's property in plain view of the whole town? You give them your sovereignty declaration. See what they do."

Claude weaves a tension bar through the openings in the wire mesh and attaches it to the bands on top of the metal posts. "There."

Dwight unrolls about twenty-five feet of the mesh, weaves another tension bar through the openings, and attaches it to the next post. In this manner he and Claude make their way down the western perimeter, then the northern edge, until chain-link fencing encloses the entire property. The sun begins its descent, both men soaked in sweat.

"We'll put the barbwire on top tomorrow. I'm beat." Dwight goes into the house and comes back with a six-pack and some frozen water bottles. He pulls off a can of Budweiser for Claude and one for himself, then puts the rest in the cooler along with the frozen water bottles.

"Too bad you didn't come to me and the guys before you met that Wilkins character and his lawyer."

"Why?"

"Guys like them are part of the system. That lawyer sees an eviction notice, sees there's no title, and thinks everything's all settled and final. Shane knows folks that could have tied up the legal end for a long time. Doesn't matter what the law says. The strategy is to tie things up, drag it out with fine legal points."

"Well, too late now."

"What about your driveway? How're you going to block that off?"

"I've been thinking about that." Dwight gestures toward the yellow school bus. "It runs. I can drive it over there and park it sideways and close off most of the driveway."

"Might work."

"We'll rig up barbwire in the gaps."

Dwight surveys the property. Feels better than he did when they started the fencing. "Maybe the authorities will back off."

"Maybe." Claude looks doubtful. "But don't count on it."

After Claude leaves, Dwight goes into his gun shed. He pulls out a Waylon Jennings CD and starts to load it into the player, stops, sets it on the counter, and listens to the silence of the night as he hand-loads some bullet casings.

The day after Ruth's funeral, he went to Ironwood, camped for eight days, waiting for grief to release him. The void left by Ruth's death hung over him like a curtain of heavy fog; he begged the sun to burn it off. He walked on and off the trails all day, not paying much attention to where he was, losing sense of time, but miraculously finding the way back to his campsite against the base of Ragged Top before nightfall. One morning as he sat on a boulder just outside his tent drinking instant coffee, a rattler slithered across the desert floor in front of him and stopped within a few feet of where he sat. His gun lay next to his sleeping bag back in the tent. He watched the snake approach. It got close enough for Dwight to see the tiny pits on either side of its head; it was looking at him. Then it curled into a circle. Dwight didn't move. He thought of slowly standing up, making for the tent and his gun, but something told him to keep still, stay where he was. Maybe the snake would strike, maybe it wouldn't. It lay coiled in front of him for about an hour, then slid away.

Against all rational thought, a feeling had possessed Dwight out there at Ironwood. If he just stayed long enough, life would return to normal. He'd go back home and Ruth would be waiting for him. He held hope or illusion somewhere in his psyche for those eight days but felt it diminish as he trekked out and drove back to Phoenix.

19

Emily runs her hand over the barrel of the Glock 17 in her lap. She turns eighteen in two days; Paula, three days later. Dwight gave each of them the same gun as a birthday gift. Emily checks the chamber. Empty. Of course. Dwight wouldn't give them loaded guns. Paula's lies in her lap, and she looks at it as if it's a bomb waiting to go off.

"Best handgun around." Dwight looks like the old Dwight, before the argument with Grandma Marilee about that professor guy wanting some of their land, before he and Claude started barricading the property. "You girls are already smart about guns. And old enough to protect yourselves." Dwight passes Emily a box of bullets.

"Are we getting ready for some kind of invasion here?" Emily means it as a joke. Sort of.

Dwight doesn't smile. A mix of resolve and defeat colors his face. "They might try to take this place from us."

"We know, Dad," Paula says. "We've known for a long time. We heard you and Grandma Marilee talking about that guy who wanted some of this property."

"Well, that didn't work out. Now the government wants the whole place."

Emily can barely stand to look at Dwight when he says this. She looks at the gun in her lap. "What's going to happen?"

"I'm not sure, Emily. But we're not letting them take it."

"Are you going to take us shooting so we can try them?"

"Maybe when all this is over," Dwight says and leaves them alone in the trailer.

All this means the new chain-link fencing and the barbed wire. A mood hangs in the hot summer air. It creeps into her bones. Something's changing. The rolls of cash they took out of the suitcase amounted to $5,500. She and Paula continue to argue about what to do with it.

"This is a shitload of money, Paula. Way more than we got from the IDs and cell phones. Or Mic Stone's suitcase jobs."

"Yeah. And we should give it back to Jeanette Karl."

"You don't even know if she's a real person." Emily stuffed all the money in an envelope and put it under the makeshift night table on her side of the bed. "C'mon, Paula. We can go anywhere now. Go live by the ocean."

"We've never seen the ocean."

"The air there smells different."

"Like what?" Paula doesn't ask how Emily knows what the air by the ocean smells like.

"Moist, of course, and clean. Musty in a good way, like rain, even when it's not raining. Grass and plants, stuff growing, blooming all the time. It smells green and cool like a breeze brushing past you. It seeps into your body to every single part of your insides. Makes the hard edges softer. Your mind too, smooths it out. Like meditation." Emily stops. For a moment she and Paula look at each other. Paula has a wistful look on her face, as if imagining the ocean. Then Emily laughs and Paula does the same.

"Fuck, I don't know what the air by the ocean smells like. That's just how I imagine it."

"It sounds nice," Paula says.

"It is nice. Look at the postcard." Emily pointed to the Eureka postcard.

"We could go without keeping all that money."

Emily ignores Paula's words. No way is she going to do anything but keep it. "We've got to plan this out."

"What about my dad? And Grandma Marilee?"

"What about them?"

"They'll be sad if we leave, especially now."

"I know. But we'll be eighteen in a few days. Do you want to stay here forever?"

Paula shrugs. "It doesn't look like anyone's going to stay here forever."

"Maybe this is the best time to leave. If we're on our own, that'll be one less thing for them to worry about."

Maybe Dwight already knows she and Paula are going to leave. Maybe that's what he means when he says *old enough to protect yourselves.*

"Stone wants to talk to you girls," Jay says on the other end of Emily's cell phone.

"Oh yeah, stranger? Where have you been?"

"I've been around."

"Ever since you got that car."

"I'm buying it from Steve. He's got a new one."

"Cool." She puts the phone on speaker, motions for Paula to listen.

"So, like I said, Steve wants to talk to you girls. Stone does too."

"It's been a while. Does he think we just jump when he calls?"

"Does he have another job for us?" Paula asks.

"Maybe. They didn't tell me what it's all about. I'll pick you two up at the lake parking lot at noon tomorrow."

"What makes you think we're interested?"

"Okay, Emily, *are* you guys interested?"

Emily looks at Paula.

"Fine. You talk to Dwight?"

"Not for a while."

"Claude's helped him build a fence. You know about the eviction thing?"

"Yeah. Government's been trying to get our property for a long time."

"Things feel weird, Jay. Dwight seems different. Everything seems different now."

"I know. Be at the parking lot at noon."

After they hang up, Paula says, "I hope Steve or Stone didn't find out about the suitcases we took, Emily."

"How could they? Besides, they don't own the airport. It's not like we stole something from them."

"I know, but they'd be totally pissed if they knew."

"I guess we'll find out."

"If we get some more money from a Stone job, we can give that money from the suitcase back."

"Whatever, Paula. Let's just see what he wants."

Jay picks them up in the parking lot.

"So where have you been staying?" Emily asks.

"Steve's sometimes. Mostly Stone's place. He don't actually live there and he likes having someone around to keep an eye on things."

"Things?"

"Yeah, it's a sketchy neighborhood."

"You forgot our birthdays."

"I'm sorry."

Emily hadn't expected him to say he was sorry about their birthdays. "I'm just kidding. You never remember our birthdays."

Jay's calm and relaxed. And serious. His legs aren't dancing around the way they usually do.

A Camaro and new-looking Honda Accord are parked on the street in front of the house on Linden.

"The Honda is Steve's," Jay says.

"So, that's why you get to drive the Camry."

"I told you I'm buying it."

They enter through the front gate. Steve opens the door and they go inside. Stone is there. He wears the same fancy shirt he had on when they first met him, but this time with old-man Bermuda shorts and sparkling white Nikes. The getup gives him the appearance of being two people—one person from the waist up, an entirely different person from the waist down. There's a large sofa in the previously empty living room. Stone gestures toward the sofa. Emily and Paula sit down, Jay next to them.

Stone pulls up a metal kitchen chair, sits on it backwards, and looks at them. Steve hovers behind him.

"How you girls doing?" Stone grins.

Maybe he does know about the suitcases they took on their own. He sounds like he's going to play with them a little. Steve's face is expressionless as always, his wandering eye subdued.

"We're doing fine," Emily says.

"Mic's got a job for you," Steve says as if on cue.

Stone nods. "You know what a courier is?"

"A messenger, right?" Emily says. "Like a pigeon."

Stone laughs. "Yeah, like a pigeon." He lights up a cigarette. "A suitcase needs to get to L.A. How'd you like to be a pigeon and fly to Los Angeles?"

"Maybe. What do we get out of it?"

"Sharp girl, Emily." Stone drags deeply on his cigarette, lets the ash fall to the floor. "How would you girls like to be twenty-one?"

"What do you mean?" Paula asks.

"It's a question. It means what it means."

"We're already eighteen," she says.

"Twenty-one's better than eighteen." Stone smiles.

"How do we get to be twenty-one?" Paula asks.

Emily watches Paula. She usually lets Emily ask all the questions.

"You take the suitcase to L.A., I make you twenty-one."

"ID," Steve says.

Emily waits for Paula to say something, but she doesn't.

"We've already got IDs. Did you forget we're the ones who sold you all those IDs? In fact, we're already twenty-one in our IDs." Both of their stolen IDs say they're nineteen years old. Emily looks quickly at Paula, who remains quiet.

"These IDs will be better," Steve says.

"We're talking about the whole works here. Driver's license, passport, birth certificate, social security card. A whole new person that looks just like you," Stone says to Emily, then shifts his gaze to Paula. "And you." His eyes bore into Emily's. "The passports and driver's licenses will have your own photos on them. No chance of anyone thinking they're fake."

"I never thought the ones we have now look like us, Emily."

"So, what's the plan?" Emily says.

"Early morning flight to L.A.," Stone says. "Check the bag in Phoenix."

"And pick it up at baggage claim in L.A.?" Emily's mind races. What does he want them to do with the bag after they pick it up in L.A.?

"Nope. Just go to baggage claim and make sure it arrives. Make sure you see it come off the belt. Someone will be there to pick it up."

"Then what?"

"Nothing. Hang around the airport until your flight back to Phoenix or go downtown, see L.A. You're a big girl. You decide."

"Sounds easy." Emily looks at Paula. "It'll be fun. We've never been on a plane before."

Stone stands and pushes the chair away. "Only one of you go."

"No. Both of us."

"Only one of you flies to L.A. You, Emily."

"It's fine, Emily," Paula says.

"This really sucks."

"Yeah, well," Stone says.

"Emily," Paula says. "It's okay."

"When do I go?"

"August 31st, next Wednesday."

"When do we get our IDs?"

"Jay will take you to get photos now. Your IDs will be ready the day before you leave."

"What's in the suitcase?"

Stone ignores Emily's question and walks out of the room. She hears a car start up and sees the Camaro pull away from the sidewalk.

"No need to know, Emily," Steve says. "Just check the bag at the airport and you're done."

20

Jay steps inside the Airstream. Emily pulls the door shut behind him, then reattaches the rope.

"Your new ID." He passes her the envelope.

Emily dumps the contents on the bed. Two bundles, red rubber bands around each, tumble out. She picks up one of the IDs. Paula's face stares back at her from the new driver's license on top and she passes this one to Paula. She examines the other bundle—license, passport, and social security card. Elizabeth Jackson, 2600 Paradise Way, Scottsdale, Arizona. Date of birth: March 15, 1989. "These are perfect."

"Yeah." Paula holds up her license. "It looks just like me."

"It is you." Jay laughs.

"My new name is Jennifer. Jennifer Lippman from Phoenix." Paula looks at Emily. "Should we use our new names when we move to California?"

"You girls going somewhere?"

"The coast. Someday."

Paula frowns. "What if my dad or Grandma Marilee asks where you are tomorrow?"

"Say she's with me," Jay says. "But I guarantee Dwight won't ask. He's going to be too preoccupied with those guys coming here tomorrow. Mom might ask though. You guys know what he's doing with the bus?"

"He's going to use it to block the entrance, so those assholes can't get in," Emily says.

"Are you helping Dad tomorrow, Jay?"

"He said I should stay away. I already did my time in Florence."

"Do you think they'll arrest him?"

"Why the hell would they arrest him?" Emily bundles up her IDs and puts the rubber band back around them. "I bet it's a big bluff. Like Grandma Marilee says they've been doing for a long time." She looks at Jay. "Right?"

"Who knows?"

"He must think they're serious. Look at what he and Claude have done to this place. All the barbed wire and new fences."

"They just want to be prepared. Don't worry," Emily says. "Your dad wouldn't do anything stupid."

Jay turns to the door. "Emily, I'll pick you up on that street behind the old Sombreros tomorrow morning, 5:45 a.m. Flight leaves at 7:30."

"Where's my ticket?"

"I'll have it with me tomorrow," Jay says.

Emily flips through the blank pages of her passport. "How come we get the IDs before I even take the suitcase to LA? I figured Stone would have waited."

"I'm the one with the IDs and I'm giving them to you now."

Something about Jay seems different. Maybe more confident. She can't put a finger on it.

He leaves and Emily sees him step up into the school bus.

"Our old selves will just disappear, Paula. We'll be brand-new people."

"Yeah."

"Seriously. Like the old Emily and Paula never existed."

"I kind of liked them."

"Yeah, they were pretty chill."

"Emily, what if they force us out tomorrow and everyone's gone when you get back from L.A.?"

"We can't go to that place with all the 'what ifs.' Think positive. That won't happen. I'll come back from L.A. and we'll have our IDs and all that money. And Eureka, here we come."

"I told you I don't want Jeanette Karl's money."

"Let's not get into it now."

"You're the one who brought it up. Are you taking it with you?"

"I can't take all that money on the plane. Those security people might find it when I go through the checkpoint. Steve said you go through some X-ray. Remember that line we saw at the airport? And they can search you."

"What if those eviction people try to go through our stuff? You could ask Jay to hold onto it."

"No way. I don't want him to even know we have it. I'll take some, leave most of it here."

"Whatever, Emily. It's not mine."

Paula places the packet with her new identification under the bed.

"I wish you were coming with me tomorrow," Emily says.

"Me too."

Wind pounds the Airstream all night. Balsa wood over the back window thumps against the frame; hot air and dust blow in through crevices. The little trailer shakes as if it might be swept up into the gusts and carried away. By morning, the wind dies down, but when Emily steps out of the Airstream the branches of the mesquite sway as if the storm could start up again. Debris covers the patio. A brownish tinge colors the air.

The yellow school bus blocks the entrance to the property except for three feet between the front of the bus and the block fence. Several rows of barbed wire hang from the bus's bumper to the ground. Dwight's tools for securing the wire to the fence lie on the ground nearby. At the top of the driveway, Emily looks back at Paula standing in the doorway of the Airstream and waves. She slips by the bus and walks the three blocks to meet Jay.

On the way, she sees True Lord church. Beer cans litter the ground around it. Dry brown Bermuda grass grows in an interlaced pattern like a system of arteries and veins. It seems like a long time since that morning in May when Paula sat on the front steps, disappointed about the retreat. Even longer since the Easter Sunday when they went to the service and the free brunch and the weird sermon by the preacher in the purple robe who took Paula's money. How would things have turned out if the church building hadn't gotten repossessed? Maybe

Paula would have been one of those born-again people and given them more money. Maybe she'd never have agreed to go along with Stone's airport jobs. Stone is not to be trusted, nor Steve, but as long as you know who you're dealing with, you're prepared. And so far, Steve and Stone hadn't tried to screw them over. Not like the preacher.

Emily wonders if when she comes home this evening, she'll find a repossessed sign at home like the one on the church. She hasn't a clue what she'll do if everybody's gone. Where would she even go to try and find them? She should have suggested Paula go with Jay today, away from the property.

Jay pulls up on time, and Emily gets in the car.

"There's the suitcase." Jay nods toward the back seat.

The suitcase is a medium-sized beige canvas Samsonite.

"Do you know what's in it?"

Jay shakes his head. "Beats me. Maybe IDs, maybe money."

"Drugs?"

"I don't think so. Too many scent dogs at airports."

"I guess it doesn't matter."

"No, it doesn't. Just check it and make sure it gets to L.A. Then your job's done."

"I could just check it and not take the flight. It'd still get there, right?" Why does Stone care if she even gets on the flight to LA?

"Maybe, maybe not. Too risky. There might be some way security monitors stuff like that. Maybe they match up checked bags with who gets on the plane. I don't know. Plus, you wouldn't be able to make sure it got to baggage claim in L.A. if you didn't take the flight. Besides, you want to go, don't you?"

"Of course. Why wouldn't Stone let both of us go?"

"Who knows? But why pay for two tickets? It's a one-person job. Two people, twice the risk. Stone's a business guy. That's how he thinks."

Traffic slows nearly to a stop about a mile before the airport exit. Jay fidgets with the radio, switches from one station to the next, then turns it off.

"Jay?"

"Yeah?"

"What did you get sent to Florence for? What was the Circle K thing?"

"Where did that come from?"

"I don't know." Emily gazes at traffic around them, inching forward. "I've just always wondered."

"Look. I'll tell you some other time."

"Do you worry about getting caught and getting sent back?"

Jay's quiet for a minute, and then says, "Naw, I'm okay. I'm careful."

The traffic moves and picks up to normal speed.

"Will you check on things at the property today?"

Jay shakes his head. "I told you, Dwight said it wasn't necessary."

"Why didn't he want you to help him and those sovereign guys defend the property?"

Jay takes a cigarette from the pack on the dash, presses the car's lighter. "Maybe he wanted one of us on the outside in case something goes down." He looks at Emily, more serious than she's ever seen him. "I don't think it's going to work. I don't know what's going to happen at our place, but the authorities ain't going to just give up. When I said this to Dwight, he got pissed. Was it quiet when you left?"

"Yeah. No one saw me leave, except Paula."

Jay takes the airport exit and pulls in front of Terminal 4. "Here we are."

Emily gets out. She opens the back door, grips the suitcase by its handle, and slides it across the seat.

"I'll be at the Southwest pickup area at 5:30 this evening to get you."

"Okay." Emily shuts the back door and starts to walk away from the car. Then she stops and knocks on the front passenger window. Jay rolls it down.

"What?"

"Paula shouldn't be there."

"It's too late now, Emily."

"Drive by later. Even if you can't get in, you could see what's happening. Check on Paula. Okay?"

"I'll try."

Inside the terminal, Emily carries the suitcase to the women's room and into the stall farthest from the door. She lays it flat on the floor, squats down, and tries to unzip it. No lock, but the zipper won't budge. Of course not. Stone wouldn't take any chances. She picks it up, turns it to one side and then the other. Nothing moves inside. She lays it flat and presses on the canvas with her palms, but it's too thick to give. Fuck it. Who cares what's inside. She takes it to the check-in line. Three people are in front of her, but the line moves quickly. As she passes her ticket to the woman at the counter, she looks at it briefly. Her new name's on the ticket, Elizabeth Jackson. The woman enters something into the computer and asks for Emily's ID. She lays the fake driver's license on the counter.

"Are you checking a bag?" the woman says. Emily hesitates and then she lifts the beige Samsonite and places it in the slot next to the counter.

21

The barbed wire on top of the new chain-link fence shimmers in the morning sun. It catches Marilee's eye when she steps onto the patio, reminding her of the harsh flicker of the fence at Florence, which always sent a chill through her when she visited Jay. All these strangers on the property. She counts eleven. Guys with guns on their hips; a woman in a sundress wearing an ankle holster, all standing around like they're waiting for something. Dwight and Claude are stringing more barbed wire around the school bus. Marilee wonders where Emily and Paula are. She puts her coffee cup on the table next to her recliner and heads to the graveyard.

Shamrocks beneath the mesquite lie wilted and brown, beyond saving, even with all her watering. Oranges blown from the tree in last night's storm litter the ground and give off a sweet citrus smell. The weather's clear now but a scent of monsoon lingers. It'll be back. A Union Pacific rumbles by as Marilee reaches the graveyard. She stands before Jack's stone and closes her eyes. What's going to happen to his grave and all the others if the authorities force them out?

The destruction of San Pablo looms in her mind. This morning has the feel of that day she walked with Maria to watch as the community fell. Marilee was twenty-one years old, engaged to Jack. She looks up at the modern buildings of downtown Tempe, and beyond to the small mountain. They came in with bulldozers, ran roughshod over homes, stores, churches, wiping out the whole neighborhood. One by one owners sold their property for the small amount of money offered, their houses razed, trees toppled, gardens ground back into the earth. Herded out like cattle, pushed into another neighborhood several miles away. The university wanted more space. San Pablo was in their way. Maria's friend Magdalena stood beside them. "There goes ours," she said as the bulldozers demolished the pale blue adobe house that stood at the base of what became "A" mountain. Magdalena's face looked as if that piece of machinery was ripping through her own body, crushing her limbs into rubble. Eminent domain.

Covered now by light-rail tracks, a sports stadium, four-story dorms, and university offices, nothing remains of the people who made their lives on that land. Like they were never there. That's what they want to do to her family: send in the bulldozers, level everything, haul the debris away. Erase those who settled on it, raised their kids, and buried their dead there. Would the state dig up the graves and bury them somewhere else? There is no place else. Marilee kneels on the ground in front of Jack's stone, runs her hand over it, closes her eyes, and tries to imagine the whole property mess settled, everything back to how it should be, all the strangers gone, the eviction notice a bad dream.

Her memory of the San Pablo destruction has remained vivid all these years. She's repeated the story so often to Emily and Paula, they're probably tired of hearing it, though it always seems to fascinate Emily and make her angry. But something else about that day has remained vague, a blurry spot in Marilee's mind that occasionally feels as if it might reveal itself to her, only to slip away again. Now on her knees in front of the graves, her property full of people she doesn't know, the fog in her mind begins to lift a little. She whispers the words she remembers from Maria's prayers. "Pray for us sinners now and at the hour of our death." To whom she whispers this plea, she doesn't know.

Maria had shown her an envelope she kept in a box in her bedroom closet, the bedroom that is now Marilee's. The envelope contained some papers that had to do with the property.

"My parents—your great-grandparents, Constance and Jimmy Baker—bought this property from Constance's brothers, Albert and Martino," Maria had said as she pulled out an official-looking document from the envelope and showed to

Marilee. "Albert and Martino sold it to them real cheap, a wedding gift along with the house they built for them. That house is our little adobe."

Marilee sees those papers in her head and the names on them—Albert and Martino, Constance and Jimmy, and another name she can't remember, didn't recognize at the time—the papers Dwight doesn't believe exist, that she too has begun to doubt. This is the first time she's had this vision, this remembrance. The names are as vivid now as those carved into the gravestones she kneels before. It's the first time in a very long time she recalls the time and circumstance. This has to be a good thing. A sign from Jack. Like the roses. What happened to the envelope, the box it was in? Did Maria give it to her? Did she give it to Jack when they got married? It's not on the shelf in the closet. She's looked; so has Dwight when he thought she was dozing on the patio. What would those assholes who call them squatters do if she found that envelope? Would they leave them alone? No, of course not. Did those bulldozers in San Pablo leave the rightful owners alone?

Marilee turns from the gravestones and opens the door to the shed where the statue of the Virgin Mary stands. Something scampers from behind the statue. A large rat? A stray cat? Gone before she can tell for sure. She braces herself against the statue and reaches to the low shelves behind it. The Virgin Mary tips forward and crashes to the ground, but Marilee catches herself on the shelf, which is thick with grime accumulated over many years. There are old tools, near-crumbling boxes of papers she's searched through, and books, all covered with thick layers of dust. And the .22 rifle Jack gave her so long ago. Marilee takes the rifle from the shelf. It's been a long time since she shot it, and rust runs along the barrel. She checks to see that it's still loaded then walks back to the patio.

She lays the gun on the concrete and sits in her recliner. Her breath comes rapidly. The end of the prayer flags has come undone again.

"What are you doing with that, Grandma?"

Paula steps out of the Airstream and points to the gun.

"Nothing, Paula. Just want it near."

"It looks old. Does it even work?"

"I don't see why it wouldn't. Where's Emily? Did she go somewhere?"

"She'll be back later."

"How will she get in?" Marilee gazes at the blockade that now surrounds the property.

"Don't worry. She's okay. She'll get back in."

The rumble of an engine sounds above the buzz of voices on the grounds. It's a big moving truck with Wilson Brothers Moving and Storage painted on the side.

Marilee sips her now-cold coffee. "What the hell do they think they're going to move?"

"I don't know. Us?" Paula says and points to Marilee's cup. "You want me to heat that up for you?"

"No, Paula, honey. Just fix those prayer flags."

Paula picks up the flags that hang from the overhead beam and for the thousandth time twists them around the vertical patio post. Marilee notices that one of the guys in the yard watches Paula. What did Dwight say they called themselves? True something. The guy's got spiky hair, deep yellow like a sunflower. And a gun in a hip holster. He's so skinny it's a wonder that holster doesn't slip down to his ankles. He steps to the patio, stands in front of Marilee. Is that a swastika on his face? He extends his hand to her.

"Name's Mike, ma'am. It's a pleasure to meet you."

Marilee nods, her cold coffee in one hand, a cigarette in the other. She stares at the swastika and doesn't offer him her hand.

22

Shane and Shawna drove up with Deland and Jerry McFaul, two cases of beer, a Safeway bag full of food and several gallon-sized plastic containers of water. "In case this thing lasts awhile," Shane said. Dwight's still not exactly sure what "this thing" will turn out to be. Cops storming his property? Forcing his mom and the girls to leave? Dragging him out? It could happen, but he doesn't let his mind linger there. A little bit later Terry Lee and Russ, with his number fourteen tattoo, pulled up in a rusty Chevy Blazer with the back window missing. They brought another guy named Mike, who looks like a cross between one of those punk rockers and a skinhead. He's got a tattoo on his left check with the words Phoenix and a swastika underneath it. There are three others Dwight's never met. Shane refers to them as "the Phoenix guys," an assortment of armed men who've come to save his property.

Dwight nods to the group. "This it?" he asks Claude.

"Yep." Claude looks around. "All here."

"Okay, let's finish this up."

Dwight and Claude close the gap between the bus and the wall with strands of barbed wire. One by one they twist strands around the screws they've drilled into the concrete fence. They run more strands from the bus's front wheels to the back so nobody can crawl under it. No way in or out. Feels like they're in a barricaded war zone.

Dwight hasn't seen the girls yet this morning. His mom came out to the patio about forty-five minutes ago and eyeballed the whole scene. Didn't say a word.

"Why don't you stick around the patio, Mom?" Dwight called after her as she headed out to the graveyard like she does every morning.

She turned around and scowled at him, then walked away.

She's so upset about the whole situation, she's going to do what she's going to do.

"Hey, Dwight," Claude says. "Hear that?"

A rumbling engine outside the front of the place, sounds like a diesel. All Dwight can see over the fence is the very top of a truck parked across the street. He steps inside the school bus with Claude right behind him. Thick dust covers the windows, but he can see out. It's a moving van. Two men are inside, but neither seems to be making a move to open the door and get out.

"Sheriff's department probably contracted with them," Claude says. "That's how they evict people. Haul their stuff off and put it in storage. Or on the street."

"Jesus Christ. They're not taking any fucking thing from here." From inside the bus he's got a good view of what's going on out front. "I'm going to check around the property and see if anybody's trying to get in."

"Okay. I told the others to give a shout if they see anything. I'll keep an eye on the truck."

Dwight walks along the chain-link fence. All is quiet. He nods to Shane and one of the Phoenix guys standing over by the mesquite. The door to his mom's Virgin Mary shed is open; he catches a glimpse of her inside and moves on. He peers over the fence behind the house and looks beyond it to the railroad tracks, catching fragments of traffic on Mill Avenue. When he returns to the bus, the moving van is still idling. Maybe no authorities are coming after all. Maybe they figured he'd just let those moving guys come on in and take all their stuff, and he'd hand over his property. It's still early though, a few minutes after nine.

"You think anything's gonna go down here?"

Dwight turns and sees the guy with the yellow-spiked hair—Mike. Up close he's older than Dwight thought, close to his own age. His threadbare sleeveless denim jacket hangs open over a skinny hairless chest tattooed with the same number fourteen as Russ's. And that fucking swastika on his face. Dwight could do without this guy. "That's why you're here, isn't it? Just hold tight and we'll see what goes down."

Fucking racist asshole. Dwight returns to the patio. Marilee's in her recliner, Paula next to her. Dwight puts his cigarette out and lights another. He's about to ask Paula where Emily is when he notices the rifle lying on the patio beside the recliner.

"What are you doing with that, Mom?"

"I'm not doing anything."

"I haven't seen that rifle for a long time. Where was it?"

"Out in the shed." Marilee picks up the butt that Dwight just put out in the ashtray and relights it.

"It's not a good idea to use an old gun like that. I'll take a look at it some other time."

"I'm just fine with it, Dwight. I handled guns way before you ever saw one. Before you were even born."

"I know that, Mom. I know."

"Then you and your citizen boys take care of your business and let me take care of mine."

Spiked-hair Mike, who'd been standing a few feet from them, approaches the patio. Is the guy following him? Mike smiles at Marilee, gives a wink, and then smiles at Paula.

"You want something here?" Dwight says.

"No, man. Just being friendly." Mike points his chin to Marilee's rifle. "That a Winchester?"

"Sure is," Marilee says.

"Hey, Dwight, come over here," Claude calls from the driveway.

"Just a sec." Dwight walks up close to Mike and nods toward Paula "She's my daughter. Stay the fuck away from her."

On the street a Maricopa County Sheriff's Office car has parked behind the moving truck. The sun plays off its red siren, a dagger of light shoots from the car's roof. Two MCSO officers are in the front seat. They get out and approach the driveway. One is tall and slim and looks about thirty; the other is overweight and pudgy, could be fifty. Dwight watches them. The officers must see them, but they are focused on the barbed wire and ignore Claude and Dwight. They scan the sidewalk in front of the property and then move closer, just a few feet from where Dwight and Claude stand.

"You folks are ordered to leave this property." The pudgy one holds up a sheet of paper with the words *Notice of Eviction* printed in bold red capital letters across the top. He presses it up to the barbed wire. In smaller type below, it says *By Order of the State of Arizona*, and then *No Trespassing* in black letters at the bottom. He holds it there like he's waiting for Dwight to read it before taping it to the fence.

Claude nudges Dwight. "Where's your declaration of sovereignty?"

"Right here." Dwight reaches into his back pocket and unfolds the declaration. He holds it up to the fence the same way the officer held his notice. "I got a piece of paper too. This is my family's property. Been here a hundred years and nobody's going anywhere."

"Who are all those guys?" The younger officer nods toward the other guys who are at various spots on the property.

"Friends. And that's my mom and daughter over there on the patio."

"Look, we don't want any trouble here."

"Then, why don't you tell that moving truck to follow you out of here?"

"We've got orders to evict you." The pudgy one takes a handkerchief out of his shirt pocket and wipes sweat from his forehead. The underarms of his shirt are wet. "That truck will take your stuff and put it in storage."

Dwight looks around the property and for a minute imagines them trying to load everything into that van. He pictures all their belongings on the street, sees his mom and the girls in one of those run-down motels on Van Buren. "Like I said, nobody's going anywhere. We don't need to store anything."

The cops glance at one another and position themselves as if they're guarding the place. They can guard it all the fuck they want, Dwight thinks. The fat one doesn't look like he's in great shape. Another MCSO car pulls up behind them and two more officers get out. Claude's pacing around near the entrance. Dwight turns and heads to the patio where Marilee and Paula still sit.

"You can't win at this, son," the older one calls to him.

Who the fuck is he calling *son*? Dwight ignores him.

By early afternoon, heat hangs heavy and moist over the valley. Shawna makes sandwiches and brings them to the patio. Paula's in and out of the Airstream. Dwight still hasn't asked her about Emily. He should have sent them both away. They could have hung out at Claude's.

Two more officers arrive, and Dwight steps into the bus for a better view. The officers walk to the west corner and turn toward the lake, out of Dwight's field of vision. He steps out of the bus and watches them through the chain-link fence. They eyeball the property and the construction site across the street, then turn around and come back and join the others near the front entrance.

What the fuck are they going to do? Dwight wonders.

As if Claude read his mind, he says, "Looks like we're going to have a standoff." He points to a fourth cop car that has just parked on the west side.

"I guess so."

"Keep an eye out," Claude says to Shane and the other guys. "Don't say anything to the cops or anyone else. Dwight does all the talking. And keep your hands away from your guns."

The men disperse around the property. Some of the construction workers from the condos have gathered to watch what's going on. The air grows thicker and hotter by the second. Dwight steps back into the school bus. One of the guys in the Wilson Brothers truck gets out and talks to the tall skinny officer. Dwight can't hear what they say to each other, but the guy gets back in the truck and drives away.

"Here. You look like you could use one of these." Claude hands him a beer.

"Thanks. That van's leaving."

"Yeah. I don't know if that's good or bad."

The first sip of beer cools Dwight. The sun has nearly disappeared, but the air swelters. Marilee's tied a bandana around her head to absorb the sweat. Paula sits a few feet away from her. The misting system Dwight rigged up drips water behind them.

"Look over there, Dwight." Claude points to where the construction workers are milling about. A fifth sheriff's car has parked in front of his motorcycle and two more officers get out. Ten cops now.

"What the hell are they going to do?"

"Who knows," Claude says. "Our guns probably made those first two nervous. I told you how much law enforcement came out to my uncle's place."

For a second Dwight tries to imagine Claude's uncle's ranch. Acres of land surrounded by acres of more land, nothing upscale. He'd like that place. He watches the two new officers walk up and down the street, peruse his property. Dust hangs from the sky and spreads as wide as he can see. It looms out there as if watching him, waiting to see what's going to happen. The dark mass is too far for him to tell in what direction it's moving. Every once in a while the wind picks up and vibrates the barbed wire on the top of the fence.

"You think that's gonna hit us?" Claude says.

"It could break up."

Marilee's gotten up from her recliner. She stands next to Dwight and Claude, looking out at the dust storm.

"That's not going to break up," she says. "Not something that big."

23

Emily follows the other passengers down the ramp and through the gate area at LAX. She finds the baggage claim carousel for her flight and watches from a distance for the suitcase. Passengers congregate around the carousel, blocking her view. She moves closer. A few bags begin to shoot onto the conveyor belt. A man wearing a Los Angeles Dodgers baseball cap stands in front of her. Is he the one picking up the suitcase she checked back in Phoenix? Or maybe the guy in the three-piece gray suit or the woman next to him? The carousel is crowded with suitcases falling against one another. She spots the beige Samsonite crammed between two bigger ones. Passengers retrieve their bags and gradually the number diminishes. The belt is nearly empty. Emily looks around to see who will come forward for the Samsonite. The man in the gray suit watches the few remaining bags disappear and then circle around again. Emily backs away a little but keeps the beige suitcase in view. The Dodgers-cap guy grabs it, then moves quickly away from the carousel. She catches a glimpse of his face as he heads to the exit. Dark sunglasses, roundish face. That's all she can see. He disappears into a crowd of people.

Her return flight to Phoenix isn't until 4:30 p.m., over eight hours from now. She exits the terminal, follows the yellow taxi signs, and stands outside in a short line at a kiosk. An official-looking woman in a white shirt gives her a ticket and points to another short line a few feet away. The air is warm and pleasant against her skin, not baking like Phoenix. Emily breathes it in, imagines the smell of the ocean. In a few minutes a black and yellow City Cab pulls in front of her and a man standing near the curb opens the back door.

"Where to, young lady?" The driver looks at her through his rearview mirror.

"The beach."

He turns around, rests his right arm over the back of his seat. His light brown hair is pulled tightly into a ponytail that hangs past his shoulders. About Jay's age, maybe a little younger, his skin, tanned a soft, shimmery color, looks slippery like butter. He smiles. "We got at least fifteen beaches in L.A. County. How about we get a little more specific?"

Of course. How stupid of her. "I have to be back here for a four-thirty flight. Which one would be best?"

"Venice is about an hour and a half. Santa Monica thirty minutes to an hour. Then you got Hermosa, Redondo, Marina Del Rey. All about an hour, depending on traffic." He checks the clock on the dash: 8:45 a.m. "It's Tuesday, we're going to hit at least the tail end of morning rush hour. Venice is the farthest, but you might like that one."

"Okay." Emily smiles. "I want to go to Venice Beach." She likes the name. It sounds like another planet.

The driver puts the car in gear and pulls away from the curb. The traffic is bumper to bumper as they leave the airport but lightens the farther away they get. He exits at Lincoln Boulevard, takes that to Venice Beach Boulevard, and pulls over to the curb.

"There's Ocean Front Boulevard." He points to a pedestrian walkway running parallel to the beach. "That's a good spot to get a flavor of this place."

Emily starts to get out, then remembers she needs to pay him. "How much?"

The driver points to the meter, it reads $37.03. She reaches into her purse, counts out the money, and passes it to him. He takes the money and waits.

"Passengers typically leave a tip."

Emily takes a five and a one from her purse and gives it to him, again feeling stupid. "Sorry. Can I call you to take me back to the airport?"

The driver passes her a card with City Cab printed in gold letters across the top. "Just call this number. You might get me or somebody else. Depends on who's in the area. There'll be plenty of other taxis around."

"Thanks."

He nods. "They shouldn't charge you any more than thirty-seven to thirty-eight dollars, so don't let them rip you off."

Vendors, skateboarders, skaters, and joggers crowd the boardwalk. A giant bong hangs in the window of a head shop. There's a tattoo shop. To the left, the beach and the ocean. It's early but already towels are spread on the sand, and girls in bikinis rub lotion into their skin, tanned and glimmery like the taxi driver's. Emily takes her shoes off and steps onto the sand. Soft and warm, it works its way between her toes. The ocean isn't blue like in the Eureka postcard. Instead, it's dark gray, almost black, with tinges of deep green. Silver-white waves dance on its surface, flickering in the sun. The water glows like a field of stars. Emily stops and gazes over the ocean, hypnotized, her breath shallow with the vastness of what lies before her, the eternity beyond the surfers and boats and ships in the distance. Nothing but ocean and sky, impossible to distinguish one from the other. The air smells of salt and grass and coconut suntan lotion. Even the fishy odor seems wonderful. She looks up the coastline to what she thinks must be north. How far is Eureka?

"I've got to tell Paula. She's got to see this." Emily says this out loud to no one.

She strolls for over an hour at the water's edge. The tide smacks her ankles and legs as waves tug and pull the sand from under her. Farther down the beach, she walks to a pier. It's long and dirty and filled with bird poop, which she tries to step around in her bare feet. No matter, she'll wash it off in the ocean. Fishermen line the edges. She reaches the end of the pier and looks back at the beach. A huge Ferris wheel spins in the distance. It must be the same one the taxi driver pointed to. *Santa Monica*, he said. She returns to the boardwalk, finds a gift shop, and buys a postcard of Venice Beach for Paula. She sits on the edge of the boardwalk, takes out her phone, and calls Paula. The sound of voices on the beach and water hitting the shore fills the background as she waits for Paula to answer. Tempe, the property, Stone, and the suitcases feel a world away from her. Those jagged, moonscape mountaintops surrounded by barren brown desert she saw from the plane's window as they made their way to L.A. seem like another world.

"Hey."

"Emily. Where are you?"

"I'm in Los Angeles. Where do you think?"

"I know that. I mean where? In the airport? Did everything go okay with the suitcase?"

"I'm at the beach. You won't believe it, Paula. The ocean is so much better in person. It's not even blue, really. And, yeah, everything went fine. I'll tell you about it when I get back. You've got to ride a plane. Maybe we should just fly to Eureka. And I bought you a postcard."

"Cool. Emily, things are crazy here."

"And the mountains here." She barely hears Paula. "Bigger than in Phoenix and the whole place is huge and busy and full of cool-looking people. The air is like silk on your brain."

"Nice."

"And guess what time I landed? 7:40. Ten minutes after the plane left Phoenix. Because of the time difference. L.A. is an hour earlier than Phoenix, so you gain time. Is that fucking crazy or what? And so many cool people here. I know, I said that already. But god, I love it here, Paula. The beach is filled with people our age. It's like they fucking shine. And oh my god, you should see this Ferris wheel. I can see it right now, it's at another beach. There's beaches all over the place. What's going on there, Paula?"

"Sheriffs' cars out front and on the side street. A moving van came this morning but left. They wanted to put our stuff in the van and store it somewhere."

"Assholes. Your dad must be so pissed."

"Claude's here. And that guy from Marana and a bunch of other guys with guns. And the woman with the tattoo and boots. And a weird guy with a swastika on his face. Grandma Marilee says we're going to get a big dust storm. She said it's an omen."

"Has Jay come by?"

"Who knows. I can only see through the chain-link fence and that side is filled with cop cars. He wouldn't drive over there."

"He said he'd try to stop by. Check on things."

"Emily, he won't be able to get onto the property. And I wouldn't know if he was checking on anything or not. We're all blockaded in here."

"Yeah, I know, I know."

"Grandma Marilee has an old gun on the patio beside her."

Grandma Marilee's not going to let anyone take their property, that's for sure. She'd never budge. They'd have to carry her off. Maybe she'll just shoot them.

"Paula, I don't think it's a good idea for you to be there."

"My dad wouldn't let anyone do anything stupid."

"I know. But it just seems like it'd be better if you weren't there. We should have thought of this before. I don't even know how I'm going to get back in."

"You can't get back in. And I don't think I can get out."

"Call Jay and see if he can come get you. He's going to pick me up in a few hours at the airport."

"I just told you I don't think I can get out with all the fences and barbed wire. And all those cops."

"Maybe there's a place where you can climb over the fence. A spot you can move the barbed wire away. Where there's no cops. Try to find a way. And take your new ID. And the money. Just try it and call Jay to pick you up. No, I'll call Jay. You just try to get out."

"I don't know, Emily."

"And bring that postcard of Eureka that's on our wall. Find a spot. You have to."

24

Dwight watches as one of the cops at the front entrance moves closer to the barbed wire. He's got something in his hand. Not a gun. He wouldn't handle a gun like that, too loose of a grip. Some sort of tool.

"What is it?" Claude says.

"Fuck if I know." Dwight touches the grip of his Glock and walks over to the fence. Claude follows.

"Bolt cutters," Claude says. "Motherfuckers are going to cut that barbed wire."

"Get the hell away from that wire. This is my property. Back the fuck off."

"You need to evacuate this property." It's the older, pudgy one. His shirt is soaked. He snips the first strand. "We don't want any trouble. We're just doing our job here."

Marilee pulls herself up from the recliner on the patio. She braces herself on its arm, then reaches to the concrete for the old gun. The cop's getting ready to cut the next strand. Marilee picks up the rifle; her eyes narrow and bore into the cop.

What the hell's she doing? He's got enough to worry about. "Mom. Leave it."

The wind picks up; Marilee's long gray hair whips about her face. Dwight doesn't take his eyes off her. The brown wall of dust has moved closer, a haze already hanging over the property; his view of Marilee is muddled, as if she's behind dirty gauze. She holds the rifle by her side, pointed at the ground, as she approaches the front end of the bus where the cop has just clipped the second barbed wire. Only three strands left.

"What are you doing, Grandma?" Paula says.

"Mom. Let me handle this." Dwight walks toward her.

"Ma'am, please put that down," the pudgy cop says. "We don't want anyone getting hurt today."

"Then why don't you stop cutting up my fence and trying to get onto my private property."

"I told you, ma'am, we've got orders."

"This is my property. We've been here over a hundred years. All my family's buried over there." She nods toward the graveyard. "And we're not leaving."

Debris blows about the property; loose dirt kicks up. The highway in Iraq flashes in Dwight's mind. He loses focus for a minute but shakes it off. Marilee lifts the rifle. She struggles to hold it in position.

"Mom, put it down."

The pudgy cop drops the wire cutters and draws his gun. "Stand down, ma'am."

The skinny one behind him draws his gun, and then a third cop. They hold weapons ready with both hands.

"It doesn't work," Dwight yells to them through the blowing dust. "That gun hasn't been fired for over ten years. It won't shoot." He doesn't know this for sure.

They ignore him, eyes and weapons on Marilee.

"Jesus Christ." Claude's voice.

"Drop your weapon, ma'am."

"Get away from my property."

"Mom, put it down."

"Grandma Marilee."

Marilee lowers the rifle, but holds on to it, no longer aimed at the officers.

"Please, Grandma. Put it down."

"Paula." Dwight squints in the direction of her voice. "Get away from the patio. Inside the Airstream. Claude, get her away from here."

Claude takes a step toward Paula, then stops. "Dwight, over there." He points toward the west sidewalk.

Two more police cars. Through the brown haze Dwight counts six cops at the fence, a wall of dust behind them, the high-rises across the street nearly invisible. He catches a glimpse of Shane and Deland out by the orange tree, McFaul at the northwest corner. Mike is a few feet from Jay's lean-to. He glances back to the entrance. Marilee's backed away from the fence to the patio, rifle at her side, barrel pointed at the concrete. Paula's gone, he hopes, inside the Airstream.

One of the cops at the west fence begins to cut the chain-link; two others push on the posts. A fourth has a canister in his hand, aimed like he's going to toss it onto the property. Two others push the fence posts farther down the perimeter. The cops out front have lowered their weapons, but the tall skinny one's also got a canister in his hand, ready to throw. That wall of dust is making it hard to see.

"Tear gas." Claude's voice in the fog. "For fuck's sake."

Tear gas with all this dust in the air? Assholes, goddamned assholes. The cop tosses the tear gas canister. A white cloud rises from the ground where it falls and spreads to the surrounding area. Another one. At first, they smell like gunpowder, then the scent vanishes. Nearby, a large section of the chain-link tumbles forward and lands with a clang. Gray smoke blends with dust and burns Dwight's nostrils. Marilee is blurry, but he sees the rifle still at her side.

"Paula," he yells, without taking his eyes off his mother. He steps off the patio, moves to a spot under the mesquite tree, and looks around for Paula. He can barely see.

When his unit arrived on that highway back in February 1991, visibility was bad, the worst he'd ever experienced. Heavy rain and dust storms had swept over the area outside of Kuwait City for days. Not even the most powerful monsoon in Phoenix compared. When it cleared, Dwight saw the vehicles spread across the highway. Miles and miles of Iraqi military and civilians, attempting to get out of Kuwait, trapped by anti-armor mines laid across the highway by Air Force and Navy pilots. Bombs rained down from the sky. Ground troops attacked from the hillsides. Dwight and Leroy were in one of the M1-A1 tanks, their orders to cover the Iraqi soldiers with piles of sand after others in armored personnel carriers fired on them. The plows of the tanks were like giant teeth. "Jesus, we're burying them alive," he said to Leroy.

It went on all night, into the next morning until a cease-fire was called and the extent of the carnage became visible. Blown-up bodies. Mummified charcoal-men. Trenches full of sand with arms and legs sticking out of them. Windshields melted by fire into blobs of silicone.

Dwight and Leroy walked through the scorched desert sand, around pools of blood and piles of bodies burnt beyond recognition. Here and there a leg, an arm, oddly undamaged. An untouched face, young smooth skin, almost pretty and with eyes that seemed to stare at the blue sky. *Some of these Iraqi soldiers are only thirteen, fourteen years old*, Leroy said so softly it was almost a whisper. A few feet away was a boot that looked new.

Dwight's eyes were riveted on the corpse of an incinerated Iraqi soldier. He must have pulled himself over the dashboard, trying to get out as flames engulfed his truck. Dwight went closer.

As he neared the truck, he felt Leroy behind him. *C'mon, Dwight. What are you doing?*

Dwight continued walking until he was a few feet from the truck and the man inside. The man's hands reached out of the shattered windshield, his face and chest seared the same color as the rusted metal around him. His face was burned and he had no eyes, but still it felt as if he was staring at Dwight. Pleading, accusing. Who was this man? What was his name? Had he joined the Iraqi army just like Dwight had joined the U.S. army? Was someone like Ruth waiting for him somewhere? What kind of person does this to another person? *Guys like me*, Dwight thought.

A hand on his shoulder. *C'mon, man*, Leroy said. *It don't pay to look too long.*

Dwight turned and looked at him. Leroy had tears in his eyes. Leroy was three years younger than Dwight; he was only twenty-four but sometimes he seemed like an older brother. He kept his hand on Dwight's shoulder as they made their way back to the jeep, the smell of burnt flesh surrounding them. When they reached the vehicle, Dwight dropped to the ground. The sand was still hot; it felt as if it would burn right through his pants. But he stayed kneeling and puked his guts out, puked and puked until nothing was left inside of him. Nothing but death.

"Dwight." Claude's voice, somewhere over by the patio, brings him back. A click and then the crunch of dry soil. A commotion of people running through the property. Cops. A shot. Who the hell fired that? Did Marilee fire that old rifle? Dwight can no longer see her or anyone else, the air is too thick and brown, a curtain has fallen over the world. He leans his back against the mesquite tree, breathing hard, tasting dust in the air, dirt scouring his skin. He chokes on the dense, blinding air, thick with tear gas and dust and dirt stirred up from all the trampling of feet on the property. His eyes are on fire. He rubs them with the back of his hand but that makes it worse. His lungs burn. Where is Paula. And Marilee? And Emily? He's not seen Emily all day.

"Drop your weapons." The words seem to come from several directions at once, from the entrance by the school bus, from behind him, from the western side of the property. Another shot. Dwight looks around but can't see who has their weapon drawn. He holds his gun in his right hand, his chest on fire. More shots. Dwight slides down the trunk of the tree, leans his head against it, closes his eyes, and see's Ruth's face.

25

Paula knows she should try to get off the property. Her dad won't do anything stupid, but what about all the other guys? What about Grandma Marilee and that old gun? Paula obeys when Dwight tells her to get inside the Airstream. She takes her new ID from under the bed and puts it and the guns he gave her and Emily in one of the backpacks they'd stolen. It seems like a long time ago, those ASU thefts. She pulls the Eureka postcard off the wall, puts it in the front zipper pocket, and thinks about leaving the money from Jeanette Karl's suitcase. That would end her arguments with Emily about what do to with it. But Jeanette Karl still wouldn't get it back—if a Jeanette Karl really did exist. And Emily would be devastated. Maybe she's right, maybe there is no Jeanette Karl. Maybe no little kid. Paula puts the money in the pocket with the postcard.

She slips her arms through the backpack straps, opens the Airstream door, and walks past the patio to the eastern edge of the property. The storm's kicking up like crazy. Grandma Marilee was right, it's a big one. A spot behind the house looks like a possibility. Three old truck tires are stacked right next to the fence. Paula braces herself and stands on the tires. She examines the barbed wire, but it's hard to see anything. She uses the cell phone flashlight to check the top of the fence. There are no loose spots, no way to pry the wire from the fence. No way out on that side. As she steps off the stack of tires her lower left arm scrapes a piece of barbed wire, which leaves a gash on her lower arm. Blood bubbles up, but she ignores it.

She hears her dad shouting for her to get inside the Airstream, but she ignores him and goes to the other side of the property. From where she stands she sees Grandma Marilee, who holds the rifle as if she's going to fire. The cops have their pistols drawn. The guy with the yellow spiky hair is hiding behind the lean-to.

Paula keeps moving but can't see a way out. The cops are cutting at the chain-link with some big tool. The wall of dust from the southwest moves quickly and engulfs the property just as the section of chain-link falls with a clang. The whole place goes crazy; cops pour in through the downed fence; empty beer and soda cans skitter across the ground; branches from the paloverde snap off and blow away. The tear gas burns her eyes and nose, and her chest is on fire.

Her eyes sting and water. Everything blurs. Maybe the cops can't see either. They won't fire if they can't see, will they? *Don't fire until you have a clear target.* She remembers these words from all the times her dad had schooled her and Emily on firearms. All the times she missed her target. She wishes she hadn't missed so much. Maybe if she'd tried harder.

Her dad walks to the mesquite tree, leaning his back against it. His gun is still in its holster, his hand positioned the way he's shown her right before he pulls it out to shoot. Sadness comes over her as she looks at her dad's dark outline against his favorite tree. Something about the lean of his body into the bark. He's lost in this mess, unable to save the things he needs to hold on to. She wants to go over to him, stand beside him under the mesquite, but there's no time.

As she's about to walk away, her dad turns toward her. Time is running out. A voice tells her she has to go, just go, get away from this place. She sees the downed section of fence, her only escape. As she runs, a shot rings out, then another, and another. She runs faster than she's ever run, past the homeless camp and toward Tempe Town Lake. It sounds like a helicopter overhead. She doesn't look up, wouldn't be able to see anyway, with all the dust. With every footfall against the sidewalk, she anticipates being caught by one of the cops. But no one comes after her.

When she reaches the sidewalk along the lake she keeps going, doesn't slow her pace until she comes to the end, close to Priest Road and Route 202. She stops, bends over, and places her hands on her knees, her breath coming in short, rapid spurts, her heart beating so hard it might explode right through her chest. Her lungs and throat sting from the tear gas. She's soaked with sweat and covered with dust. Her breath slows and the brown air lightens. The storm is moving off to the east.

"You dropped this." A dim figure in the haze approaches.

Paula stands and looks at the man with a cell phone in his hand. It's Billy. He holds the phone out to her. She takes it. It must have fallen out of her back pocket. The glass on its face is cracked and looks about to shatter, but it's intact. She presses the button at the bottom of the screen; the icons appear. Five missed calls.

"What's going on back there?" Billy says.

"You weren't there at all today?"

"No. Me and Hank left when that MCSO car pulled up this morning, thought they might be there to tell us to clear out of our camp. I was on my way back and seen all them cops and the smoke."

"They're taking away our property, Billy. Kicking us off."

Billy shakes his head. "Assholes. Anybody hurt?"

"I don't know."

"There's an ambulance and fire truck just pulled up."

Billy walks away, and Paula calls after him. "Thanks for finding my phone."

Paula hits the green phone icon. Three missed calls from Emily, two from Jay. She presses the one from Emily, who picks up immediately.

"Where are you? I've been calling and calling."

"Are you still in LA?"

"I'm in the car with Jay. He just picked me up at the airport."

"It's five thirty already?"

"It's almost seven thirty. We landed late because of the dust storm."

"Jay's been trying to get a hold of you too. He drove by the neighborhood and couldn't get anywhere near our place. What's happening? And where are you?"

"Just come get me. I'm at the end of the lake sidewalk. At Priest."

"We're on our way now. What happened there?"

"Guns and tear gas and the cops went crazy. Knocked parts of the fence down. I don't know where Dad and Grandma Marilee are. Billy said there's an ambulance and fire trucks." Paula looks back at the property. Two helicopters circle the area overhead. Sirens shriek. She thinks of the chaos that enveloped the place, the swarm of cops, and wonders what's happening there now.

Paula waits for Emily and Jay. She checks the backpack. Her ID and the money are still there. She thinks of tossing the guns but decides against it. She zips it back up.

The Camry pulls up and Paula runs to it. Emily leans her body over the seat and opens the back door. Paula tosses the backpack on the floor and gets in. Jay pulls away and heads back to the 202.

"Where are we going?"

"Back to Linden, I guess," Jay says. "Where else can we go?"

"Wait a minute," Emily says. "Try to get near the property again. I want to see what's going on."

"Let's just get out of here," Paula says.

"Don't you want to see what's happening now?"

"I just saw what was happening. I saw what was happening all day. I don't want to go back. There's cops all over the place. And we won't be able to see anything anyway." Paula's lungs and throat still burn. Truth is, she's afraid to find out what happened.

"Are you okay?" Emily says.

"Yes. I mean, I don't know. There were gunshots and I couldn't see straight."

"We have to find out if Dwight and Marilee are okay."

"Those cops were aiming toward the patio."

"Oh, Jesus fuck. We have to find out about them. What happened to your arm?"

Paula examines the gash on her arm, the blood nearly dry. "Nothing."

Jay looks at Paula through the rearview mirror. "Let's see how close we can get," he says. "They've likely still got the place surrounded."

Jay makes a right on Van Buren, drives over the lake bridge and through downtown Tempe. He circles back toward the property and slows down when he gets to True Lord Church. Two helicopters circle overhead. He pulls over to the curb, puts the car in park, and rolls down his window. He leans out and looks up at the sky. The sun has gone down, and the sky has cleared, but the smell of dust still fills the air.

"One of those choppers must be the cops, the other may be local news."

"Go closer," Emily says.

Jay drives to the next block, but the street is blocked off. The whole area crawls with police vehicles. A Channel 5 news van parks on a side street near the property. He drives back to Mill Avenue and approaches from another street, but that street is also blocked. "This is fucked," Emily says.

"I told you," Paula says.

Jay turns on the radio and switches stations until he finds the news, but they hear nothing about what's happened. There's only talk about the record-setting dust storm that whipped through Phoenix and moved off to the northeast.

"Let's go back to Linden. Maybe there's something about it on TV."

By the time they get to the house on Linden it's a little after nine-thirty.

Paula sits down on the sofa. "Shit."

"Where's Steve and Stone?" Emily says.

"Steve's down in Tucson for something. I don't know what. I don't know where Stone is. They don't tell me shit. Except they won't be back for a couple, three days."

Channel 5 TV News headline: *Squatters' Stand-off Results in Two Deaths and one wounded Maricopa County Sheriff's officer.*

"Jesus." Jay moves closer to the little twelve-inch TV on the floor. Emily and Paula crouch around him.

The newscaster doesn't tell them much more than the headline. No names. The wounded officer is in serious condition. Paula stares blankly at the screen.

"Grandma Marilee and Dwight are probably okay," Emily says.

"Grandma Marilee raised her rifle once, that I saw. And I think those cops were aiming at her and at Dad."

"We can go back over there later."

"What will that tell us?"

"I don't know. But it's better than just sitting here."

The three of them are quiet. They stare at a commercial, where some guy with a skewed toupee advertises payday loans.

"Okay," Jay says. "Let's go back tomorrow night. Things will have died down a little by then."

26

At two a.m. the next night, they return to the property. Yellow police tape cordons off the western perimeter of the property where the cops cut the chain-link. Sections of it lie on the ground. No police in sight. Dwight's truck is still parked on the street with some other vehicles and a motorcycle. Emily raises the tape and steps under it. Paula and Jay follow.

A dim streetlight gives a yellowish illumination to the patio; smudges of brown streak the concrete. Grandma Marilee's book lies on the ground next to her chair, as if resting there while she's in the kitchen getting more coffee. It's covered with dust. Emily picks it up, a hardcover: *Percival's Planet* by Michael Byers. She flips through the pages. She read the story about the discovery of Pluto at the observatory in Flagstaff. A bunch of edgy young people, all crazy, her favorite character a woman who believed a large tusk grew out of her neck. The woman walked around trying to avoid bumping into things. A few feet from the book, Marilee's turquoise barrette. Emily puts it in her pocket.

Paula stands on a chair and unravels the prayer flags from the patio posts and disconnects them from the hooks on the overhead beam. She folds them and tucks them into the waistband of her shorts.

The door to the Airstream hangs open. More police tape forms a large X across the door to the adobe house. Emily pulls it off, turns the doorknob. Locked. She kicks the door, but it doesn't budge.

"What the fuck! They don't own what's inside."

"They own everything now, Emily."

Jay kicks the door until it opens.

Nothing's changed inside: shelves full of books in the living room and Grandma Marilee's room; a photo of Dwight and Jay and Phyllis when they were kids; another of Dwight and Ruth; a black-and-white one of Grandpa Jack and Marilee. Emily takes the photos and places them by the door.

"All these books," she says. "They're Grandma Marilee's treasures. We should take them for her."

"We can't take all of them," Jay says.

Emily picks books randomly from the shelves and puts them with the photos. By the time she's finished, two stacks sit at the door. She adds the book from the patio, then joins Paula in Dwight's room.

"Anything you want to take?"

"Not much here, except this." Paula pulls a ring out of her pocket. "It was in his top drawer. It must be my mom's wedding ring." She passes it to Emily.

Emily turns the simple gold band over in her palm. "It's nice. She'd probably want you to have it."

"And there's some photos and papers in this shoe box. I'll take those too. And this key."

"Let's check the rest of the property." Jay stands in the doorway. "But be quick, in case anyone comes."

Dwight's gun shed is locked. Paula passes the key she found in his room to Jay. It unlocks the shed door.

"They didn't take Dad's guns."

"Probably didn't know they were here. These are worth money." Jay picks up a .22 long rifle from Dwight's worktable.

"He always brought that one when he took us shooting," Paula says.

Emily surveys the shed and counts seventeen guns. "We need to take them."

"Yeah. My dad wouldn't want the government to get them."

They take them to the car.

"It's gonna be a tight fit," Jay says. "We should put a blanket around them so they don't rattle all over the place."

Paula brings some towels and a blanket from the house. She lays some on the back seat, some in the trunk.

"We should take Dad's truck too." She walks over to the truck, tries the door, but it's locked. "They'll probably take it if we leave it here."

"How are we going to get in?"

"I've got a key." Jay takes his key ring out of his back pocket.

"I can drive it," Emily says.

"Okay." Jay takes the key to the truck off the ring and gives it to Emily. "Let's load up and get out of here."

"I'll be back in a minute," Emily says.

"Where are you going?"

"I want to take a look at the graveyard."

"Why?"

"I don't know. It just seems like I should. For Grandma Marilee. So we can tell her everything's okay. Do you want to come?"

Paula shakes her head. "I'll help load Dad's guns in the car."

Bone-dry crabgrass shoots up around the edges of the stones, so tall some of the graves are barely visible. It feels like Grandma Marilee is right next to her. She remembers all the times she watched her grandmother stand over those stones, and the way Marilee used to pull weeds from around them when Emily was little and her grandmother was younger and free of arthritis. Emily squats on the ground and brushes the weeds away from Maria's stone. What's going to happen to all these stones, to those buried beneath this ground? Where the hell are Marilee and Dwight?

The door to the Virgin Mary shed swings in the intermittent wind. Emily goes inside. The door slowly swings shut and it's nearly black inside except for cracks of light through seams in the corrugated metal roof. Emily props the door open with a rock.

The statue lies on the ground in front of the bookshelves. Broken into three large sections with several smaller pieces scattered around them, the Virgin's face looks up to the ceiling. A dusty, near-disintegrated cardboard box has fallen from a shelf and spilled its contents onto the dirt floor. Books and papers lie scattered next to the box. A manila envelope protrudes from a large book, a photo history of the Arizona Territory. Emily can barely see inside the shed even with the door propped open. She gathers the papers and envelope, takes them to the patio, and sits on the concrete where the streetlight shines the brightest. Old letters addressed to Marilee. Some with Dwight's name as the sender and a military base return address. Receipts from APS, the City of Tempe. Faded sepia-colored photographs of the dock, looking just the way Marilee described it to her. Several newspaper clippings: a story about the San Pablo neighborhood and the expansion of the university; a local news story about Tempe men going off to fight World War I, Boyd Stewart, Maria's husband's name, among them. The manila envelope, faded and torn at the corners, feels so dry it could crack and disintegrate into dust.

Emily carefully removes papers from inside. There's a handwritten document with the names of Constance and Jimmy Baker, the address of the property, and a description—two acres bordered on the north by the Salt River, the east by the Union Pacific railroad. Behind the document is another piece of paper with the handwritten names of Martino and Albert Sandoval. Grandma Marilee mentioned those names before, some old relatives. There's another paper, dated 1864, with a name Emily doesn't recognize: Harmon Valenti. Are these what Marilee's been looking for all this time? Does this mean those assholes from the state are wrong? Emily imagines giving these to Grandma Marilee and Dwight and seeing the looks on their faces. She puts it all back in the envelope.

When she gets to the car Paula says, "What's all that?"

"Some letters to Grandma Marilee from your dad when he was in the military. And stuff about the property."

"Are you shitting us?" Jay stands behind Paula. "We need to look at them. Let's get out of here. You know how to get back to Linden?"

"I think so," Emily says. "But don't get too far ahead. Keep us in sight."

Emily gets into the driver's side of the truck.

Paula opens the passenger-side door but stops. "Wait. I need to get my backpack from the trunk."

"Your backpack is under all the guns," Jay says. "Can't you wait till we get back to the house?"

"No. I want it."

"Jesus, why can't it wait?" But Jay opens the trunk and begins moving the guns aside so Paula can reach the backpack.

Emily puts the envelope between her seat and the console and then remembers the stacks of books and photos back in the house. "I need to go back for those books."

Paula slips her arms through the straps of the backpack and the three of them go back to retrieve the stacks of books and photos.

After they load the books into the bed of Dwight's pickup, Emily and Paula follow Jay away from the property.

"The money's in here." Paula nods toward her backpack at her feet. "I thought you would have asked me about it yesterday."

"Well, with everything that happened, you were upset. Let's just leave it in your backpack for now."

"I remembered your postcard." Paula pulls out the Eureka postcard and shows Emily.

They head toward Route 202.

"I like this," Emily says.

"What?"

"Driving the truck. It feels like shooting a gun." Emily presses her foot hard on the gas pedal and accelerates. "Oh, I have a postcard for you too. Of the beach in L.A. It's called Venice Beach. I'll give it to you later."

She merges onto Interstate 10 and after a few miles, exits at Nineteenth Avenue. She follows Jay through the dark, industrial neighborhood to the house on Linden.

"We need to go down to the county sheriff's office tomorrow," Jay says. "There's no other way to find out about Dwight and Mom."

"I can't go," Paula says.

"You're right," Emily says. "They'll ask where you were yesterday. You're a witness. I can't go either."

"Why not?" Paula says.

"What am I going to say? I was in L.A. after I put a suitcase on the flight for this guy named Mic Stone? Something illegal? Maybe drugs? Who knows?"

"Well, I guess that leaves me." Jay lights up a cigarette.

"You can't go, Jay."

"Why the fuck not? I'm just checking on where the hell my mom and brother are."

"They'll ask who you are."

"So?"

"They'll ask where you live," she says. "Where you were yesterday. You want to call attention to this house on Linden and whatever the fuck goes on here? Mic Stone and Steve wouldn't be happy about that."

"Well, fuck. How are we going to find out?"

"Let me try that." Emily points to Jay's cigarette.

Jay passes it to Emily. "Since when do you smoke?"

She doesn't answer him, but inhales and coughs, then takes another drag and gives it back to him. Outside, sounds from the mechanic's shop across the street, a dog barking, metal hitting concrete, and someone running past, break the silence.

"Phyllis," Paula says, and looks at Emily. "She could call the sheriff's office, say she's been trying to get ahold of her brother."

"Dwight told me about your guys' trip up there," Jay says.

Emily thinks about the letter from Phyllis. She hasn't mentioned it to Paula. She wants to forget about it and the second letter that came a couple of weeks after the first. Short. Same Clown Motel stationery. *I have no excuses, Emily. I'm sorry. Phyllis.*

"And if she doesn't want to call the sheriff here," Paula says. "She could talk to that cop guy in Tonopah who's friends with Dad. She could see if he can find out anything."

"I don't want to call her." Phyllis is the last person Emily wants to talk to about Dwight and Marilee. Or anything. And she'd probably screw things up somehow.

"Okay. Give me the number," Jay says.

Emily takes out her cell phone, looks up Phyllis's number, which she'd taken from the first letter, and gives it to Jay.

"I'll call in the morning. What about those papers you found in the shed, Emily?"

Emily opens the manila envelope and takes out the papers. "Be careful. They're really old." She passes them to Jay.

Jay reads through the documents. "Sure as shit looks like something that might be legal. Some kind of bills of sale. And a deed." He hands them both to Paula.

"How could the state do it then? Send those cops out to our place, try to take it back?"

Jay shrugs. "I don't know. Maybe no one knows about these documents. Maybe the state didn't file them. Maybe they conveniently forgot about them. Who the hell knows."

Paula passes the papers back to her. "What good is this stuff now?"

"I don't know. We need to ask somebody."

"Who? Who do we ask? We can't even find out about my dad and Grandma Marilee."

Emily tries to sleep, but she's still awake when blue-gray light, which creeps through the slits in the sheet that hangs over the dirty front window, signals the approach of sunrise. A loud truck engine roars outside and dogs begin to bark.

27

The phone goes to a prerecorded voice mail: Phyllis's laugh and then, *Leave a message.* Jay's already called Phyllis's number three times. The first two times he hung up. The third time he left a message. "This is your brother Jay. We got some problems down here. Give me a call."

Emily's glad she's never tried to call Phyllis. Her call probably would have gone to voice mail too. She pictures Phyllis working at the Clown Motel café, smiling at customers, trying to cover her missing teeth, going to the Bug Bar at night. The Bug Bar. What a stupid name. Why did she even bother writing those letters? She was probably drunk at that bar when she wrote them. Phyllis doesn't give a shit. Never did, never will. Can't even bother to call and find out what's wrong.

No calls from Stone or Steve, either. Emily and Paula can't stay in this house forever. Emily lies on the floor and looks at the postcard of Eureka. She examines the details for the umpteenth time. How long would it take to get there? Maybe a three- or four-day drive. She's lost in the blue of the ocean water. It reminds her of the water at Venice Beach. "We could fly," she says softly.

"Fly where?" Jay says.

"Nothing." Emily refolds the postcard and stuffs it back in her pocket.

"Try again," Paula says. "Call Phyllis again."

"I just called less that twenty minutes ago." But Jay punches in Phyllis's number on his cell. The same recording. He puts the phone back in his pocket. "We're gonna have to do something. We need to find out about Dwight and Mom."

"I should be the one to call," Paula says. "He's my dad. I'll go down there if they won't tell us anything on the phone. They've got nothing on me."

"You're right," Emily says. "We were being a little paranoid before. Even if they ask you questions, just say you ran when the shooting started. You don't even know those guys who came out to the property."

"Who should I call?"

"You said their cars were Maricopa County Sheriff's Office." Emily looks at Jay. "She should call them, right?"

"I guess," Jays says. "Start with them. Don't say who you are."

Jay's phone rings. Emily's heart jumps despite herself. Maybe it's Phyllis. But a male voice comes from the other end.

"What's up, Steve?"

Emily can't make out what Steve says but she pictures his roaming eye and hears the word "property."

"Yeah, it is." Jay looks at Emily and Paula. "It's my family's place. Long story, Steve."

Emily presses her index fingers over her lips, and mouths, *Don't tell him anything.*

Jay nods. "Yeah, yeah, I'm staying at the house on Linden. No problem."

Steve says something Emily can't make out and Jay nods into the phone. "Got it," he says before hanging up.

"He's gonna be down in Tucson another few days. Stone's traveling, won't be back for a while."

Jay's quiet for a few minutes and then says, "When I heard that male voice, at first I thought it might be Dwight." He tries Phyllis's number for a fourth time, leaves another message.

"What's in there?" Emily says. The room that held all the suitcases that first day Steve brought them to the house is locked. "More suitcases?"

"No need to know, Emily."

"C'mon. Cut the shit. There must be something important in there."

"Like I said."

"It's got to do with the IDs, doesn't it?" It hits Emily, how Stone got her and Paula's fake IDs so quickly. She has no idea what's needed to make a driver's license, a passport, and fake social security cards. But you don't just make them from nothing. There's gotta be some kind of equipment. A computer? Stolen IDs like she and Paula sold to Steve? Or maybe they just make up names and license numbers. Jay might not even know for sure what's going on.

"You know what, Jay?" Emily says. "I think there's some big shit going on here."

"Could be." Jay lights up a cigarette, gets up from the sofa, and paces around the living room.

"So, what is it?"

Jay gazes out the window. "Okay, I know they've got something new. Steve brought another guy over who worked in that room for a few days. He's the one who made your guys' IDs. They didn't tell me much else. Just gave me the IDs to give you."

"That sounds like important stuff."

"Yeah, I know. Fake IDs are big business."

"Is that what was in the suitcase I took to LA? Fake IDs?"

"I don't know. Like I told you, they don't tell me everything. They don't tell me shit really. Just what I need to know."

"When is Stone coming back?"

"Who knows? But you guys don't want to be here when they get back."

"Yeah, tell me about it," Paula says. "This place creeps me out. But where can we go?"

"I don't know. We've got to find out about Dwight and Mom."

"You should call the sheriff's office from a public phone," Emily says to Paula. "So they don't see your phone number."

"There's a Circle K over on McDowell and I-10."

"And those papers about the property. We need to do something," Emily says.

"We can ask my dad, when we find him."

"Yeah, but in the meantime, can't we just take them to some

government person?"

Jay shrugs. "I don't know who."

"What about the weird dude? The professor guy? Maybe he could help."

"Yeah," Paula says. "Do you remember his name? Did Dad even tell us his name?"

"I don't know, but if he did I don't remember. Maybe there's something in Dwight's room with his name or number. A card or something. We should go back and look."

"Okay," Jay says. "Let's go call MCSO and then we'll drive over to the property.

The phone at the Circle K is just outside the entrance. Traffic noise from McDowell and I-10 creates a background buzz. Emily and Jay stand on either side of Paula as she inserts coins into the pay phone and presses the MCSO phone number.

A woman answers the phone. "Maricopa County Sheriff's Office. Can I help you?"

Paula hesitates, then says, "I'm calling about the shootings at the property in Tempe two days ago. Can you tell me who was killed there?"

"Can I have your name please?"

Emily shakes her head.

"I can't give my name," Paula says.

"Just one minute," the woman says.

Emily puts her ear close to Paula's. Silence. For a second she thinks maybe they got disconnected, and then a male voice. "We're going to need your name to give out any information. If you have any information on this case, you need to inform us."

"I just want to know who was killed," Paula says.

"I'm going to need your name. If you could—"

Emily presses the silver bar and hangs up the phone.

"What'd you do that for?"

"They're asking too many questions. They're not going to tell you anything. They just want to keep you on the line.'"

"Let's get out of here," Jay says.

28

The street's empty; the construction crew is finished for the day. The yellow tape Jay carefully refastened two nights ago still covers the door to the adobe house. Emily undoes it and they go inside.

"Did you see any papers or business cards in Dwight's room?"

Paula shakes her head. "I wasn't looking for anything in particular."

Jay goes into Marilee's room, Emily and Paula into Dwight's. Emily opens the closet door and peruses the shelf. Nothing. Paula opens and closes drawers. "Maybe there's something in Dad's gun shed."

"Hey, you guys. I think I found something," Jay calls from Grandma Marilee's bedroom. He holds a piece of paper in his hand, smoothing it out. "Looks like a contract Dwight was going to sign with that guy. His name's Wilkins, Eugene Wilkins."

"She probably got pissed and crumpled it up. Let me see it."

Jay passes the paper to Emily.

"He was a professor. I remember Dwight telling Grandma Marilee."

"That's right," Paula says. "She didn't think Dad should trust him. They argued about it, remember?"

"Yeah." Emily passes the contract back to Jay.

"There's no phone number for him," Jay says.

"We can go over to the library and check the ASU website."

"Okay, let's get out of here," Jay says. "Cops could still come around."

As they head back to the car, a man walks along the sidewalk. The afternoon sun reflects off his black vest and creates an otherworldly quality, as if he's floating through the heat. The man steps around the downed fence and stops, gazing at the property. He looks familiar.

"It's dad's friend. He was here when all the cops came."

"Claude," Emily says.

He waves when he sees them.

"What are you doing here?"

"Picking up my bike." He points to his motorcycle parked at the end of the street.

"Where's my dad? Did they arrest all of you?"

"They took us all in. Just let us go this morning."

"Did they arrest Grandma Marilee too?"

Claude nods.

"Where are they?"

Claude's face is drawn. He swallows hard, hesitates.

"No one told you guys?"

"Told us what?" Jay says.

"Dwight's gone."

"Where?" demands Paula. "Gone where? He wouldn't just leave our grandmother. Did those cops take them somewhere? Where's my dad?"

Jay places his hand on Paula's arm. When he looks at Emily, he looks like a scared kid.

"They shot your mother, Jay. And Dwight," Claude says.

"I knew it. Goddamnit. I knew when I saw that blood on the patio. I fucking knew it."

The blood flashes before Emily. She turns toward the patio and Grandma Marilee's recliner. Her ashtray is shattered on the concrete. She looks to the graveyard and the row of headstones. Grandma Marilee should be there, kneeling in front of Jack's stone. She'll set this thing straight, show them Claude is mistaken. But no one is there.

Jay wipes his eyes with the back of his hand. "I should have been here."

Paula's face is scrunched into a little clump of sadness, the way it was the night Ruth died. She's crying. Intensely. Silently. Emily feels herself begin to crumble, parts of her dropping away. She wraps her arms around herself as if to hold her body intact.

"Kept us all locked up until they determined whose gun shot that cop." Claude pauses. "I asked to see Dwight when they released me this morning. Thought they were still holding him. Maybe it was his gun that killed that cop."

"Was it? Was it my brother's gun?"

Claude shakes his head. "No, they told me it wasn't his gun."

"They just fucking killed him and Mom for no reason." Jay stalks away and then returns.

"That asshole, Mike, fired at the cops. Got the whole thing going. He was standing so close to your mom, I think they thought she was the one who fired. They fired back."

"Mike?" Jay says.

"Asshole skinhead. Dwight wasn't comfortable with him. We should have made him leave."

"I saw him," Paula's voice is barely audible. "That Mike guy. By the patio, when I was leaving."

"Dwight pulled out his gun when they fired at Marilee. But I don't know if he ever even fired it. It was a fucking mess." Claude runs his palm over his forehead. "But it was Mike's gun that shot that cop."

Paula looks anxiously around the property as if she too is looking for Dwight and Grandma Marilee, as if they might appear and tell her they're okay, if she focuses strongly enough.

"My dad too. Standing under that tree. I think he looked right at me before I ran." Paula's body shakes with sobs.

Emily should have told Stone it had to be another day for L.A. She shouldn't have left Paula alone. She wants to hug her but doesn't.

The white-noise buzz of downtown Tempe and the Union Pacific rumbling by seems very distant, muffled.

"Emily!" Paula shouts as if she can't see Emily standing right beside her.

"I'm right here." Emily touches Paula's arm and turns to Jay. "We need to get out of here."

Jay puts his right arm around Paula's shoulder. "Okay. We'll go in a second." He turns to Claude. "Do you know who we should contact about Dwight and Marilee? How we claim them?"

Claude shrugs. "You could try MCSO. You're next of kin. Might be better to just go down there."

Jay nods.

"Dwight was my closest friend. If you guys need anything. Anything at all." He gives Jay his phone number.

"I think Dwight would want his ashes scattered." Jay says.

"Ironwood," Paula whispers. "That place he took us."

"We can do that, Paula," Jay says.

"He loved it out there," Paula says.

"If we get the property back, we can put Grandma Marilee's ashes next to Grandpa Jack. She'd want that," Emily says. "Maybe some of Dwight's next to her."

At All Souls Mortuary, the lawn is green and manicured, and neatly trimmed oleanders are planted along the front on either side of the small brick building. Inside the reception area, a poster on the wall displays various services and products along with their prices: urns, $25-$995; prayer cards in packets of fifty, $45; rosary beads, $15; crucifix, $35. A glass bowl on the desk is full of cinnamon candies.

All Souls charges only $1,000. Jay puts in $600; Emily takes $400 from the money in the suitcase to make up the rest. Jay doesn't even ask where she got it.

The mortician, a tall, heavyset man, with awkward movements as if he's sensitive to disturbing his customers, greets them. His jowls seem to sag with sorrow for all the deaths over the years. He leads Emily, Paula, and Jay into a room with an oblong table and wall shelves full of colorful, themed urns; a heart stone, an angel, a football player, one that looks like a coffee mug with the Arizona Diamondbacks logo, a cowboy boot.

He explains the process: how the containers disintegrate in the furnace, and how, if by chance anything remains, like a bone fragment, it will be crushed. Metal pins and any other non-body elements will be separated out so that what is left will be uncontaminated cremains. Cremains. The word sounds like the name of a candy, those cinnamon ones in the bowl in the reception area.

"Our next group goes in tomorrow afternoon." He looks at the paper on the table in front of him.

Emily cringes, pictures a conveyor belt with corpses moving toward giant, leaping flames. She looks at Paula. She's always reminded Emily of Ruth, but now she sees Dwight.

"Then what?" Jay says.

"We can mail the ashes to you. Or you can pick them up."

They choose the cheapest urns, two small brass ones shaped like vases.

Back in the car Jay's hands grip the steering wheel. "Jesus." His face looks as if a grenade has exploded in front of him. Emily's always thought of Grandma Marilee as someone who took care of her when she was little, not so much about her role as Dwight and Jay's mother. And Phyllis's. Jay's lost his mother. And his brother.

She reaches over, lightly touches his arm. "Do you want me to drive?"

"No, I'm okay."

29

Emily scrolls through the computer screen in Tempe Library. Paula and Jay sit on either side of her. The article in the *Superior Sun* quotes the mayor. *Not an unpleasant man.* There are photos of the abandoned hotels and schools that Wilkins promised to renovate or tear down and replace with something new. Residents thought he was a real-estate expert looking to restore their town.

There are several additional stories in the *Arizona Republic* and a student-run university paper about Wilkins. He also owns properties in other rural communities that have struggled since the decline of copper mining and were hit by the 2008 recession. And rental houses and apartments in the Phoenix area. Ninety-seven properties in all. Emily reads through one of the longer stories, going back over it several times. Wilkins manages his properties through different real estate companies he owns, which makes it difficult to trace ownership. Jay and Paula read over her shoulder.

"This guy's a real piece of work," Jays says.

"We can't trust him," Paula says.

"No, we can't," Emily says. "But he might be able to help us."

They walk back to the car. Emily is still dazed—about Dwight and Marilee. About Wilkins. About the general fucked-up situation. She can tell Jay and Paula are too. In the car Jay turns on the AC and it blasts through the car. They sit in silence for several minutes, as if this is the funeral service.

"Dwight couldn't have known this stuff," Jay says. "He'd never have trusted Wilkins."

"What are we going to do now?"

"Just what we planned to do," Emily says. "Get ahold of Wilkins."

"After all that stuff in those articles?"

"Does it really matter if we can trust him? He can get something out of this," Emily says. "That's why he wanted to make a deal with Dwight. Same thing with us."

Wilkins suggested meeting them at one of his currently unoccupied rental properties. Jay exits US 60 at Goldfield Road at Apache Junction and heads toward the Superstitions. He stops at a small two-bedroom with a carport, on a quarter acre of land that backs up to a new gated subdivision near the base of the Superstition Mountains. Wilkins comes out of the house as Jay pulls into the driveway.

Emily's never seen him close up. Just his tall bird-body when he came around the property and sat under the mesquite with Dwight. He's a vulture. Feeds off the dead and desperate. This would be clear even if she hadn't seen those news stories.

Wilkins extends his hand to each one of them in turn, Jay first. He nods toward the subdivision. "Property out here's not going to do anything but appreciate," he says, then looks at the three of them. "Go up in value."

They go inside. Emily takes the papers out of the envelope and passes them to Wilkins. He reads through them.

"Who's Harmon Valenti?" He points to the name on one of the documents.

"We don't know," Emily says.

Wilkins looks at them. "That's quite a story. The stand-off at your place. They know who shot that cop?"

They ignore his question.

"So, what do you think? Can this get our property back?" Jay says.

"I'm not a lawyer."

"And the one you hired wasn't much of one either. Or else none of this would have happened," Jay says.

Emily takes the papers from Wilkins and puts them back in the envelope.

"Well, given the situation and without documents like what you've got there." Wilkins shrugs. "There wasn't much to be done. This changes things quite a bit, I would imagine."

"So?"

"So, I offer you the same deal as before. And where's Dwight anyway? They got him locked up?"

Emily and Paula and Jay exchange glances. "My dad's dead," Paula says. "Grandma Marilee too."

Emily can't read Wilkins's scavenger face, but he appears taken aback.

"I'm sorry to hear that. I liked Dwight." He sounds almost sincere. No matter.

Emily's always thought of the property as Dwight's, but of course, it's equally Jay's and Phyllis's and now partly Paula's too, since she's Dwight's daughter. And hers.

"My brother's not around anymore. We need a new deal. And we'll just hang on to this title."

"Alyward, the lawyer, will have to see it."

"Of course he can see it."

"Okay." Wilkins seems to ignore Jay's comment on a new deal and again extends his hand to each one of them. "I'll have Alyward draw up a contract."

"Just so everything's on the table," Jay says. "We know about your little real-estate empire and those slum properties you own."

Wilkins smooths his hair. "I was hurt by those stories. I've never done anything illegal."

"Didn't say you did. Just wanted you to know we're not stupid."

"Never thought you were stupid."

"One more thing," Jay says.

Emily looks at him. *What's he doing?*

"What's that?" Wilkins says.

"You got an empty place here, right?"

"Yes, I do." He looks puzzled. "For now. It's a rental."

"How about you let these girls stay here until the property thing gets settled."

Wilkins is taken off guard. "This isn't a homeless shelter."

"They've got no place to live right now. Just until you rent it or whatever you plan to do with it," Jay says.

"What the hell are you doing, Jay? I'm not staying out here in the middle of nowhere. There's nothing here but a couple of strip malls."

"He's right," Paula says. "We can't stay at Stone's house. We've got no place to go."

Emily knows she's right. They can't stay at the house on Linden much longer. An image of the man eating grapes on the light-rail comes to Emily. And Billy and the other homeless guys who stay on the property.

"Just until I rent it," Wilkins says.

"Until the property gets settled," Jay says. "Or no deal. We'll get our own lawyer. Now that we've got documents."

"Okay, okay," Wilkins says. "The authorities have to let you get your stuff off the property. Whether you get it back or not. I know that for sure."

"Thanks for the info," Jay says. "And one more thing about the contract." He's in his element, like he's playing a TV role.

"What's that?"

"You figure that spot on the property's going to bring you some good money with whatever you put up there?"

Again Emily wonders what the hell he's doing.

Wilkins nods. "That's the hope."

"Seems like that ups the ante a little."

"What do you mean?"

Jay's eyes go to Emily and Paula. "I mean that little piece of property might be worth more than the cost of a lawyer."

"That's the deal I made with Dwight."

"Like I said, my brother's dead now. That counts for something. And there isn't any signed contract with us yet."

"Yeah," Emily pipes in. "Maybe if that lawyer of yours had used a little more diligence, been a little more persistent—"

"We give you a section of the property," Jay says. "You provide the lawyer. And we find out how much that piece of property's worth and you pay us. We'll cut you a good deal."

"Okay," Wilkins says. "But let's settle the price now. I provide the lawyer and pay you twenty-five thousand."

"Let's not rush it," Jay says. "We'll do a little research on the value of that land and then we'll talk."

30

Jesus Christ. What in God's name are all those?" Wilkins's neck juts forward, his nose a beak pecking at something in the air.

"What do they look like?" Emily picks up a long-range rifle from the Camry's trunk.

"My dad was a collector," Paula says. "We couldn't just leave them on the property."

Wilkins takes a couple of steps back. "Don't point that thing."

"She's not pointing it." A cigarette dangles from Jay's lips, his right hand on the open trunk. "Besides, the safety's on."

"What are you going to do with them?"

Jay nods toward a door at the end of the carport.

"You want to keep all those weapons here? I'm not a big fan of firearms. In fact, I strongly believe in strict control."

"We don't give a shit if you like guns or what you believe in, we need a place to keep these until the property thing gets settled."

Emily put the rifle against the wall and tries the knob. "It's locked."

Wilkins reaches in his pocket, pulls out his key chain, and unlocks the door. He gives the key to Emily. "Same key as for the house."

Emily, Jay, and Paula unload the guns and lay them in the storage room. Wilkins stands next to his Austin as if protecting it. He smooths the car cover. Jay lets his smoked cigarette fall from his lips, snuffs it out on the concrete in front of the storage room. Wilkins reaches down and picks up the butt, holding it between his thumb and index finger.

"We got some stuff in the truck too," Emily says when they finish. "Some books and other things."

"You can put them in the house. When are you going to move in?"

"May as well do it tomorrow." Jay looks at Emily and Paula. "No point you two staying at the Linden house any longer than you have to."

Wilkins seems creepier each time Emily sees him. "He's not going to be hanging around here when we move in, is he?" She looks at Jay for the answer, though she's still not used to his new take-charge attitude. Wilkins shakes his head.

"Make sure of that." Jay lights up another cigarette. "And we're gonna leave the truck here for now."

Wilkins shrugs. "Whatever, as they say."

"What time's that lawyer going to be here?"

Wilkins checks his watch. "He said ten a.m. He should be here soon."

Shortly after they finish unloading the truck bed, a shiny white Prius pulls into the drive behind it. A man gets out. He wears beige khakis and holds his briefcase at his side, an extension of his body. His pale blond hair is parted on the side and combed back. It stays in place like a toupee.

The man extends his hand to Jay, then Emily and Paula. "Jeffrey Alyward. Gene tells me you have some documents."

"They're inside," Emily says.

In the living room Emily opens the manila envelope and takes out the papers. Alyward holds them carefully by the edges, examines one and then the other. Wilkins stands over his shoulder. Emily reaches for the papers and Alyward returns them to her.

"Who all are the heirs?" Alyward directs the question to Jay.

"The heirs?"

"Of Constance and Jimmy Baker, the names on the second bill of sale?"

"My mom would have been their great-granddaughter. Cops killed her. Then there's my brother, Dwight. Cops killed him too. So it's me, and Paula here is Dwight's daughter, and Emily's my sister Phyllis's girl."

"So, you and Phyllis are next in line."

"No one's seen Phyllis for fifteen years," Jay says, even though Emily knows it's a lie.

Alyward nods. "So, you're next in line. Then Emily and Paula."

Jay looks at Emily and Paula. "The property belongs to all of us. We don't care about next-in-line shit."

"Regardless. We're going to have to verify the authenticity of the deed. And investigate why the state doesn't have a copy filed. Looks like Valenti claimed the land when Arizona was still a territory. Things could've gotten murky."

"How do you know the state doesn't have a copy? Did you already check that out before?" Emily says.

"I did. That's why I didn't take the case. It seemed pointless. A waste of time for all of us." Alyward takes a breath. "I'm truly sorry what happened." His eyes look sincere. Maybe he's not an asshole like Wilkins.

"Can you get our property back?"

"I can't say positively. With that document, we have a decent chance, a better chance than before."

"How decent?" Wilkins asks.

Alyward shakes his head. "I can't say for sure. I've drawn up a contract here." Alyward takes out the agreement stating the portion of the property that will go to Wilkins if they get it back. The document contains a blank space to be filled in regarding the money Wilkins will pay them.

Jay and Emily and Paula examine it.

"It says you get the northwest corner." Emily looks at Wilkins. "That's where Billy and the other guys stay."

"Billy?"

"Billy's homeless," Paula says. "He's been sleeping on the property since me and Emily were little. My dad let him."

Wilkins shrugs. "Dwight already agreed to that spot."

"We can find Billy another spot," Emily says to Paula.

"What about the blank space?" Jay lights up a cigarette.

"We need to fill that in," Alyward says. "You and Gene need to agree on a value."

"I offered them $25,000," Wilkins says.

Alyward looks a little surprised but doesn't say anything.

Jay laughs.

"You think we're fucking idiots, don't you?" Emily says. She's ready to hit Wilkins. "You thought Dwight was an idiot. He was just desperate because of assholes like you."

Jay touches Emily's shoulder lightly. She brushes it away.

"We did some homework." Jay speaks to Alyward, ignores Wilkins. "That piece of property's a little less than a quarter acre, right?"

Alyward nods. "Point one-eight to be exact."

"Seventy thousand," Wilkins pipes in. "That's a fair price."

"Bullshit," Emily says. "One hundred and fifty thousand." After looking up land values at the library, Emily, Paula, and Jay had agreed amongst themselves on $125,000. They weren't sure how accurate that figure was, or if it was too high or too low, but it was a hell of a lot more than the $25,000 Wilkins offered. He's a creep though. Why not ask for more?

Wilkins puts his hand to his forehead, as if he's suddenly developed a migraine. Alyward remains silent, then nudges Wilkins and nods.

"Okay," Wilkins concedes. "One hundred and fifty thousand."

Alyward prints the amount in the blank space in black ink.

"We want a copy of that," says Emily.

"Of course. And I'll need the deed and bill of sale." Alyward passes the contract to Jay. "Why don't all of you sign it. You girls are eighteen, right?"

"Yes."

They each sign their name at the bottom of the contract. Emily isn't comfortable letting the deed go, as it's her last connection to Grandma Marilee. Jay reaches for it. "C'mon, Emily. He needs to take it."

Alyward waits, then says, "I noticed an Office Max at one of the strip malls on the way over. Let's go down there and I'll make copies for you."

31

The property looks like it died too. Dwight and Grandma Marilee breathed life into it; their blood pumped through every inch. Now the adobe house seems on the verge of collapse. Large chunks of plaster have broken away from the brick wall and lie on the ground. Did it always look this way? An AC unit protrudes from Grandma Marilee's bedroom window and another from the kitchen window. Rust covers them both, their frames partially pulled away from the exterior wall. Without Dwight, his projects appear nothing more than junk. Even the mesquite tree has lost a lot of leaves.

The school bus door hangs open, strands of barbed wire still attached to the front bumper. Emily steps up and goes inside. Paula follows.

"Remember when we used to play in here? Pretend we were on that trip your dad always talked about?"

Paula sits in the driver's seat, places her hands on the steering wheel. "Yeah. He loved it. Or the idea of it."

It's the most Paula's said about the deaths.

"I know." Emily stands behind her and touches her shoulder.

"I saw him sitting behind the wheel of the bus one afternoon. He looked at me and smiled, then turned away, like he made a mistake. I wondered why he did that. Now I'm thinking he must have thought for a second I was my mom."

"You look a lot like your mom. Maybe he was thinking about her."

"That card game at the hotel in Tonopah was the happiest I'd seen him in a long time. He laughed the way he did when Mom was alive. I never realized how much he missed her. I never thought of his grief. Only mine."

"You were just a kid, Paula."

"I guess. I don't even know if he knew how much I loved him."

How does a person know if someone loves them? Love isn't a word Emily likes to think about. Who did she love? Who loved her? Grandma Marilee used to tell her when she was little that she loved her. And Emily saw something in her grandmother's eyes. Dwight must have loved her; he was like a father, whatever that means. Did they know how she felt about them? She wants to say to Paula that he knew, Dwight knew how much she loved him, but she doesn't.

"You can keep the bus. Fix it up the way your dad wanted to."

"Maybe."

Paula rises from the driver's seat and they both step out. Billy is standing over by the paloverde trees. He waves.

"Hi, Billy." Paula smiles. "How are you doing."

"Okay. I've been keeping an eye on your place."

"Are you guys sleeping here again?" Emily gestures toward the three sleeping bags rolled up on the ground under the trees.

"Came back last night. We've been over at a camp in Papago Park. Cops kicked us out of there. Where's Dwight? And your grandma?"

Paula tells him. He walks over to Paula and gives her a hug and then Emily. *He smells bad*, they said to Grandma Marilee one time, holding their noses and giggling. They were seven or eight years old. Marilee had looked at them as sternly as she ever did. *I don't want to hear that again from you girls*, she said. *Don't you ever take away someone's dignity.* She explained to them what the word dignity meant.

Billy's not like that man eating grapes on the light-rail. He walks like he's worth the space he takes up on the earth. A little bounce in his step.

"We're gonna get this place back," Emily says to him.

Jay walks toward them from the house, a box in his arms. "You girls ready?"

They nod.

"What's in the box?"

"Mom's old photo albums."

Jay stops at a QuikTrip gas station before they head back to AJ. He hands Paula a twenty. "You want to go in and tell them fifteen dollars on pump number four."

Paula returns a few minutes later with the *Arizona Republic* folded to a story at the bottom of the front page.

"Look at this." She hands the paper to Jay.

He takes it with his left hand, pumps the gas with his right. "Two arrested in identity thefts," he reads. "Holy donkey balls! Jesus Christ!" He passes the pump handle to Emily.

She squeezes the nozzle, looks over her shoulder at the paper.

"They've busted Stone." Jay shakes his head. "And this other guy. Larry Banks."

He opens the paper, turns the page. The article continues on the next page, along with two photos. One is Stone, minus his hat.

"Who's that other guy with the baseball cap?" Paula points to the photo next to Stone.

"I don't know who the hell the other guy is."

"Let me see." Jay holds the paper so she can see it. "I know the other guy. He's the one who picked up the suitcase in LA."

In the car, Emily reads the article aloud. Holy crap. It could have been her. Did those security cameras at LAX see her? It doesn't matter about the cameras. She wasn't even near Larry Bonds.

Jay rubs his head. "Wonder where Steve is."

"Didn't he call you from Tucson?"

"Yeah, yeah. That's where he said he was."

"So he wasn't with Stone?"

"No. Said Stone was off somewhere. Didn't tell me where."

"Well, we know where Stone is now." Paula looks at Emily. "Caught and up shit's creek. Like we could have been."

"Did Steve really give you this car?"

"I told you I'm buying it from him. Why?"

"Is it in your name?"

"Yeah. What's that got to do with anything?"

"I don't know. I'm just thinking if the cops know about Steve, they might be looking for anyone connected to him, and to Stone. Like maybe they'd check out cars and stuff in his name."

"It's in my name. But I still owe him money."

"He trusted you to not take off with it?"

"I can't read Steve's mind. But he thinks I'm a dumb fuck who'd be too scared to take off with his car. Where would I go anyway? He was always worried I'd screw up on something, cause an accident, wreck his car, get caught with something illegal in it. He'd be responsible. He's the one who insisted on putting it in my name after he got that new one."

"You're not a dumb fuck, Jay." Paula points to Stone and the guy in the baseball cap. "There's the dumb fucks."

"It's good the car is yours. If the cops get Steve, they won't be looking for the Camry." Emily folds the paper and lays it on the floor.

"I hope they get him. I'm glad Stone's locked up," Paula says. "Let's just forget them."

"I don't have much over there anyway." Jay backs out of the parking spot. "Nothing worth anything. I'll just have to stay out at Wilkins's place with you guys."

32

The Superstitions loom so close you could almost touch them, the only thing worth looking at in all of Apache Junction. Emily's pulled a couple of kitchen chairs onto the small concrete slab at Wilkins's rental property. His backyard, barren and full of weeds, becomes a swirl of dust when the wind comes. This afternoon it whips furiously and stirs up loose dirt from the new retirement communities under construction. Grit works its way onto Emily's bare feet. They've been here two and a half weeks now. Nothing more in the news about Stone. No calls from Steve. Alyward brought some papers for them to sign over a week ago. "This is going to take some time," he said.

The outside air still swelters in mid-September but being inside Wilkins's house makes Emily antsy. "We need to start thinking about California."

"Maybe we should wait until things get settled."

"Why? There's no reason to stay here. Jay can handle stuff. The property thing could go on forever. Nothing's left for us."

"I know."

Emily and Paula haven't said a word more about Dwight or Marilee since they stood in the school bus. Neither has Jay, which is fine with Emily. She works to check her grief. It feels like once it is released it will be boundless, overwhelming.

"How would we go?" Paula says.

"We've been through all this before. We can fly. We've got that money."

"Then what? How do we get around after we get there? Where will we live? We don't know anybody there."

"We don't know anybody here. Except Jay. Maybe we could take the truck. Jay's got the Camry."

"Maybe."

"I bet your dad would've liked us taking off for a new life with his truck. Let's look at the maps in the glove box." She watches Paula's face for any reaction to her mention of Dwight. Nothing.

Emily stands up. "C'mon. Let's see how far it is and what route we should take."

Paula doesn't make a move.

The Rand McNally is still in the glove box along with smaller individual state maps for Arizona, Nevada, New Mexico, and California. Emily pulls out the Arizona and California maps, takes them into the house, and spreads them out on the living room floor next to one another.

She slides open the patio door. "Paula. C'mon." Emily leaves the door open, returns to the maps in the living room, and kneels on the floor in front of them. She hears Paula close the patio door, her bare feet padding on the kitchen tile.

"Look." Emily places her index finger on Eureka.

"That looks far. Farther than Tonopah." Paula squats next to her.

"We can do it. Look, on the way there's Los Angeles and San Francisco. We could stop there. Remember that song Grandma Marilee used to sing? About wearing flowers in your hair if you go to San Francisco?"

"Yeah, I do." Paula's eyes are glassy.

Emily looks at Paula and then back to the map. "Let's go soon. This place is getting to me."

"Go where?" Jay walks into the room, stands over them and the maps.

"We're going to California. To Eureka."

"Where the hell is Eureka?" Jay crouches next them.

Emily points. "Here."

"You need a shit-pile of money to go somewhere brand new like that. You don't know anybody there. And why Eureka?"

"It's just a place to go, that's all."

"She saw it on a postcard," Paula says.

Emily tells Jay about the suitcase and the money. No point in him not knowing now. And maybe she wants to let him know they can take care of themselves, that they're as smart as Steve and Stone. Smarter.

"Holy goat shit," Jay says. "You two are something. How much do you have?" He laughs his old dumb laugh that used to annoy Emily, but now she's glad to hear it.

"Enough."

"Fifty-one hundred," Paula says. "After the four hundred for the mortuary."

"And if we get that one hundred and fifty thousand from Wilkins when the property shit gets settled, some of it belongs to you two."

"See." Emily looks at Paula. "We'll be rolling in money. No worries."

Jay's cell phone rings. "Hey."

A woman's voice on the other end. Jay puts the call on speaker phone.

"Phyllis. We've been trying to get ahold of you. For a long time."

Jay's face is pained when he tells her what happened, as if he's reliving the news himself. That's how Emily feels, like Dwight and Grandma Marilee have died three times. First when Claude told them, then at the mortuary, now the telling of it to Phyllis. How many more times will there be?

"How are the girls?" Phyllis's voice on the other end of the line. "Is Emily there?"

Emily shakes her head to Jay, mouths the word *no.* She doesn't want to talk to Phyllis. What the fuck took her so long to call?

"She's not here right now."

Nothing on the other end. Maybe Phyllis is crying. She should cry. Her mother's dead, her brother's dead. She should just fucking cry the rest of her life.

"Leave real early tomorrow morning," Jay says when he comes out of the QuikTrip with a Styrofoam cooler, ice, a twelve-pack of plastic water bottles, and two more one-gallon jugs. "Get through the desert before the worst heat."

He'd driven the truck, Emily and Paula beside him. He'd filled the tank, then opened the hood and checked the oil. Dwight had shown Emily and Paula how to do it all, but they didn't say anything.

"It's hot as hell driving through that desert until you get to LA. We'll put some of these water bottles in the freezer tonight, get 'em good and cold." He reaches into the glove box and pulls out an envelope. "You don't want to get stopped and not have a registration."

He takes the registration out. Still in Dwight's name. "It's good for six more months."

"I'm surprised he registered it," Paula says. "The way he hated the government and their rules."

"He used this truck for his business. I think he just went along on this one."

Just before dusk they sit on Wilkins's patio, the air clear, no wind, the sky like blue glass.

"What will you do?" Emily asks Jay.

"What do you mean?"

She doesn't know what she means, it just seems like a thing to say. What she wants to say is, *Will you be okay?* "Without us. What will you do without us around?" She laughs as if she's joking, but she's not.

Jay shrugs and smiles. "I'll think of something."

Emily watches the glass sky melt into dark, interrupted by a smattering of lights from developments in the foothills.

The next morning Emily's up before dawn. Her selection of Grandma Marilee's books is already in the truck, along with some clothes and odds and ends. She stuffs the rest of her clothes into her backpack and wakes Paula.

"We want to get going early, like Jay said."

Paula rolls over and places a pillow over her head for a minute, then gets up.

"It's almost six," Emily says. "We need to beat the heat."

"Okay." Paula pulls on a pair of shorts and slips her feet into her sneakers, leaving them untied. "Let me brush my teeth and I'm ready."

Jay's at the kitchen table. Emily watches him before he notices her. He's the only family they have now. Phyllis has never counted. "You could come with us, Jay." She sets her backpack by the front door. She knows he can't.

Paula brings her backpack in and sets it next to Emily's.

"Appreciate the invite," Jay says. "I do. But you girls will have a brand-new life ahead of you up there. And I need to stay here for the property stuff."

"You too, Jay," Paula says. "You can have a brand-new life. When you get the property back. A new life without Steve and Stone."

Jay nods. The three of them remain quiet for a couple of minutes, as if they need the stillness to settle over them before it's okay to move. Then Emily picks up her backpack, opens the front door, and walks to the truck. She slings it behind the seat in the pickup. Paula stands just outside the front door, her backpack on the ground beside her. Jay walks around the truck, checking the tires, then checks them again.

"You going to put that in the truck?" Emily points to Paula's backpack.

Paula hesitates.

"C'mon, Paula. Let's go."

Something's off. Paula bites her lower lip, runs the fingers of her right hand through her curls, and exhales as if she's been holding her breath for a long time and can't keep it in anymore.

"I'm not going."

"What? What the fuck?"

"I'm not going, Emily."

"Everything's planned. We've talked about it for so long. Now we can really do it."

"You've talked about it mostly. It's always been your dream, not mine."

"But you said you wanted to go."

"I know. And I did."

"So, what the fuck's going on?" Emily walks to the front door of the house, then back to the truck. "You're fucking backing out at the last minute? Jesus Christ, Paula."

"It just doesn't feel right for me. Not now. Maybe later. Maybe in a few months. I don't know."

Emily's on the verge of saying *fuck you*, getting into the truck, and slamming off.

"You go ahead. Take Dad's truck. And here, take the money." Paula reaches into her backpack and takes out the envelope with the money, handing it to Emily.

Emily hates the feeling that's welling up inside her. She counts out half and hands it back to Paula. "It's half yours. I'm sure you can use it for something."

"It's not half mine. I never wanted it in the first place."

Emily backs away as Paula attempts to return the money to her. She raises her hands into the air to refuse it.

"Take it!" Paula screams. Tears well up. "You always thought everything my dad did was so great. But you're not like him. He never took stuff from people—not stuff they needed, not their money. He wouldn't like this, Emily. Nothing that we've done."

Paula forces the money into the space between Emily's folded arms.

"Fuck you, Paula." Emily throws the money at her. It falls to the ground and splays around the house's front entrance.

"Cut the shit, you guys." Jay gathers up the bills and passes them back to Emily. "Just take it."

"What-the-fuck-ever." Emily takes the money, stuffs it in her two back pockets.

"I'm not sure you should go alone, Emily," Jay says. "You've never driven—"

Emily cuts him off, tears running down her face. "I'm going, Jay. I'm fucking going."

"Okay, okay."

She gets in the truck, slams the door, and starts the engine.

She grasps the steering wheel with both hands as the AC blows cool air onto her face.

Paula runs to the truck and taps on the window. "Wait."

Emily doesn't react, sits motionless staring out the front window.

"I'm sorry, Emily. Let the window down."

Just go to hell. Emily turns, still crying. Paula's still crying too. She hasn't thought about it for a long time, but the night Phyllis left, after Grandma Marilee held her for so long, she and Paula lay side by side in their little sleeping bags on the living room floor. Paula crawled into Emily's sleeping bag, the two of them stretching it at the seams. Paula put her arms around Emily and stayed there the whole night. She lets the window down. Paula reaches both arms inside the truck and hugs Emily. Emily hugs her back, notices that Jay stands right behind Paula.

"I'm sorry," Paula says. "I just can't go with you."

"I know. It's okay." But it's not okay.

Paula steps away from the truck. Jay comes to the window and rests his elbows on the door. He just looks at Emily without saying anything.

"What?"

"That Circle K thing you asked about?" He's nervous and shifts his weight from one leg to the other and back again.

"Yeah?"

"We tried to rob the place. Me and a guy I hung out with back then. Told the clerk to empty the register."

"Did he?"

"No. He just stood there with a blank look on his face. But he must have pressed an alarm or something 'cause the cops showed up real quick."

Emily imagines Jay standing awkwardly at a Circle K counter.

"The guy I was with had a gun. He never fired it. No one got hurt."

She examines Jay's face. Why is he telling her this now? It feels like a lesson. Jay's new role.

"Thanks for telling me."

"They could have, though. Someone could have gotten hurt."

Neither of them says anything. Emily looks away from Jay. "I need to go now."

She pulls out of the driveway. Jay stands there waving, like a parent, Paula next to him. Her family. Emily watches in the rearview mirror until she can no longer see them. She turns at the corner and heads for US 60.

Her fake driver's license is in her wallet behind the real one, along with the passport and birth certificate in her backpack. Maybe she'll toss them, use her own. But they might come in handy. Emily presses the gas pedal hard, visualizes the open desert, and imagines the truck racing through it. Then the glisten of the California ocean. Maybe she can make it in less than three days. She'll find a cheap motel, maybe sleep in the truck. The window is still down and Emily inhales the heat of Phoenix along with the fumes of freeway exhaust. She rolls it back up and presses a little harder on the accelerator. She's flying, riding the air.

She drives for nearly six hours, straight through L.A., her brain on fire. Maybe she can make it all the way to Eureka after all. She stops on the outskirts of L.A., fills the gas tank, pees, and buys a Pepsi, then drives another two hundred miles and pulls into a rest stop in Coalinga. She sits in the parking lot, eating the chips and drinking the Coke she'd bought from the vending machine outside of the rest stop. Semis pull in and out. A car full of kids in the back seat parks next to her, a van with an elderly couple in front on the other side. The deaths of Grandma Marilee and Dwight hit her again. The fact that she will never see them again, never watch Dwight working on his projects, never hear his voice telling her how to shoot, never see Marilee out by the graveyard, her fragile body bent over the stones, seems unreal. When will she see Paula again? Jay? Will Paula be okay? They've always been together. Their entire lives.

The kids in the car next to her get out and run to the vending machines. A boy and two girls. The girls look about six. They come away with some snacks and sit on a concrete bench. Emily watches, wonders where they're traveling to. The little girls get up, take each other's hands, and run through the grass in front of the building, dancing and giggling.

It's early evening, nearly five p.m. Emily feels like she's been gone from Phoenix for a long time. She remembers the postcard from Venice Beach. The magic of the ocean flashes before her. She never gave it to Paula. She reaches over into her backpack and unzips the front pocket. It's still there. Behind it, the baggage claim from the L.A. suitcase. The same day Dwight and Marilee died. She takes out her cell phone to call Paula but changes her mind. Puts it back in her pocket and drives out of the rest stop.

One Year Later

Emily pulls weeds from around Marilee's grave, next to Jack's. Her eyes go to the next one: Dwight Larson 1964-2010. Claude chiseled their names into the stones. Grandma Marilee used to tell her how the dead weren't truly dead, they just live in a dimension you can't touch the way you do regular objects or people in the world. *They walk right next to us*, she used to say. When Ruth died, Emily tried to feel her presence but never could, even though she assured Paula that Ruth was always with her. She thinks she believes it now, though, with Marilee and Dwight gone. Sometimes she almost glimpses that parallel space. Mostly they live inside her, that's how she keeps them alive. She understands why the graveyard was so important to Grandma Marilee. Paula stays away from it, but every once in a while, Emily sees her standing over Dwight's stone. Claude took them out to Ironwood, found the spot where Dwight liked to shoot. Paula tossed most of his ashes into the desert, but they saved a little to bury.

The property's full of deep green growth from the winter rain that deluged the valley. It's mostly weeds, but some hollyhocks popped up, and two more branches of that rose bush Marilee said came from Jack after he died. The street on the western side of the property is a buzz of activity from morning to night, a weird mix of old people and young.

Vehicles come and go all day long, the condos completed and filled with tenants. Retired people who look like they have lots of money. The building's called Maravilla. Trees grow on the rooftops and each apartment has a little patio protruding from the building. Jay said there's a movie theater inside. ASU provides a special bus from Maravilla over to the campus. It pulls up three times a day. Emily thinks of Grandma Marilee when she sees the retired people. Sometimes they walk along the sidewalk, down to the lake with little dogs on leashes.

It took nearly a year for the property settlement. Emily still gets a headache thinking of the details, but they've got the title. In her name, Jay's, and Paula's. Turns out Harmon Valenti filed a homestead claim way back before Arizona was even a state. He worked with Albert and Martino at Hayden's Ferry and sold them the property. That was one of the bills of sale she found, along with a handwritten deed. Albert and Martino sold it cheap to their sister and her husband, Constance and Jimmy Baker, as a wedding gift. Alyward said the deed was either never filed or filed improperly or lost, maybe purposely lost. Who knows?

A lot of corruption in the state land office back then, he told them. *And the city was already claiming part of it for the railroad, even before Valenti sold it.*

When Valenti, who had no family, died, the federal government claimed his land and didn't have a record of any claim when Arizona was still a territory. They set aside a strip of the land along the eastern edge for the Union Pacific railroad and gave the rest of it to Arizona upon statehood, in 1912. The state ran a chain-link fence along the railroad tracks and put up a No Trespassing sign. Emily grew up looking at that sign as she watched the trains go by.

Even with the documents verified, the state claimed a portion along the northern edge facing Tempe Town Lake, the section with the big citrus tree Grandma Marilee used to brag about. And the corner with the paloverde. Alyward's advice had been to accept the state's claim. *You're lucky they're not going to try to take all of it,* he said. *Just let it go.* And they did. The state sold part of it to a private developer, and there's a restaurant under construction.

Wilkins wanted to buy more to make his section bigger, but Jay said no. Emily and Paula agreed. His piece still stands empty, but he cordoned it off with a chain-link a couple of weeks ago, so something must be coming soon. Emily hasn't mentioned it to Jay or Paula yet, but she got an idea when Wilkins wanted additional property. They could sell off another section and still have a lot left over for themselves. Give Wilkins some competition from whoever else might want to put up something. She imagines Dwight saying the whole western edge has already gone to shit anyway. Maybe they'll build a tall fence so they won't even have to see whatever comes along. But she sort of likes the activity, the comings and goings. A new bar just went up on the southwest corner across from the condos; a lot of young people hang out there. Three big TV screens in the bar are visible from the property.

She told Paula they should go there sometime and use the IDs that made them twenty-one, but Paula said no, that she didn't even remember where hers was. Paula's probably right. After Stone's bust, the authorities might be watching out for certain fake IDs. Maybe they had a way to trace them. Who knows? She couldn't bring herself to throw hers out though. She knows exactly where it is. Sometimes she looks at the fake license and passport, imagining a parallel self who didn't turn around in Coalinga but drove all the way to Eureka and started a new life there. Maybe someday she'll try again.

They moved the school bus over to the southeast corner and told Billy he could keep his stuff inside it, sleep in it if he wanted. Jay moved into Dwight's old room. Marilee's is still full of her stuff. Paula offered Emily Marilee's room, and she would stay in the Airstream, but neither of them has made a move yet. Too many changes to deal with.

As Emily turns away from the graveyard and walks back toward the patio, the irrigation comes on. Nobody ever discovered the system Dwight and Claude rigged up for getting the water running again. Not until Jay asked the city of Tempe to turn on the irrigation. Then they had to pay all the back bills and a fine. They also had to pay the state a bunch of back taxes on the property. Alyward said someone had to pay them. Once the paperwork got straightened out, the title was fixed to back when Harmon first sold it, which meant the state was entitled to back taxes. *Sounds fucked to me*, Jay said. But they went ahead

ACKNOWLEDGMENTS

I would like to thank the members of my writing group, whose advice, feedback, and encouragement were invaluable in completing this project: Keith Anderson, Natasha Anderson, Martha Blue, Jonathan Bond, Ray Carns, Ruth Chavez, Trish Cox, Kate Cross, Lynn Galvin, Amy McClane, Marty Murphy, Amy Nichols, LaDonna Ockinga, Karen Reed, Pat Rudnyk, and Charlotte Schodrok. I would also like to thank my friend and mentor Jim Sallis for his encouragement and faith in me as a writer and from whom I have learned so much more than I can say.

Author's Note: This story was inspired by actual events. All names, characters, and incidents are products of the author's imagination and are fictitious and should not be construed as real.